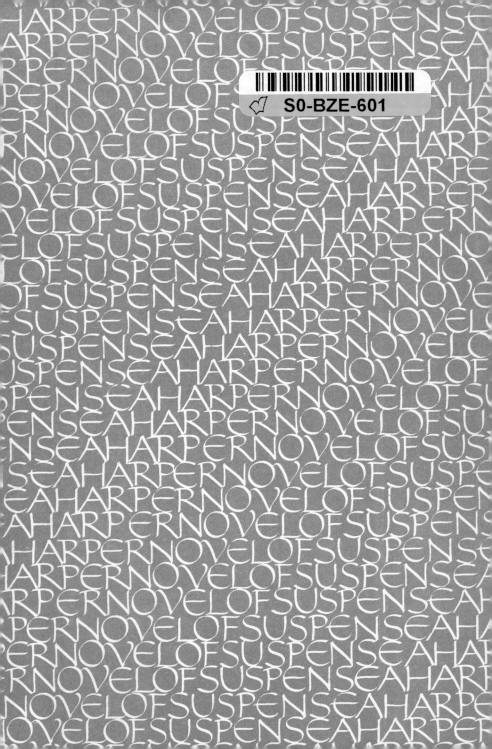

THE CASE
IS *ALTERED*

THE CASE
IS *ALTERED*

SARA WOODS

HARPER & ROW, PUBLISHERS
NEW YORK AND EVANSTON

FIRST U.S. EDITION

LIBRARY OF CONGRESS CATALOG CARD NUMBER: 67-28827

M-R

THE CASE
IS *ALTERED*

PROLOGUE

The little man who sat by the table was beginning to have a dogged look. He said stubbornly, "They didn't promise nothing." And his counsel, already gowned because they were due in court in five minutes, took a quick turn down the full length of the interview room and came back to say with exaggerated patience:

"Of course they didn't. But you know as well as I do, if you'd just say what you've done with your haul—"

"Well, I ain't a-telling you that, guv'nor, not if it was ever so."

"You know perfectly well you'll get the maximum this time," said Antony Maitland, exasperated.

"My business, ain't it?" He looked up and added kindly, "Of course, you means well."

"That's more than can be said for you, Jim. What about your wife? And the kids?"

"I shall miss them," said the little man reflectively. He was very neat in a blue serge suit, and had an ineffectual air that stood him in good stead, except with people who knew him.

Unfortunately, over the years the police had come to know him very well indeed.

"That isn't what I meant, and you know it!" Maitland told him. He wasn't even trying to sound patient now.

"Oh, well now, they'll be looked after all right."

"I see! And when you come out—"

"You don't have to worry about that," said Jim. "I'm retiring after this."

"Pensioned off, I suppose?" asked Maitland sarcastically. He leaned forward with a sudden movement, and Jim looked up unwillingly to meet his eye. "You've found a buyer already," he said.

"Now, you know, guv'nor, I never said I done it."

Counsel ignored this. "Can you trust him?" he said; and added in a tone of enlightenment, when Jim's eyes shifted uneasily away from his own, "Now I know what it is. You're afraid!"

"Do you wonder?" the little man grumbled. "All this talk!"

"I didn't mean the judge. It might be better if you were." But Jim seemed to have recovered his spirits.

"I'm an innocent man . . . remember?" he said with dignity. "Why should I be scared?"

"Have it your own way." Maitland's tone was grim now. "Don't say I didn't warn you, that's all."

"I know you done your best." The soothing note in his voice was too much for counsel, who said, "Heaven and earth!" in an overwrought way, and strode across the room again to fling open the door. "I hope you get twelve years," he remarked, pausing an instant, and departed with a swirl of his gown. Jim turned to look at his solicitor, who had got up from a chair at the far end of the table and picked up his briefcase.

"He doesn't mean nothing, you know," he confided.

"You'd be well advised to listen to him." The solicitor, a stolid-looking young man with red hair, seemed neither surprised nor perturbed by the somewhat unusual nature of Maitland's valediction.

Jim seemed to consider this, and then shook his head. "Five years," he said philosophically. "Couldn't be less, as I see it.

Won't be more, not after *he's* had his say. Extenuating circumstances," he added carefully, "and all like that."

Geoffrey Horton returned his grin. He had known Maitland for all of ten years now, and his present client almost as long. "I shouldn't have thought there were any," he said unsympathetically; and watched with amusement the reproachful look that dawned on Jim's face in answer to his bluntness.

CHAPTER 1

He noticed the girl at once as he came round the corner of the gardens in the center of the square. She was just turning away from the door of number five, and even at a distance there was a disconsolate air about her as she came down the steps and stood hesitating on the pavement, obviously undecided which way to go.

He came up with her before she had made up her mind: a slim girl with silky, fair hair almost to her shoulders and a pale, clear complexion. And young, very young; she might even be still at school. Her beige coat was noncommittal, and she wasn't wearing a hat. He said, "Were you looking for Jenny?" because it didn't seem kind to pass her without a word.

She turned sharply at the sound of his voice, and gave him a quick, nervous smile. "No . . . at least, I don't know who Jenny is. I wanted to see Mr. Maitland."

"Then it's lucky I came along." His tone didn't reflect his disappointment; the court had sat late, and it couldn't be said his case was going well.

"Are *you* Antony Maitland?" He had already seen that her eyes were deeply blue; now he saw too that they were unusually expressive. "Oh, I beg your pardon, but I mean . . . the one I want is a barrister, a Q.C."

He grinned at that. "I admit it looks as if there'd been an oversight somewhere. But you could hardly expect me to come home in my wig."

"I didn't, of course." She was on her dignity for a moment, but his smile was disarming. "It's just that I thought you'd be older."

"Does it matter? I mean, can I help you in some way, or would you rather wait a year or two?"

Her eyes were fixed on his face, almost painfully intent. Now she closed them, licked her lips, and said so hastily that the words were slurred, "Mr. Horton sent me."

"Did he, though?" He sounded thoughtful, but when she opened her eyes again he still had his amused look. "Then you'd better come in, hadn't you, and tell me what you want?" He went up the steps as he spoke, and turned at the top with his latchkey in his hand, waiting for her to join him.

She followed slowly. "I don't want to be a nuisance."

"Why didn't you wait?" he asked, ignoring this. "Gibbs knew I shouldn't be long."

"I didn't quite like to suggest it."

So Gibbs was in one of his surly moods. He pushed open the door, and waited for her to precede him across the threshold. As he expected, the butler was hovering at the back of the hall. "Did Mrs. Maitland get back, Gibbs?"

"I haven't heard her come in, sir." Which was as good as to say she hadn't; the old man missed very little that went on in his orbit. At the moment he was looking censoriously at Antony's companion, disapproving of her, disapproving of both of them; but that was only to be expected.

"Never mind. Two flights up, I'm afraid," he added to the girl, leading the way towards the stairs and speaking over his shoulder as he went. "This is my uncle's house—Sir Nicholas Harding. We have a flat at the top; it's very convenient really."

He waited until they reached the second-floor landing and added, as he pushed open the door to his own quarters, "You haven't told me your name."

"Jo Marston."

"Straight ahead, Miss Marston. The living room door's open. Shall I take your coat?"

The big room was shadowy already, and much cooler than was comfortable. He pulled down the window, turned on the lamp in the corner near the writing table, and knelt to put a match to the fire. As he turned he saw that she was still hesitating, and gestured invitingly towards the chairs that were grouped round the hearth. "As this isn't a professional consultation we may as well be comfortable."

"No . . . of course . . . how do you know?" she asked confusedly.

"Geoffrey would have come with you. Aren't you going to sit down?" She seated herself on the sofa opposite the fire, looking down at the grate now, not at her companion any longer. "Will you smoke?"

"I should like . . . I should just like to try one," she said, raising her eyes as far as the box he was holding out for her, and no further.

Maitland grinned, and said appreciatively, "It's a good act . . . really! But at least thirty years out of date."

That brought her eyes back to his face again, and when she saw his smile her lips quivered responsively. "That's what I told Angelo." She seemed pleased by the remark, rather than discomposed by it. "Of course, I've smoked for years. And you couldn't call this a public place, could you?"

"Not exactly."

"You see, it's in my contract," she said, as though that made everything plain. "I thought a lawyer would understand that."

"Perhaps I might, if you explain very carefully," said Antony, with a note of apology in his voice. "But why——?"

"I thought all lawyers were stuffy. I thought it would go down well. But now I see you're not like that at all."

"I hope not." The idea seemed to startle him. "But you've met Geoffrey Horton. Did you find him stuffy?"

"Terribly . . . terribly."

"When he *sent* you to see me?"

"He didn't. You've guessed that, haven't you? He told me about you . . . when I asked him. It wasn't *exactly* a lie."

"No, I see." But where was this getting them, after all? "What do you want of me, Miss Marston?" he asked; and was angry with himself immediately for the brusqueness of his tone. But she answered him steadily enough.

"I want your help."

"In what way?"

"For a friend . . . well, we're engaged to be married."

"A matter of litigation?"

"He was accused of theft, but he didn't do it . . . truly!"

If his thoughts at this point were a little cynical, he was perhaps not very much to blame. "Who is his solicitor?" he asked.

"Mr. Horton . . . I thought you understood that."

"Then why the . . . then why—?"

"He wanted to—to brief you, but you were too busy, or something." The scornful note in her voice dismissed as paltry the difficulty a man might experience in being in two places at once. "And so then I thought it was too late, because Roy has been in prison for—for nearly a month. But afterwards, when I told Roddy—"

"Oh, Roddy." He sounded relieved; as indeed he was, that a minor mystery had been explained. "If you're going to believe everything Roddy tells you—"

"What should I believe, then?" she flashed at him. "That you're selfish, and hardhearted, and untrustworthy?"

"I'm certainly not *soft*hearted," said Antony, revolted by the idea. "Roddy never told you that."

"Not—not exactly. I inferred it," she added, on her dignity again. "But he did say you sometimes helped people, and Mr. Horton agreed that was true."

"I suppose he told you I had sometimes been engaged— professionally—on cases that weren't altogether straightforward," said Maitland. His tone was meant to be damping, and he was disconcerted when she nodded quite cheerfully in agreement. "But this is different, don't you see? I mean, it's all over."

"It's an injustice," she said, watching his expression. "And it isn't nice, being in prison. The judge said some quite horrible things, and he gave him three years."

Having had a difficult afternoon in court, Antony might well have condemned the whole bench indiscriminately as a heartless lot, but somehow he didn't think it was quite as simple as that. A silence spread itself between them; an uncomfortable silence on his part, because he didn't want to hurt her and it seemed so very likely that her trust was misplaced, that she would find the truth—if only she could be brought to face it— harsh and unkind. For her part, Jo was looking at him critically. She saw a dark man, tall and rather thin, with a casual air that might have deceived her if she hadn't been prepared for it. Until a few moments ago there had been an amused look in his eyes; now he seemed uneasy, as if her own nervousness had communicated itself to him. It would have made more sense if he had been angry with her for coming. "I wouldn't have bothered you, just for myself," she said; and was annoyed to hear that her voice sounded hurt and a little resentful.

"No, of course you wouldn't," he agreed quickly. "But you mustn't count on me. You mustn't count on anything."

Jo gave him a rather uncertain smile. "I know what you mean. You think Roy's guilty, and unless I can make you believe me—"

"I've nothing to go on yet," he protested. "But I suppose the police had a case."

"Yes. Oh, yes. A very good one. It was at a party, you see, and they found the emeralds in his pocket."

"Did they indeed?" Something in his tone touched her to anger again.

"It isn't only me who says he's innocent. Mr. Horton would tell you the same thing."

"I see." The doubtful way he spoke made nonsense of the assurance; for himself, he'd never found Geoffrey of a particularly credulous disposition. But even . . . "Even if I accept that fact, Miss Marston, what do you think I can do about it?"

"I thought perhaps—I thought perhaps you could prove it."

She met his eye defiantly as she said this, but the nervousness he had noted before was very evident now.

"Just like that!" He spoke lightly, and was met suddenly with a blaze of anger.

"I never said it was easy, and I know I've no right . . . but do you think it was easy for me to come here, to ask you—?"

"Tell me about it," he said, temporizing. "After that, we'll see."

"Oh, very well then." She sounded ungracious. But the tempest died as quickly as it had arisen. "I'm sorry. I know it's an—an imposition."

"Forget it," he advised. "Would you like a drink? I think I need one."

"Thank you." She still sounded subdued.

"Is that in the contract too? I won't tell anyone," he promised, smiling at her. "What will you have?"

"Sherry, please."

"Are you sure?" He was moving across the room as he spoke, and it occurred to her as she watched him that he held himself a little stiffly.

"I happen to prefer it." She was being dignified again, but when he turned his head and raised an eyebrow inquiringly she added, almost apologetically, "My grandfather can't tolerate cocktails, so I sort of got used to sherry, you see."

"Sweet?"

"Oh, dear me, no," she told him primly. And received her glass, when he returned to the fireside, with all the aplomb of a duchess.

"You'd better start," he said, "by telling me about yourself." He gave the fire a critical look before he sat down in one of the wing chairs and eyed her expectantly.

"I'm an actress," Jo told him, and thought her voice sounded loud and overassertive. "Well, films," she added. "Some people say it isn't the same thing."

"Yes, of course; that contract," said Antony, enlightened.

"It's for five years. *Five!*"

"Isn't that a good thing?"

"I thought so at first, but in some ways it's rather—rather

nauseating, you know. No smoking or drinking in public, no makeup *ever* . . . well, just a very little powder, and enough lipstick not to look like a beatnik, which would be too mildewed; even Angelo admits that."

"I don't quite see—"

"It's hard, isn't it?" She took his sympathy for granted. "If I'd been just a year or two older I'd have been in time for sex; but as it is, it's completely antiquated, don't you think?"

"Is it, though?" said Antony, startled.

"Oh, yes. At least, that's what Angelo says. He prides himself on being an—an innovator. And he says there's bound to be a reaction, and one should lead the trend, not follow it. So he's making a lot of rather pure films—"

"Who the devil is Angelo?" asked Maitland; his irritation was understandable, even if it might have been more appropriately expressed.

"Angelo Valenti."

"A film director?"

"*The* film director." She seemed to find his ignorance unreasonable. "He's Anglo-Italian Films, and really good. At least," she added, perhaps feeling that a greater measure of accuracy was needed when dealing with the law, "good at his job."

"I see. Now, this friend of yours—Roy, did you call him? Is he with the film company too?"

"Oh, no." The idea seemed to amuse her. "We're rogues and vagabonds—"

"You mustn't say that, Miss Marston; not to a lawyer. It might put the wrong sort of ideas into his head."

"I only thought . . . well, it doesn't matter. Roy works in a bank . . . I mean, he did. The Head Office of the Northumbrian and Wessex." She sipped her wine, and he saw that her hand shook a little as she put down the glass; and was aware in that moment of the first stirrings of sympathy.

"How old are you?"

She opened her eyes a little at the roughness of his tone. "Eighteen . . . if it matters."

"Have you known Roy for long?"

"Nearly six months. It's quite long enough," she added, meeting an objection that she obviously took for granted. "Well, it was four and a half months, nearly, when we got engaged. That was just before the party when—when it happened."

"You mentioned your grandfather. Do you live with him?"

"Yes, he brought me up." She was smiling again, reminiscently; and again he was angry at his own reaction to her mood.

"Does he approve of this contract of yours? Does he like you being a film star?"

"Oh, I'm not a star . . . that's Giuditta. And of course, he hates the whole thing. He said he'd agree if I was really determined . . . well, he had to, because he thought I'd throw a fit if he didn't. But he said if I went through with it he'd—he'd repudiate me."

"I thought you didn't get your vocabulary from Angelo," said Antony, with some small satisfaction apparent in his tone.

"From Angelo? Oh, you mean . . . well, Grandfather does use long words, rather. But he didn't cast me off, after all."

"Did he approve of your engagement? What is the fellow's name, anyway?" he added, with a return of irritation.

"Roy Bromley. And Grandfather would have liked it all right if all this hadn't happened."

"Would have—?"

"I hadn't actually got round to telling him," she admitted.

"Does he know you're here?"

She shook her head. "He'd never have let me come alone."

"I see. Tell me about the theft, then."

"I suppose you mean, from the beginning," said Jo cautiously.

"From the beginning, certainly."

She wasn't looking at him now. Her eyes were downcast, and she was twisting the ring on her left hand; he noticed that it was a plain gold signet. "I told you about Roy. He's twenty-seven, as you're so interested in ages, and he's been about three years in London. Before that he was in Manchester, I think."

"Is that his home town?"

"No. That wouldn't be bank policy." The words were obviously a quotation. "He was brought up by an uncle and aunt, in Reading; but I don't know much about them."

"Well, what happened when the emeralds were stolen?"

"It was at a party to celebrate the film we'd just finished, and it was on February tenth . . . Shrove Tuesday . . . because of Lent," said Jo, not very lucidly. "Angelo was quite pleased when I said I wanted to bring Roy—"

"Why was that?"

"He worked in Advance Department, on the section that deals with the Anglo-Italian Films account." She sipped her sherry, still avoiding his eye; and he wondered again if the dryness was really to her taste, or if that was something else she thought would go down well with a lawyer. "Angelo's a great one for public relations; he wanted David Warren to come, but luckily he wouldn't. So he thought Roy would be second best, and he asked Larry Truscott too, who works with him."

"Who is David Warren?"

"The Chief Controller . . . on Roy's section, you know. Bank people have to be very careful. They're expected to be sociable, but not to accept invitations that might—that might make them feel indebted in any way. It all sounds very silly to me."

"But it was all right for the other two?"

"Roy and Larry. They were junior enough for it not to matter. And Angelo was pleased, because I don't think he realizes at all how banks are organized," she added thoughtfully.

"You got your information from Bromley, I suppose."

"And from Grandfather. He's one of the General Managers."

"Oh, is he?" Maitland sounded vague. "Is that how you met—?"

"No, of course not. He wouldn't even know Roy existed."

He waited a moment, but she seemed to have no intention of amplifying this. "Then that brings us back to Shrove Tuesday, doesn't it?"

"I suppose so." She had been holding her glass between her hands, looking down at the wine as though there was a story to be read there; but now she raised her head, and met his eyes steadily. "The party was at the studio . . . on the set. Roy and I got there about nine o'clock."

"Who was there?"

"Everyone! All the people connected with the film in any way, and special friends, and people Angelo thought would be useful. I could tell you some of them, but nothing like a proper list."

"Never mind. Just tell me what happened."

"There was lots to drink, of course, and everyone talking at once, and a few people dancing down at one end of the studio. All very informal. Giuditta was wearing her emeralds; that was because some of her friends were there—people who are just as big stars as she is—and a few society people, the ones who think it's chic to know someone in films." She paused, considering what she had said. "I expect I sound catty, but it's true. And I wouldn't mean it nastily about Giuditta, because I love her."

"Why?"

Jo seemed taken aback by the question. "Why do you love people? She's a darling . . . I can't explain. And it's quite sensible really to want to keep her end up."

"And the emeralds—"

"There's a tale they were given her by Royalty in Exile. She always denies it, so it may be true. But I think it was probably Angelo, and perhaps they were more of an investment than a gift."

"Are they married?"

"They live together," said Jo, very offhand.

"Anyway, the emeralds are valuable."

"Frightfully valuable. They're the d'Albret necklace, you know."

"*Are* they?" said Antony. And then, more honestly, "I'm afraid I never heard of them."

"They're very famous," Jo told him reprovingly. "The necklace was made for Cesare Borgia to give to one of his mistresses. I forget which one. But then when his father died and he had to leave Rome . . . you remember the Pope was his father?"

"That and the Battle of Hastings," he assured her.

"Well, when things got too difficult he went to Navarre. And I suppose he stole the emeralds back from his mistress to take to his wife. A sort of peace offering, you see."

"I can see he might have needed one. I don't imagine he was a model husband."

"He was married to Charlotte d'Albret, whose brother was the King of Navarre. I suppose it was really him he wanted to— to ingratiate himself with."

"So Charlotte got the emeralds. I hope she felt her bargain was a good one."

"She didn't have to put up with Cesare very long, anyway. I don't know what happened to her, or the emeralds, after that."

"No curse?"

Jo shook her head. "It's a pity, isn't it? I expect they'd be even more valuable with a proper curse."

"You can't have everything," said Antony regretfully. "And on Shrove Tuesday, Giuditta was wearing this very famous necklace."

"Yes." Jo sighed. "There she was, positively glowing . . . glad to be done with the film. Angelo gets difficult, you know, towards the end. And there we all were," she concluded lamely; and sat looking at him in a helpless way.

"You're going to have to tell me what happened, you know. If she was wearing the emeralds, how did they get themselves stolen?"

"She went to her dressing room. That was at ten-thirty-six, as far as the police could make out from the statements. Just eight minutes later she was found, unconscious. Someone had hit her on the head, and the emeralds were gone."

"When she came round—"

"She didn't know anything. She'd heard someone come in, and thought it was Angelo. She was sitting at the mirror, and when she looked up she just saw the reflection of a man with a black sort of mask thing pulled right over his head. And then he knocked her out."

"Did she make any identification?"

"No . . . no, she didn't." She hesitated, and then added firmly, "I think she thought it was Roy, but she never said that to the police."

"Who found her?"

"Angelo. And it was all so quick, you see. He came out and grabbed Dr. Carr, but no one noticed or got fussed. And the doctor made him call the police, and they arrived before anyone knew what had happened. And it was Frank who suggested everyone should be searched."

"Frank?"

"Frank Eversley. You must have heard of him. He's starred with Giuditta ever so often."

"Yes, of course."

"He said it would save a lot of bother, so no one felt like admitting they didn't like the idea; in fact they rather treated it as a joke, you know, because they didn't realize Giuditta had been hurt. But then the policeman found the emeralds."

"You said, in Bromley's pocket."

"Yes. I wish you knew Roy," she added inconsequently.

"That can be remedied. Go on."

"Well, they thought he'd meant to make a getaway, but things had happened too quickly. And Giuditta had already described the man she saw—about five foot ten, but with broad shoulders and moved like an athlete. It could have been Roy . . . except that it wasn't."

"You weren't able to say he hadn't left your side?"

"No. You see, I was a sort of hostess too, because of being in the film. So I couldn't just concentrate on him. I'd been dancing with a man who came with Sue Brown—she does continuity. When the music stopped and I went back to Roy, Angelo was just going out towards the dressing rooms."

"Did Bromley say he'd been in the studio all the time?"

"Yes, but he was moving about, talking to different people. Nobody could remember exactly."

"Was anyone with him when you went back?"

"Frank Eversley." She gave him another of her appraising looks. "And Larry joined us almost immediately, and Michael

. . . Michael Ross. No, Michael got there first, before I did. Any of them could have slipped the emeralds into Roy's pocket; that's what you're thinking, isn't it?"

"With so many people milling around——"

"Someone else *could* have come near without my noticing, though we were standing a little apart, as it happens. I don't think they did, but they could have done."

"You're saying, then, that one of those three men——"

"I don't know. I'm sorry, I don't know!" Her vehemence was the first really open sign of distress, and for a moment her eyes met his with an almost frantic appeal. "It wasn't Roy, but I can't accuse anyone else. It wouldn't be fair."

"How much does the necklace weigh?"

"Oh, it isn't one of those great heavy things," she told him eagerly. "The emeralds are—well—big for emeralds; I never can remember about carats and things. But the chain is very delicate workmanship, nothing clumsy. I do think, truly, you could have them in your pocket and never know."

"I see. And all that happened before eleven o'clock."

"Yes . . . I told you."

"What time would the party have gone on to in the normal way?"

"Two o'clock . . . three o'clock. Late."

"You say Frank Eversley starred opposite Giuditta."

"Yes, he did."

"Have you any reason to think he's hard up?"

"He doesn't seem to be." She paused, not looking at him. "I ought to tell you, Roy was short of money. And he owed quite a lot to a bookmaker."

"Had he been gambling for long?"

"No. No, I don't think so." She was staring down at the fire now, and he thought she flushed, but it might have been only the reflection of the flames. "They said he—he cultivated me because he'd found out about the emeralds through information given to the Bank; and he thought I'd introduce him to Giuditta, you see."

"I'm afraid I do." His tone was grim, and her eyes flew back to his face again.

"I thought I ought to tell you the worst," she said, with an attempt at dignity that he didn't find laughable any longer, but only pathetic.

"I appreciate that, believe me." The trouble was, it made the inevitable refusal so much the more difficult. "I'd like to help you, Miss Marston—"

"But you won't?"

"I don't see how I can."

"Never mind." Her sudden capitulation was disturbing. She finished her sherry and put down the glass with a gesture that was somehow final and decisive; and he knew as he watched her that it was intended to be deliberately misleading, that she was still casting about for the means to get her own way. She picked up her gloves, and began to smooth them out on her knee. "Would you just—would you just do one very small thing for me?" she asked.

"What?" said Antony cautiously, and the blue eyes were raised reproachfully to his.

"Nothing very dreadful. If you'd have a talk with Grandfather . . . it needn't take half an hour."

"But what good do you think it would do?"

"I don't mind him thinking Roy's a thief, because he doesn't know him. But he thinks he's a fortune hunter, and that's just too much."

"I don't quite see—"

"I'm going to marry Roy—of course I am!—when he comes out of prison. So if you could persuade Grandfather it's no use hoping—" She broke off there, and finished the sentence with an odd, ungraceful gesture.

"What isn't he to hope for?" Maitland asked, after a moment's silence.

"Oh, just that—that I shall change my mind."

It seemed likely that Grandfather had, perhaps, some other, more eligible candidate up his sleeve. "I could certainly tell him no ulterior motive would be necessary for someone to want to marry you."

"I didn't think you were *stupid*," she said angrily.

"You shouldn't have listened to Roddy," he told her. But he

relented when he saw her expression and added gently, "I could tell him that circumstantial evidence can sometimes be misleading . . . which is true. But why should he believe me?"

"He's heard of you, Mr. Maitland. And if you could only accept Roy's story—"

"What is his story? A straight denial?"

She flinched a little from his tone, but answered steadily enough. "If he could have proved anything he wouldn't be in prison."

"No," said Maitland, flatly.

"If you'd only talk to Roy . . . talk to some of the people who know him."

"It isn't so easy."

"It could be arranged."

"I didn't mean that." He smiled at her suddenly, and added, more honestly than he had intended, "I don't want you to be hurt any more."

"I don't care about that."

"Perhaps not, but . . . it isn't fair even to let you hope."

"Then I won't. I promise." She was carefully holding her eagerness in check. "If you'd only try."

He got up with an abrupt movement, turned his back on the grate, and stood looking down at her. "You say Geoffrey Horton believes in Bromley's innocence?"

"That wasn't a lie, Mr. Maitland. It's perfectly true."

"Then I'll talk to him." This time there was no doubt that she flushed, and he added quickly, "Not to check up. He may have some suggestions."

"You won't let him discourage you."

He grinned at that, and shook his head. "But you mustn't expect too much."

"Oh, no!"

"I'm afraid—" He broke off, listening. "That will be Jenny," he said. "She must have forgotten her key."

But when he crossed the narrow hall and pulled the door open, it was his uncle who stood at the top of the stairs. "I'm coming to dinner," Sir Nicholas explained, meeting a rather blank look. "Had you forgotten it's Tuesday?"

"You'll be lucky." Antony backed away from the door. "Jenny isn't home yet."

"I doubt if she's deserted us," said Sir Nicholas placidly, and followed him into the hall. "Meanwhile, Gibbs informs me—"

"He would! I'm entertaining a blonde, and she's in the living room looking at my etchings," said Antony bitterly. "You'd better come in. Miss Josephine Marston," he added, as his uncle accepted the invitation. "She's a friend of Roddy and Liz." He was already regretting the impulse that had taken him, a moment before, to a halfhearted agreement with her request.

Jo was making a conquest of Sir Nicholas, who took all women at face value except when he encountered them in court. Her manner seemed carefully calculated to appeal, which annoyed Maitland for a moment, until he saw the little flicker of uncertainty in her eyes and was again aware of a reluctant sympathy. "You'd better sit down again," he said, "and drink to our bargain."

She obeyed without comment, but Sir Nicholas's eyebrows went up at the roughness in his nephew's tone. "Have I interrupted you?" He went across to the wing chair that faced the window, seated himself in a leisurely way, and accepted a glass with a grateful grunt. It was difficult to believe in the relationship, Jo thought. He was as tall as Maitland, but that seemed to be almost the only point of comparison. His build was heavier, his features more regular, his manner far more decided; and his fair hair—so fair that you couldn't tell whether there was any gray in it—was a good deal tidier.

"Not at all. I'd like your advice, sir," said Antony, not without malice. "If Miss Marston doesn't mind—"

"I'm too grateful to mind anything," she told him. But added thoughtfully, after a moment, "Except being called Josephine."

"Isn't it your name? My nephew was never noted for his exactness."

"I just mean, it isn't what I'm *called*. Don't you think 'Jo' is much nicer?"

"Much nicer." He was observing the sherry at her elbow with some apprehension, and frowned a little as he caught Antony's eye. "Er—do you really think—?"

"I'm not a schoolgirl," said Jo; it seemed only too likely that he was about to recommend a nice glass of milk instead. But suddenly her eyes were dancing, as though her own solemn tone amused her. Sir Nicholas inclined his head, in polite, though unconvinced, acceptance of her statement, and she thought all at once that the two men were really very alike after all, but the likeness was one of expression only. "I really ought to be going now," she said. "It must be getting awfully late."

Maitland turned and went back towards the desk again. "Finish your drink," he recommended, "while I phone for a cab."

Ten minutes after Jo had left them Sir Nicholas put down his empty glass and surveyed his nephew thoughtfully. "Aren't you being a little rash?" he inquired. *"Can* you help her?"

Antony had taken his favorite position, back to the fire, with one shoulder propped against the high mantel. He scowled now, because the question echoed too precisely his own misgivings. "I don't see what I can do, but I told her that."

"Do you suppose she listened?"

"No."

"And when you have to explain at last that there's nothing to be done?"

Maitland made no attempt to answer this directly. He shifted a little out of the direct range of the fire and said moodily, "Has it occurred to you that she may be right about Bromley?"

"It has not." Sir Nicholas sounded startled. He watched his nephew's expression for a moment, and then added bracingly, "Come now, Antony; a girl in love!"

"There was one thing that worried me," said Maitland stubbornly. "She said she was a sort of hostess."

"Well?"

"As her escort, Bromley could hardly be expecting to leave the party early, unless he pleaded illness or something of the sort. And no one in his senses would have hung around indefinitely with the emeralds in his pocket."

"I don't think much of that," said Sir Nicholas in a judicial tone. "He didn't expect the theft to be discovered so quickly;

and, anyway, if criminals never made mistakes the police force might as well be disbanded."

"Yes, I know."

"The point means nothing, alone," insisted Sir Nicholas, rubbing it in.

"Damn it all, I don't *want* to believe him."

"No, but . . . I've seen all this before. And I wouldn't give a penny, myself, for that child's opinion."

"Nor I."

"Besides, I understood from Mallory—"

"I *am* busy," Maitland conceded.

"Are you in court?"

"We should be through tomorrow. I say, Uncle Nick, that Baxter woman—"

"Is she the one who went on drawing her mother's old age pension for twelve years after the old lady was dead?" asked Sir Nicholas, momentarily diverted.

"She prefers the phrase 'passed away,' but that's right."

"Doubtless she acted with the best intentions," said his uncle encouragingly. Antony laughed.

" 'She only lived a year after the pension started, and it *did* seem a waste,' " he quoted.

"There's a sort of perverted logic about that." The older man's tone was reflective.

"But I can't expect the jury to have a sense of the ridiculous," Antony complained.

"Not considered as a unit instead of as twelve individuals. All the same—" The problem had caught Sir Nicholas's interest, and they were still arguing it in comparative amity when Jenny came in five minutes later with a hair-raising story of being held up for hours at Marble Arch. Sir Nicholas said coldly, "If you could tell us that the traffic was moving freely, my dear, that would at least have the benefit of originality."

At which Jenny glanced at the clock for the first time and, startled by what she saw there, exclaimed, "You must be famished!" and departed headlong for the kitchen.

CHAPTER 2

As Maitland had expected, the verdict next day was not exactly favorable to his client; what he hadn't foreseen was that the case would keep him in court until late in the afternoon. He got back to chambers in a ruffled mood, and put through a phone call to Geoffrey Horton. His friend's evident amusement when he told him about Jo's visit did nothing to put him in a better humor.

"I might have known she'd come to you, for all I said." From his tone, Geoffrey had found a good joke and proposed to play it to death. Antony said gloomily:

"What's so funny?"

"I've known you to fall for some pretty queer stories, but this one—"

"She said you believed what Bromley told you."

"What on earth has that to do with it?" said Geoffrey, in obvious astonishment.

"This cynicism is unbecoming. I should have thought the point was material, at least."

"Well, I did believe him, on the whole. But there's no proof whatever . . . and the case against him was pretty strong."

"So I gathered."

"There's nothing to be done, and you know it." Horton's amusement was getting a little ragged now; if anything, he sounded worried.

"*I* know it," said Antony sadly, "but does Jo Marston?"

"I should have thought you'd have more sense than to let her persuade you. I know she's an attractive girl," Geoffrey added unkindly.

"She *said* you were stuffy," said Maitland in a thoughtful tone; and then grinned to himself when he heard the stiffness in Geoffrey's voice.

"If it's stuffy to give her good advice . . . which is more than you seem to have done—"

"Let's say I'm a fool, and be done with it," Antony snapped; and added, no less abruptly, "I want to see Bromley. Can you arrange it?"

"By stretching the facts a little, I suppose I can."

"Tomorrow?"

"Of all the impatient—"

"Yes, but can you?"

"I can try. But he's at Maidstone, and Joan wants the car tomorrow." He said this rather as one who trumps his opponent's ace; Maitland, as he very well knew, had not driven himself since a wartime injury to his shoulder had made the exercise painful.

"I'd even let you drive the Jag, but Jenny says she'll take us."

"Oh, very well!" It was a capitulation, though not a gracious one. "But if you want to know what I think, Antony—"

"What made you think I did? Tell me tomorrow," he added hastily; and replaced the receiver when it became apparent that Geoffrey had by no means exhausted the subject.

At about eleven-fifteen next morning they were at the prison, and waiting for Roy Bromley to be produced. Horton had seated himself placidly enough at one end of the table, but Maitland was frankly prowling, with an occasional pause to glare up at the high window through which a shaft of sunlight slanted into the room. "It's always fine as soon as the vacation is over," he complained; but the contrast in his mind was not between today's sun and the rain they had had over Easter, but between the green countryside through which they had driven and this bare unfriendly room, between freedom and captivity. Horton, who had a pretty good idea what his companion was thinking, ignored his restlessness and watched the door.

Inevitably, perhaps, Antony's first thought when the prisoner came in was a vague surprise that Jo Marston could see anything in the fellow. Bromley was a little over middle height, with hair of an indeterminate shade, hazel eyes, a sensitive mouth, and a pallor that went a good way beyond being "interesting." Incredibly, he contrived to look well dressed even in prison clothes that hung too loosely. But this was to see him at a disadvantage; you could hardly expect . . .

The door closed, a key turned in the lock. Bromley moved to the foot of the table and spoke across it to Horton, though he ignored his greeting. "You said there was no point in an appeal."

"Nor is there, as things stand." Horton's professional manner always amused Antony; he put on a perfect performance . . . which wasn't a performance at all, as it happened, because Geoffrey had not one scrap of the actor in him. He said now, as though the present meeting was the most natural thing in the world, "I should explain we've no further evidence, and I don't want to raise any hopes. But Miss Marston suggested that Maitland should talk to some of the witnesses; not in a professional capacity, but as a friend."

It didn't seem to be a time to wait on formal introductions. Bromley looked at Antony and said slowly, "I've heard of you . . . haven't I?"

The only answer to that was "I don't know," and it didn't seem to get them very far. Antony moved a little and sat down with his back to the window. "It's all very irregular, but Miss Marston is persuasive, as no doubt you're aware. I hope you won't disappoint her by refusing to talk to me."

"Why should I?" His tone was faintly surly, but no more, perhaps, than was natural in the circumstances. "On the other hand, what can you do for me?"

"Relieve the tedium of prison life for half an hour, perhaps. Beyond that . . . probably nothing."

"I see," said Roy. "Or do I?" He pulled out a chair and seated himself, but his eyes never left Maitland's face. "Are you a friend of Jo's?"

"Yes."

"But you're a lawyer." His voice went up a little on the words, giving them the effect of a protest. Antony gave his sudden smile.

"Even lawyers have friends," he said. "Will you talk to me?"

"If there's any hope at all—"

"I'm sorry, I don't think there is. It's only fair to say that, but, of course, I may be wrong."

"That means, I suppose, that you believe the evidence."

"You'd better start by taking what I say at face value, Mr. Bromley; neither more nor less."

"At least, it can't do any harm," said Roy; and looked at Horton, as though for guidance. Geoffrey contented himself with nodding, but Maitland chose to take the words as acquiescence.

"Miss Marston tells me you were wrongly convicted," he said.

"Yes, I was." As though the question reminded him of his wrongs, the sullen look returned.

"Let's go back a bit. How long had you been playing the horses?"

"Did she tell you that?"

"She had enough sense to realize there was no way of helping you except by facing adverse facts as well as pleasant ones."

"Oh, I see." He sounded startled, and Maitland said more sharply:

"It's a rare trait, and one I find admirable."

"I daresay you do, but—"

"But?"

"It's all very well for you."

"We've all made fools of ourselves, one time or another." Maitland was back to his equable tone again, but Bromley seemed to find it no more acceptable. He said with a sort of controlled violence:

"All right then! You asked when I started betting. It was two years ago . . . about."

"Did you lose consistently?"

"Pretty well. It was stupid to go on, I suppose, but I kept on hoping—"

"Of course you did. How much?"

"I owed nearly two hundred pounds. But I'd lost more than that; my deposit account was pretty well cleared out."

"What was in it, before you started?"

"About five hundred pounds."

"Did you indulge in any other form of gambling?"

"No. You sound more like the chap for the prosecution," he added discontentedly.

"I know I do. How did you propose to recoup your losses?" asked Maitland, unmoved.

"By economizing, I suppose."

"A slow business. Did your employment at the Bank give you access to any funds?"

"If it had, I wouldn't—"

"We're taking your honesty for granted for the moment. Just answer the question."

"Well then, I was in Advance Department. It's all on paper; no cash."

"Thank you. Were you worried?"

"More fed up, really."

"Did your employers know of your difficulties?"

Bromley laughed. "Do you think I was likely to tell them?"

"Since you ask me, no."

"Well, I didn't."

"And then you met Miss Marston."

"Yes; I know what the old man thinks."

"Tell me, then."

"That I'm a fortune hunter. It wasn't like that." His voice softened as he spoke, and the sullen look—which Maitland had begun to think habitual—disappeared.

"Where did you meet her?"

"At the cinema. I suppose I picked her up," he added. The idea seemed to surprise him.

"How was that?"

"Mr. Warren had given me a pass for the AngIt cinema in Leicester Square; that meant I got VIP treatment, front row of the circle. Jo was there and—well—we just got talking during the interval. They were showing an old film, one of Giuditta's early ones, and Angelo wanted her to have a look at it."

"I see." He couldn't help wondering how Giuditta fitted into the "rather pure films" that Valenti was supposedly making now. "How soon did you get to know the people at the film studio?"

"Not until the night of the party, except from Jo talking about them the whole time. And except Major Cooke, of course."

"Who is he?"

"The Major? Oh, he's the—the financial side of Anglo-Italian. And I hadn't met him, exactly; just been in the room sometimes when he was talking to Mr. Warren. And Mr. Warren," he went on, anticipating Maitland's question, "is the Chief Controller on 'B' Section—the one I was in."

"I see. Did you know about the emeralds, as the prosecution say?"

"Well, I could have done, I suppose. For that matter, I could have known about them from the press, because I gather they've been well publicized. But it isn't the sort of thing I'd notice; I'm not much interested in precious stones."

"Not a good point, you think?"

"Not particularly. But it added up . . . oh, God, how it added up!"

It didn't seem altogether tactful to agree. "Let's get on to the night of the theft, then. You were already engaged to Miss Marston by the time the film was completed?"

"Yes, I—" He broke off, looking from Maitland to Horton, and then fixing his eyes on a point between the two of them. "Unofficially, I suppose I should say. I hadn't the money to buy a ring, and I wanted to get things straight before we told the old man. And I know—you don't have to tell me—that just makes things sound worse."

"Unfortunate," said Antony, in a tone of polite indifference. Geoffrey gave him a puzzled look, and Bromley said angrily:

"I'm just trying to be honest with you."

"I know." He pulled a bundle of used envelopes from his pocket, selected one that wasn't particularly battered, and began to scribble on the back. "Go on trying."

"Well, it was a celebration . . . the party, I mean. The film was called *Sunflower*—it was symbolic, or something," he added, as Maitland raised his head and seemed about to say "Why?" again.

"It sounds good value."

"Yes, I suppose—" His smile was rather strained, and faded altogether as he went on. "Jo was talking about it forever, but I never got a chance to see it, of course."

Antony suppressed an insane desire to say, "If you're here long enough—" because he supposed they didn't show you really new films in prison. The trouble was, he didn't want to believe Bromley; because if he was telling the truth the position was no less hopeless . . . but a good deal more unpleasant to accept. He got up and took a turn down the length of the room. Horton followed him with his eyes; from his expression he seemed undecided between amusement and exasperation.

"I understand you arrived at the studio at about nine o'clock."

"Yes." Roy hesitated, and spread his hands in a helpless gesture. "What is there to tell you, really?"

"Try to think of something," Maitland advised, tart again.

"Well then, it wasn't much of a show from my point of view; Jo seemed to regard herself as being on duty, so I didn't see much of her. I didn't know anyone else; they were quite friendly, but I wasn't all that interested."

"Did you see Giuditta go out to her dressing room?"

"No."

"That's something I hadn't thought about." Maitland halted his pacing. "Would you have known where to find her?"

"Yes, because there were a couple of dressing rooms being used as cloakrooms, and they were all down the same passage. There was a big star on the door of the one nearest the studio, and Jo said not to get in there by mistake. . . . Francis Eversley's room had a star too, but it was being used as the gents."

"A guest who hadn't had that explained to him—"

"I should think it would be pretty obvious. You couldn't mistake Eversley's room; there were masses of photographs, and all inscribed to 'darling Frank,' or something like that."

"I see. Well, if you didn't see Giuditta leave we'll have to get at it another way. The last time Jo came back to you from dancing with someone else, you were talking to Eversley. What had you been doing during the previous ten minutes or so?"

"Wandering about. I stood watching the dancing for a minute or two, then I moved from one group to another; the first lot were talking about the casting of a new comedy—disagreeing with it, so far as I could tell. I hadn't anything to add to that conversation, so I moved on a bit, and tagged on to a group who had some juicy scandal, only I didn't know either of the people concerned. Then I saw Eversley standing by himself, and thought it might be more amusing to join him. And *then* Jo came back."

"And Angelo left the studio."

"I didn't notice."

Maitland turned his head. "Were those times definitely established, Geoffrey . . . when Giuditta left the studio and when Angelo followed her?"

"Near enough," Horton told him. "Eight minutes between."

"And you've considered—of course you have!—that it might have been a publicity stunt."

"Well, it couldn't. Mr. Valenti came back for the doctor, and after that they weren't out of each other's sight until the police came," said Horton positively.

"Were there any goings and comings noticed from the dressing rooms?"

"That doesn't seem to be the sort of thing people take note of, not to remember the time, anyway."

"Someone noticed Giuditta; but that doesn't count, of course, if he was watching her. Anyway, it seems obvious that the thief must have returned to the studio before Angelo went out." As he spoke his eyes returned to rest thoughtfully on Bromley's face; Roy flushed and said awkwardly:

"I can't prove I was there all the time."

"Did no one remember the conversations you overheard?"

"Oh, yes. But not when they occurred. I suppose that was natural enough," he added gloomily.

"Had Eversley been in the studio all the time?"

"I don't know."

"Could he have planted the emeralds on you?"

"I've got to say 'yes,' I suppose. I'd have said no one could without my knowing."

"Who else?"

"If you mean, who was with us during the time until the police came, there was a chap called Ross, Michael Ross. And Larry Truscott, of course."

"Of course?"

"Jo was there," said Roy, a little impatiently.

"Had they met before?"

"No. Well, I don't think so. She seemed to know Ross quite well."

"Can you tell me anything about these three men that might help?"

"Nothing at all."

"Truscott?"

"Employment in a bank ought to imply a certain basic respectability, but it hasn't kept me out of trouble," said Roy bitterly.

"You must know more of him than that."

"Very little. We've been working together for a year. His home's in Shrewsbury."

"For heaven's sake, what's he like?"

"Nice enough. Not too overburdened with brains. I can't think what he's doing in A.D., as a matter of fact." Again he answered Maitland's question before it was uttered, saying wryly, "Advance Department. Where the Bank's bright young men are groomed for stardom."

"And Ross?"

"Someone said he was a journalist. He seemed to be on terms with most of the AngIt people."

"Any particular paper?"

"Free lance . . . I think."

"And that's all you can tell me."

"If I could help, as you call it, don't you think I would?" There was the rising note of excitement again; and again Maitland felt a tightening of his own nerves in sympathetic, if reluctant, understanding.

"If you had taken the emeralds——?"

"You don't believe me, do you?" The brief excitement died; his tone was flat. "Well, it's all the same."

"In that case, there's no harm in humoring me. If you had taken the emeralds, how would you have disposed of them?"

"I haven't the faintest idea."

"What are your hobbies?" Bromley gave him a blank look. "Do you walk . . . sail . . . ski . . . go mountaineering——?"

"I play tennis in summer; that's more my financial mark."

"Where do you take your holidays?"

"Here and there. Bournemouth last year. Torquay the year before."

"Not abroad?"

"No."

"Have you any connections with the Continent . . . through your family, for instance?" he added as Roy shook his head. And for the first time Bromley grinned at him with unaffected amusement.

"This is beginning to sound like a detective story. There's just my uncle and aunt, and they go down to St. Ives every year. Anyway, I don't see much of them, these days."

"The police asked you that, of course."

"I suppose you're still looking for the worst side of everything."

"I'm afraid so."

"Well, they did. But I can't honestly say they seemed very interested in the reply."

"They didn't press the question? No . . . I see." This time the words sounded anything but casual. The look he exchanged with Horton was almost startled, certainly surprised. "Look here, Bromley," he added earnestly, after a momentary hesitation, "you're sure you want me to go on with this? Because it would be much kinder to Miss Marston——"

"If I'd admit my guilt and have done with it," said Roy in
a hard voice.

"It couldn't prejudice your position. I mean . . . here you
are."

"And it would make it so much easier for her to start forgetting me. Are you sure it was Jo who asked you to come . . .
not the old man?"

"Quite sure."

"Forgive my asking." The chair scraped as he pushed it back
and came to his feet. "As for what you do, since you ask me,
I couldn't care less. If you can't understand that that's what
makes it so damnable—not being shut up here . . . not my life
being wrecked, and the problem of starting again . . . not
what anyone thinks of me . . . except Jo."

"I'm sorry," said Antony. His eyes were steady; he did not
seem conscious of the inadequacy of the remark. Bromley stood
staring at him for a moment, and then wheeled round and made
for the door. It was a measure of the warder's alertness that it
swung open at his approach.

Outside, there was still the spring sunshine. They found Jenny
curled up on the back seat of the Jaguar, with the workshop
manual on her knee. "I've quite made up my mind," she said,
looking up at them and smiling. "The timing isn't quite right.
I'll have to do something about it."

Geoffrey held the door open. "If that's meant to be tactful,"
he said, a trifle grimly, "you're wasting your time. Because I've
got some questions, and I'm jolly well going to ask them now."

"Oh, dear." Jenny slithered out of the car to join them. "That
sounds ominous. Won't it wait?"

"No, it will not!" said Geoffrey explosively.

Jenny turned to look at her husband. Just for a moment a
spark of anxiety seemed to disturb her serenity. "Wasn't it—
wasn't it a nice interview, darling?"

"I hate prisons," Antony said flatly. There seemed to be no
emotion behind the words, but his gaze lingered on her and he
let his thoughts drift for a moment, seeking—perhaps uncon-
sciously—a release from tension. Jenny looked well in tweeds,
and the greenish shade of her new suit was just what he would

have chosen for her; with the sun tangled in her brown curls she came as near to beauty as a man had a right to ask. "What's biting you, Geoffrey?" he said, without any change of expression.

"Well, first, what do you think of him?"

"Bright," said Antony. He sounded thoughtful. "Bright enough to jump to my points before I made them. Bright enough to load his answers, for that matter."

"I could have told you that," said Horton resentfully.

"I'm sure you could." His soothing tone was probably not intended to be appeasing, but at least he was looking at the other man now.

"Did you believe him?" Geoffrey demanded. "At one point I was sure that you did."

"He seemed to be giving us a straight enough story."

"But then just at the end—"

"The point struck you too, Geoffrey; don't play the innocent. The police thought he knew how to dispose of the necklace. Was there anything in the prosecution's case to indicate that?"

"Nothing at all."

"Then we needn't let it influence our opinion. I agree with you, I don't think he stole the emeralds; and for good measure —since Jenny will inevitably ask me as soon as she gets the chance—I think he's genuinely in love with Jo Marston."

"But what do you think you can do about it?" said Geoffrey.

"About his feelings, probably nothing," said Antony, maddeningly literal. Horton glared at him.

"Do you think there's any chance of finding grounds to re-open the case?" he asked, speaking slowly as though he were suddenly doubtful of Maitland's capacity to understand.

"Nothing's impossible. Always providing we don't starve to death in the meantime," he added, and pulled open the car door for Jenny to get into the driver's seat. "I noticed a likely-looking place for lunch about five miles back down the road," he told her, and further infuriated Geoffrey by refusing to revert to the subject, either during the meal or on the way back to town.

CHAPTER 3

Maitland got back to chambers, thinking himself late, and found that his four o'clock conference had been canceled after all. He took the news with surprising calm, merely slackening his pace a little as he went down the corridor to his own room. Old Mr. Mallory looked after him suspiciously, but as there was no one under him in the clerk's office in whom he would have felt it proper to confide, he kept to himself his opinion that there was something in the wind.

As for Antony, he was aware only of relief; there'd be time enough this evening to turn his mind to the troubles of a client whom he strongly suspected of having systematically defrauded his employers over a period of twenty years or so . . . an ingenious scheme, it had to be admitted, but in the long run not quite ingenious enough. He sat down at the desk and spread out his sheaf of envelopes, and after a while succeeded in identifying the one on which he had been scribbling that morning. When he had been staring at it vaguely for several minutes he came to the conclusion that as a source of inspiration it wasn't a success, and reached instead for the telephone and asked for New Scotland Yard.

Detective Chief Inspector Sykes of the Criminal Investigation Department was almost disconcertingly ready to stop work and talk to him. "I'm free for the next hour, Mr. Maitland, if you care to step round." There was an undercurrent of amusement in the slow, north country voice.

"Not on your life. That place depresses me. If there's somewhere we can get tea—"

"Brackett's is handy."

"As soon as I can get there," Antony promised. He hesitated a moment, eyeing his notes with dislike, and then went out, leaving them scattered across the desk.

Sykes was waiting for him in the basement café that was only a few minutes' walk from his office. Antony blinked a little, coming in from the sunlit street, and it was a moment before he saw the detective seated at a corner table. The Chief Inspector was a dark, square-built man with a placid disposition and a deceptive slowness of movement. "Neutral ground, Mr. Maitland?" he said with a half-smile in reply to Antony's greeting.

"Something like that," Maitland admitted; but he knew better than to regard this as an invitation to plunge straight to the point. Sykes had a strong sense of propriety, and all the conventional inquiries must be made and the weather commented upon before he considered it seemly to touch on anything that savored of business. These preliminaries served them while the tea was served and poured. The detective commandeered the sugar bowl and said in an interested way:

"Is it true there's a question of an appeal in the Bromley case, because of fresh evidence?"

"Now, what the hell do you know about that?" said Antony, not exactly annoyed, but a trifle disconcerted at having the initiative taken away from him.

"We hear things," said Sykes modestly. "Every now and then some information trickles through."

"Well, it's all wrong, anyway." He sounded disconsolate, and Sykes gave his sedate smile.

"A bit premature, like," he said, making the words a question.

"I went to see Bromley this morning," Antony told him. "I was going to ask you if you remembered the case."

"When a lady like Signora Giuditta gets robbed," said Sykes carefully, "there's always talk."

"So you remember the details." He spoke slowly, as though the subject was distasteful to him.

"I do. But what's your interest in all this, Mr. Maitland?" asked Sykes with his usual bluntness.

"Not a professional one."

The Chief Inspector seemed to find this comprehensible enough. "Then why are you concerning yourself?"

"I'm not at all sure; because I was asked, I suppose. Bromley's engaged to be married, and Miss Marston is persuasive." He paused, frowning. "I think I should have said 'no' straight away. But now I've had a talk with Bromley—"

"And so?" prompted Sykes as Maitland hesitated again. And held out his hand for his companion's empty cup.

"That's where you come in, Chief Inspector. Thanks," he added, receiving his cup again. And went on, almost diffidently, "I hope you're not going to snub me."

"Well, as to that, it all depends," said Sykes, his native caution reasserting itself.

"It's a very simple question," Maitland told him more cheerfully. "If Bromley had stolen the emeralds, how did you think he was going to dispose of them?"

Sykes made no attempt to reply to this immediately. He stirred his tea, sipped, and added another lump of sugar. Finally he replied with a question of his own. "Have you quite made up your mind to reopen the case, Mr. Maitland?"

"That sounds too official. I shall go on until I've satisfied myself there's no more to be done, I suppose."

"I'm still wondering . . . why?"

"I told you—"

"On the face of it, rather a slender reason." He raised his eyes and added deliberately, "I'm asking you what you know."

"Oh, for heaven's sake!" said Antony, exasperated. "Is that why you were so ready to see me?"

"Not altogether." Sykes maintained his unruffled air. "But you must admit, Mr. Maitland, when you talk to me there are usually reservations."

"Well, this time—" He broke off and added helplessly, "What's the use?"

"Very well then, you've no special knowledge." It was a concession made in the interests of peace, not because he believed what he was saying. "How do you propose to set about your inquiry?"

Antony gave him a doubtful look. "Bromley's background . . . the scene of the crime. I wish you'd answer *my* question."

" 'appen I will," said Sykes thoughtfully. "And 'appen I'll have one for thee, an' all."

"What sort of a question?" said Antony, as cautiously as the detective himself might have done. He wasn't quite sure what this sudden lapse into dialect portended.

"More a request, really." In his turn, Sykes sounded doubtful. "Mutual assistance," he said, and took the last piece of toast and bit into it in an absentminded way.

"That's all very well, but what can *I* do for you?"

"I'm not at all sure I ought to be encouraging you."

"I haven't seen much sign of it yet," said Maitland, suddenly amused by the situation. This was a new departure for Sykes, who was usually comfortably sure of himself; and if he didn't want to answer the question it was easy enough to say so.

"Well, I'll tell you." But even when he had got so far the Chief Inspector seemed unwilling to proceed. "We thought Bromley had a buyer all fixed up before the theft took place."

"You're not being particularly lucid, you know," said Antony, scowling at him. "A private buyer? Someone who knew the d'Albret emeralds and coveted them?"

"Nothing like that. I'll try again. During the last few years someone has been organizing jewel robberies much as they would a legitimate business, not only in London but all over the south of England. Smash-and-grab, climbers, the lot. First the choice of objective, then a detailed survey, and after that the actual job."

"Is that something new?"

"No. No, of course not. It's the scale of the operation, you see. We call it the Association."

"Good lord! You really take it seriously."

"That," said Sykes, "is the idea I was intending to convey." He seemed to have regained his customary placidity.

"But how can you know?"

"We have our methods." Sykes disregarded the skeptical tone. "Jewel robberies have been on the increase; that's significant in itself, because unless he has a market a thief is usually only too aware of the difficulty of getting what he thinks is a fair price. One way and another, it's got beyond being amusing."

Maitland was frowning. "You're postulating two quite separate sets of people."

"That's the way we see it. I don't suppose they even know each other, the scouts and the operatives."

"I still don't see—"

"The really convincing thing, Mr. Maitland—the thing that convinces me—is what's been happening lately when we've made an arrest. There wasn't one of them willing to talk and you know yourself that isn't natural, not when it so happens we've got a clear case." Sykes had seemed absorbed in what he was saying, but he must have been watching his companion's expression; he broke off now and said shrewdly, "That rings a bell with you, doesn't it?"

"It makes me think of Jim Arnold." Maitland spoke slowly, thinking it out. "He was the last of my lay clients while I was a junior; I expect that's why he rather stuck in my mind." But that wasn't the whole truth; what had stayed with him was a momentary expression, a look of fear.

"Lady Markley's diamonds. We never found them," said Sykes, nodding in an encouraging way.

"Well, I did my best to persuade him, and I remember I got the impression he might be scared of what would happen if he talked. But—this is really the point, Chief Inspector—he definitely said his family would be looked after; and he told me he was retiring when he came out."

"All right then. I could cap that story with half a dozen

others," said Sykes, gloomily triumphant. He picked up the teapot and shook it. "Do you want another cup?"

"Yes, please. Had you any positive proof that Bromley was one of these . . . operatives, did you call them?"

"Have you heard the evidence the prosecution offered?" asked Sykes dryly.

"Yes, I see," said Antony, discouraged.

"It seemed the obvious assumption. They seem to have all sorts on their books. The chaps who can persuade a well-known jeweler to bring a selection of rings to their hotel aren't going to go out next night and shin up a drainpipe."

"I see that, of course. But in this case you say Bromley did his own scouting."

"I think the way he got to know Miss Marston was contrived, but the spadework had probably been done before. Making an opportunity was up to him."

"If you want to know, I think he's really in love with her."

"Do you now?" said Sykes, obviously incredulous.

Maitland ignored the comment. "If you're right, these people find there are certain advantages in silence, even if they're caught and it means a longer sentence. They can trust the Association to take care of their dependents, and to hand over their share of the profits when they come out."

"Exactly."

"But that isn't enough . . . is it?"

"There'll be threats used, I wouldn't wonder. Nothing else could make them show quite such solidarity."

"That's what . . . why are you telling me all this?"

"You asked me," said Sykes, gently pointing out the obvious.

"I know. I thought I'd better make sure . . . I mean, if there was anything definite against Bromley. But . . . wait a bit! You talked about mutual assistance." He looked at the detective reproachfully. "What do you want?" he asked.

"I want you to know what you're up against; that's the first thing. And then if you're still determined to go ahead I want your cooperation."

"In what way?"

"I don't think you're going to find anything to prove Bromley's innocence. Wakefield had the case, and he wasn't in any doubt. Of course, you may be able to get more out of these Italians. A proper cough drop, this Valenti chap, from what Wakefield says, while as for the lady——"

"Giuditta?"

"That's right. But you're a bit of a linguist, aren't you?"

"I never had much Italian."

"I thought perhaps during the war——" said Sykes; and watched Maitland's intent look fade to blankness.

"That's a long time ago." And then he was suddenly voluble, and again Sykes observed the fact with more interest than he displayed. "Uncle Nick's more fluent; he's rather apt to dash off to Switzerland during the long vacation, and he has friends near the border. It's rather good value, really, if you can get him going." He paused, and grinned. "He has a Churchillian disregard for the niceties of pronunciation. But I can't see him taking on Giuditta, even if I asked him."

Sykes smiled too, in his sedate way. "I don't think you're going to get anywhere," he repeated. "But if you should come across anything to suggest the identity of the buyer——"

"I don't think that's very likely, do you?"

"Stranger things have happened. I thought if I was frank with you——" He let the sentence trail invitingly, and Antony grinned at him.

"You hoped it might encourage me to an equal candor. Well, I was telling you the truth: I don't know anything beyond the evidence, though I may not interpret it in quite the same way as you do. But if at any time in the future the position changes, I'll let you know all right."

"I shall be grateful," said Sykes, suddenly formal.

"I'm much more likely to advise you that I'm giving up the struggle. But since we're allies you won't mind telling me . . . what was Giuditta coshed with?"

Sykes seemed to be considering this, or perhaps it was the question of their alliance. There was something quizzical in his look. "A homemade sandbag," he said at last.

"An amateur affair?"

"Could be."

"Small enough to be carried?"

"There are ways," said Sykes.

"I'll take your word for it. And the mask?"

"Also homemade. Black stockinette. Ku Klux Klan effect. Both it and the sandbag were discarded in the dark corner of the corridor."

"And no help from either. Do you know anything about the three men who were talking to Bromley when the police arrived?"

"Only that they exist. Do you really think he was framed?"

"It's possible . . . isn't it?" His tone was challenging, and Sykes shook his head in a deprecating way.

"I won't argue with you, Mr. Maitland, seeing as how we've concluded a treaty," he said.

"Treaty be d-damned," said Antony crossly. But his irritation faded before the amusement in his companion's eyes. After all, the situation was not without its humor. He wondered for a moment what Uncle Nick would make of it, and decided he had no special desire to find out.

When he parted from Sykes he had an hour to spare before Jenny would be expecting him, and while he was waiting to cross the road to the bus stop an empty taxi came by. He hailed it on an impulse, and had to search hurriedly through his pockets until he found the sheet of paper on which he had written, among other things, Michael Ross's address. Then he sat, while the cab moved spasmodically westwards, and wondered whether it was a good idea after all. Ross was the only one of the people he planned to see who fitted into neither camp, whom he would not find tomorrow when he visited the Bank and the film studio, according to his present plan. On the other hand, he'd no real grounds for thinking he'd find the chap at home at this hour. Better have telephoned first. . . .

Later he was to wonder if things would have worked out any differently if he'd gone straight home.

His destination was a block of bachelor apartments in the Gloucester Road, and to judge by appearances free-lance journalism must pay reasonably well; though, come to think of it, Bromley had been rather vague about that. He found Ross's name on the board, and took the lift to the third floor. Flat E was at the end of the corridor. Everything seemed very quiet; too early, perhaps, for most of the tenants to have got back from work. Or else the soundproofing was unusually good.

He was already regretting the impulse that had brought him here, taking it for granted that this was a wasted journey; so that he was momentarily startled when the door swung open almost as soon as he had pressed the bell and a voice said, "What's the matter? Forgotten your key again?"

The man in the doorway was tall and very thin, dressed with an elegance that managed to remain casual; rather handsome, in fact, in a sharp-featured way. In spite of his obvious expectation of finding a friend on the threshold he showed no sign of surprise at being confronted instead by a stranger. Antony thought he had the coldest eyes that he had ever seen. Jo hadn't mentioned Ross's age, but he'd imagined him younger than this. Even so, his query was only a formality.

"Mr. Ross? I'm afraid I've come at a bad time."

"No. I'm waiting for him." The cold eyes were intent, unfriendly. "I'll give him a message," he offered; but even this apparent helpfulness had an air of calculation. From the room behind him music poured into the hallway, something modern and overconfident. Maitland became aware of annoyance.

"If he's expected—" he began, still mildly.

"I shouldn't wait, if I were you." And again there was an afterthought to soften his abruptness. "I've no idea how long he'll be."

"I should have telephoned first." The music swelled, so that he had to raise his voice to make himself heard. "Perhaps I could leave a note."

"As you like." He backed away from the door a little, giving Maitland a footing in the room, no more. It was a comfortably masculine apartment, perhaps a little self-consciously correct in its fittings, and almost big enough for the expensive stereo equipment that had been installed. The tall man's face was expressionless still. He made no move to control the volume of the music, so that their conversation proceeded on different levels, now in normal tones, now in something approaching a shout. "I gather you're not a friend of Michael's," he said.

"We've never met. A small matter of business," said Antony. As the other man's tone became more aggressive, his seemed quieter, more diffident. He endured a further hard scrutiny before the stranger moved aside and waved a hand in indifferent invitation towards the writing table.

There was a pad there, and a pencil. "Will you be seeing Ross?" said Antony, as he wrote.

"Oh, yes, I shall wait for him."

"Then perhaps you'd ask him—" He had printed his name and telephone number, and now he turned to look up at his companion as he spoke. And unmistakably, in the thin man's eyes there was a flash of recognition as he stared down at the paper. But the look was gone in an instant.

"Why not tell me when you want to come, Mr. Maitland? Michael can phone you if it isn't convenient."

Now, what the devil had got into the man, that he should suddenly decide to be helpful? "Tomorrow evening, then . . . after dinner . . . about nine-thirty?" said Antony hesitantly. The music's dominance underlined his irresolution. For a moment the hard eyes met his with a queer intentness; it was something of an effort to look away, down at the pad on the desk. He drew a circle around his name, put down the pencil carefully, and stood.

"I'll tell him." The tall man did not seem conscious of the pause before he spoke, or of the fact that the visitor was uneasy. "Can I also tell him why you want to see him?"

"Oh, I don't think . . . I won't worry you."

"You're a lawyer." The stranger was abrupt again.

"I'm afraid you have the advantage of me, Mr.—?"

"Let's leave it that way, shall we?" His tone was openly mocking now. "So long as you don't want to serve a writ, or anything like that."

"I'm afraid that wouldn't be my province." Antony began to move towards the door. "It's just that I think he can help me," he said; and turned his head to meet the other man's cold and questioning look. "If he will," he added gently, and stepped out onto the landing.

He did not look back again as he walked towards the lift, but for some reason it was difficult to maintain even so much detachment.

Thinking about it on his way home, he decided it was the music that had set him on edge. Something with sharp corners—angular, that was a better word—he just hadn't been in the mood. The rest was imagination; why shouldn't the fellow know his name, anyway? If he really did.

All the same, when it came to telling Jenny he felt oddly disinclined to do so. Not that there was any need, he told himself, to say anything except that an appointment had been made, and Ross might phone to change it. There wasn't any need to make a production of Sykes's revelations, either. "They seem to be running a sort of underground welfare state," he said, when at last he got round to it; he'd spent the evening meditating on the misdeeds of his client, Mr. Longman, so that was a good enough excuse—if he needed one—for not having brought up the subject before.

Jenny gave him one of her long, candid looks. The serenity of her gray eyes was untroubled; there was no reason for him to add, defensively, "Rather amusing, really."

"But that's just one side of it," she objected. "If you'd said totalitarian government—"

"I expect you're right." It was obvious, of course, so why attempt to skirt the subject? "But it can't matter to us, love. I mean, this idea of Sykes's is all nonsense, you know."

"Is it?"

"Yes, of course. I suppose there's a faint chance of finding something that would help Bromley . . . and when I say faint I mean almost invisible. I've no intention of going beyond my brief."

"Poor Jo," said Jenny, and sighed extravagantly. Antony gave her a suspicious look, which she met with an innocent one that only increased his distrust. It wasn't until later, when he was on the edge of sleep, that she returned to the matter, saying drowsily, "I always thought Inspector Sykes was such a sensible man." He wasn't sure whether, on second thoughts, she was agreeing with his own estimate of the situation, but when he remembered the remark next day it was with a vague uneasiness.

CHAPTER 4

Anglo-Italian Films had set up their studio soon after the war ended on part of an airfield at Cricklewood for which neither government nor industry could find any further use. The big hangar could be adapted without much expense, and they were able to acquire enough land for their purpose before the housing boom got going. There were disadvantages, of course: the hangar, even when gaily painted, could not be regarded as a thing of beauty, and the war-surplus Nissen huts which had been acquired as "temporary" offices were always too hot or too cold. "But why do we care?" said Angelo, with his usual buoyancy. "Being artists, these things are unimportant."

Maitland went out by train on Friday morning. Jo had told him they started early when work was in progress, but he had his doubts about that and was inclined to dawdle on his way from the station. Another fine morning, but there were clouds banking up to the southwest; it would probably rain later on.

Jo came down to the gate to vouch for him. Her hair was tied back in a ponytail, and she was wearing an unlikely-looking print dress with her coat slung casually round her shoulders.

46

With the heavy makeup her face looked strange to him; he thought perhaps it was the mascara that altered her expression so completely.

He followed her back across the tarmac, past the shell of an old-fashioned pub and the facade of a Welsh chapel which stood side by side in unlikely proximity. "Giuditta's still in her dressing room; they had to change her hair style this morning. But I told Angelo . . . you won't have to explain." She was hurrying him along towards a door at the back of the main building, but she turned her head now and gave him a brief, searching look. "Did you see Roy?"

"Yesterday morning."

"Is he well?"

"Yes, quite well." The inadequacy of the words angered him, but what else could he say? He's shut away, and he's hating it. Even this little freedom our life gives us . . . to take the bus instead of the train . . . to be late if we choose . . . to buy a different newspaper, or pick up a paperback from the rack outside the bookshop . . .

He felt her hand on his arm, a light, apologetic touch. "I'm sorry," said Jo. "I didn't mean to bother you. Be careful through here, it's a bit dark."

They went from the sunshine into a narrow passage. "Is this the door you used on the night of the party?" he asked.

"No, this one was locked. We only use it when we're shooting at the west end of the studio; we shall come in behind the cameras."

He had expected a scene of frenzy, but there was a queer kind of calmness in the studio that came as a complete surprise, as though everything were being played in slow motion. Later he was to realize that this was a transient effect, the eye of the storm perhaps. The cameras seemed to be focused on a suburban dining room, but there was nobody on the set. Beyond the range of the lights a number of figures could be dimly seen; probably the actors, because they seemed to be fully dressed, while the men who were arguing halfheartedly around the cameras were all in shirt sleeves and anything but elegant. The main animation came from a small, balloon-like man with a shock of white hair, who was bounding around them in an agitated way, apparently exhorting the camera crew to greater efforts. Jo went up behind him and said "Mr. Valenti" in his ear, so that he spun round and clasped his hands on his chest in a mute parody of terror.

"Giuseppina!" he exclaimed reproachfully. And then, peering past her, "But certainly, I come."

"Thank God," said a voice, a little too audibly. Someone else muttered, *"Now* we shall get somewhere." Angelo drew himself up to his full height and directed over his shoulder a look of such burning reproach that the entire crew should have sunk through the floor for shame; then he turned, putting the whole unsavory business behind him, and stalked across to where Antony was standing. "I am Angelo Valenti," he proclaimed dramatically, leaving Jo only half the introduction to perform. *"Piacere,"* he added, with so delighted a smile that Antony should have had no excuse for doubting that he meant exactly what he said.

"I'm afraid I'm disturbing you."

"Not so much as the *signorina* will disturb me if I do not do as she ask." Angelo was philosophical. "Besides, there is trouble —always there is trouble with the camera. They are so stupid," he said, raising his voice and directing a venomous look at the shirt-sleeved men, who took no notice of him whatsoever. The actors had moved a little away, and now there was a murmur of talk. They were obviously resigned to the delay, almost apathetic.

"What a pity," said Antony unoriginally. The impulse to imitate Angelo's extravagances was almost irresistible.

"Pazienza." The little man shrugged. "If it is not this it is that." Even in the dim light his face glowed pinkly; he had a childlike look; in view of his name it was impossible to avoid the word "cherubic." A cherub with Saint Vitus's dance, Antony decided; and was silent because, for the moment, there seemed to be nothing to say.

"I'm going to get some coffee," said Jo. "I'll ask Betty to bring you some." She paused, and then added, "Don't forget, you promised." There was no way of telling which of the two men she was addressing.

"*E veramente peccato.*" Angelo was looking after her. "The young man is a bad lot, I think. Do you know him, *signore?*"

"We've met. Just once."

"Well, I admit, I did not myself think ill of him."

"That is what I want to ask you, Signor Valenti. Do you now think he stole the emeralds?"

"We will go over here," said Angelo, taking his arm in a friendly way, "and we will talk together."

"Over here" proved to be the most remote corner of the studio; there was a circle of chairs and a standard lamp which Angelo switched on with the air of one performing a successful conjuring trick. "You have been talking," said Angelo, shaking his head as over the folly of a dear friend, "with the little Giuseppina."

"She said she explained the position," said Antony hopefully.

"She talked to me, yes, a long time. *Non ne capisco niente,* but I do not want any more explanations," Angelo told him firmly.

That seemed to be invitation enough. "I'd like to know what you thought of Bromley."

"I thought him a good match for her. I thought in an English bank a man must be respectable." An expressive gesture mourned his lost illusions.

"And when you met him?"

"A nice young man. But with so many who come, there is no time to know more."

"That was the only time you met him, then . . . the night of the party?"

"I have seen him at the *tribunale,*" said Angelo mournfully. His capacity both for feeling and for expressing emotion was apparently unlimited.

"Tell me about the party, then. Miss Marston said it was a celebration."

"The end of a film . . . always we celebrate. But such a film—!"

"*Sunflower?*" said Antony intelligently.

"You have heard of it, then. A masterpiece, *signore.* Though I must admit"—he gestured widely—"this one will be better.

A greater insight, a greater sympathy . . . but this you do not
wish to know?"

"The evening the emeralds were stolen—"

"Everyone was coming. It was an event, you will agree. And
Giuditta so beautiful!" He seemed rapt for a moment in contemplation of a vision.

"Did you see her go out to her dressing room?"

"Yes, I did. And I think, now I shall tell her that Patrick
Moore is not the leading man for her next picture. Watching
him, I am sure of this . . . he is too young, you understand,
but this I do not tell her. So I am talking with a lady, and when
it is fitting for me to leave her I follow Giuditta. And it is of
no use to ask, how long was this? because I do not know."

Altogether, this seemed only too likely. "Did you see anyone
coming back into the studio as you went out?"

"No one at all." His eyes became round and tragic. "I go to
the door of the dressing room; it is open a little and so I go in.
And there on the floor, my Giuditta . . . dead!"

"Dead?" echoed Antony, startled. It seemed unlikely that no
one had thought to mention this development.

"I tell you what I think, what I feel. At that moment I am
dead too."

"So what did you do?" It seemed callous not to spend more
time on Angelo's feelings, but an idea had come to him and he
wanted to follow it through.

"I go back to the studio and I find the good Dr. Carr. It is he
who tell me I should telephone the police. And this I will say,
they are here at once . . . almost before I can put down the
receiver."

"Where are the dressing rooms?"

"Over there." Angelo gesticulated, but it was difficult to see
anything beyond the circle of lamplight.

"Could anybody have got in or out without coming through
the studio?"

"The police say no. The doors were locked and the commissionaire had the keys."

Now, why had that suddenly seemed important? "But you

found the doctor without difficulty? You did not have to look for him?"

"He was just by the door that leads to the dressing rooms."

"Do you know where Roy Bromley was standing at that time?"

Angelo shrugged; he seemed to be getting tired of what at first he had found a pleasant diversion. "So many questions. How should I know that?"

"Well, I can tell you." The pleasant voice, coming from the outer darkness, made Angelo jump again. A tall man moved into view, walking carefully with a cup in either hand. "Sugar in the saucer," he said. "I hope you don't mind *café au lait,* it's all that was going. At least it's hot."

"Ah, Francesco." Angelo's relief at the interruption was a little too obvious. "This is Signor Maitland, of whom you have heard."

"I have indeed." Francis Eversley turned, and smiled; and Antony saw with something of a shock that he was even better-looking at close quarters than he appeared on the screen, though not, perhaps, quite so young. Dark hair and a thin, aquiline face; perfect grooming; the sort of person, in fact, to make a man uneasily aware of his own limitations. Even now, in ordinary conversation, his voice had something of a caressing note, but Maitland wasn't at all sure that the smile was altogether without malice. He took the cup that was being held out to him, murmured his thanks, and awaited developments. "I gather Jo had an ulterior motive when she made me her messenger boy," said Eversley, and seated himself in the empty chair on Angelo's right.

"She cannot believe," said Angelo sadly, "that this young man of hers is a thief."

"And it seems that Mr. Maitland agrees with her? Is that right?"

"Oh, I don't know." Antony was vague. "I've not much to go on, yet."

"But you think we can help you form an opinion. We really know very little of this young man."

"You can tell me, at least, the circumstances of the crime."

"Yes. You were asking, if I remember, where Bromley was standing when the police arrived. He was with me, you know."

"So I've been told."

"Well, let's see. I've been ordered to help you. . . . Jo's a delightful girl, don't you think?"

"Delightful."

"And so refreshingly levelheaded. Or so one thought."

"He means," said Angelo, "that she does not have a crush on him, as so many young girls do." His face was as bland as ever; as always when he became colloquial, the words sounded like a quotation. And obviously their intent was spiteful.

"Well—" said Eversley. For a moment his smile was uncertain; he looked as though he had been given the wrong cue. "We were a couple of yards from where you're sitting, Mr. Maitland."

"How long had you been together when Giuditta was found?"

"I'm not much better on times than Angelo is, but I don't think we can have been together more than a minute or so before Jo came back from the dance floor."

"And then?"

"Those two other young men joined us . . . Ross and Truscott." He paused, and now his amusement was evident again. "I'm afraid it was unkind of me: Ross may have intended to join us in any event, but I saw him crossing the studio and called him over."

"Unkind?" echoed Antony vaguely.

"His attentions to Jo were so very marked, and Bromley so clearly resented them."

"Oh, I see. And then you were all together until the police arrived?"

"We were." Eversley smiled delightedly. "You're wondering how to wrap it up, Mr. Maitland. You're wondering which of us had the opportunity of planting the emeralds in Bromley's pocket."

"You read me like a book," Antony agreed amiably.

"I may as well tell you straight away, you'll have to take my word for this. The others haven't such an eye for a scene as

I have, I suppose. Jo was on Bromley's right, I was on his left; the emeralds were found in the left-hand pocket of his jacket. That much we're all agreed about." Maitland had pulled an envelope out of his pocket, and was looking at it rather helplessly. "I'll show you, shall I?" Eversley offered. "This is how we were standing."

$$\text{Bromley} \quad o$$

$$\text{Jo} \quad o \qquad\qquad o \text{ Eversley}$$

$$o \qquad\qquad o$$
$$\text{Truscott} \qquad \text{Ross}$$

"I see," said Maitland doubtfully, as he received his envelope again.

"Looks obvious, doesn't it? But at one point Truscott moved across to light a cigarette for Bromley. He's left-handed, by the way, so when he put his right hand back into his pocket with the matchbox . . . do you see?"

"Yes, but wouldn't you have noticed if he'd transferred the emeralds?"

"No, because Ross dropped his lighter. He must have had a hole in his pocket, and when he put it back it fell right through."

"You said Truscott—"

"We were all smoking. He lit Jo's cigarette, and Bromley's. Ross lit mine and his own."

"Could he have dropped his lighter deliberately, as a diversion?"

"Well, I shouldn't think so. It made a frightful clatter, and he seemed as startled as any of us. And then while he was picking it up the police arrived, and neither Bromley nor I had eyes for anything else."

"You were facing the door then; the other two men had their backs to it?"

"That's right. But someone called out—facetiously, you know, thinking it was all part of the fun—'Gee, boss, de cops' . . . or something equally unlikely. I think we must assume that whoever had the emeralds in his pocket was pretty much on the alert."

"You seem to have done a good deal of thinking about this, Mr. Eversley. Does that mean you doubt Bromley's guilt?"

"Not at all. But the police inquiries were thorough, they didn't take anything for granted. That's why I think you can take it that Jo's idea is wrong."

"All wrong, *signore*," echoed Angelo, unhappily.

"But still, I suppose, you would like the rest of the story." Eversley's eyes were thoughtful. "I moved away from the group then, to meet the Divisional Inspector—"

"Leaving Ross on Bromley's left," said Antony, consulting his envelope.

"Precisely." There was a note of satisfaction in his tone. "But the one certain thing, Mr. Maitland, is that when the police searched us it was Bromley who had the emeralds."

"The search was made at your suggestion, was it not?" Now it was Maitland who sounded reflective. And he thought that Eversley's color heightened as he answered, though in the lamplight it was hard to be sure.

"It seemed the best thing—"

"Yes, no doubt. Could anyone else have approached Bromley in the meantime?"

"He says not, and so do the others. It wasn't very long, you know. At that stage it was just a matter of turning out our pockets, and the ladies opening their handbags. And, as it happened, they didn't have to carry it any further."

"That poor Giuseppina," mourned Angelo, in a minor key.

"Yes, well . . . better to find out what the fellow's like," said Eversley.

"But, Francesco, she does not believe!"

"I wonder."

"You think she deceives herself?" This seemed to be a new idea to Angelo. "Then Signor Maitland must make her believe the truth," he added more briskly. "It is always best to know the truth, is it not, Francesco? Even when it is unpleasant."

"I suppose it is," said Eversley shortly.

"But what if she's right?" Maitland put forward the suggestion with a deprecating look from one of his companions to the other.

"You don't seriously believe that."

"I'm trying to find out," Antony reminded him.

"But the evidence—"

"What do you know about the other two men in the group?"

"Young Truscott only found himself here by chance; your idea, wasn't it, Angelo?"

"Sì," said Angelo, still despondent.

"And Michael Ross?"

"Him we have known for some time." The idea seemed to cheer him a little.

"How long?"

"Two months . . . three months . . . how long, Francesco?"

"I don't know," said Eversley impatiently.

"Is he connected with the film business?"

"No. That is, I do not think—"

"Cooke introduced him." Eversley seemed to reach a decision. "Said he was a journalist, or some such thing. Let's ask him."

"And I will go back to my camera," said Angelo, his troubles forgotten. "If it is arranged you must come, *subito*." He bounced happily to his feet. "But first, Francesco, it is for the quarrel, you remember? You must be a little untidy . . . your hands through your hair . . . your tie . . . so." His hands fluttered; obviously it gave him some obscure pleasure to suggest the changes. "You have been drinking," he added, as reproachfully as though the accusation were true. "And so you must disorder yourself a little."

"All right!" said Eversley. And then, more amiably, "You're the boss." He was smiling as he watched Angelo trot down the studio towards the set, but when he turned to Maitland again there was no trace of amusement in his eyes. After a moment he said, "Are you going to ask Truscott and Ross about me?" but somehow Antony didn't feel that the question was genuinely uppermost in his mind.

"I doubt if they could tell me what I really want to know."

The statement seemed to startle Eversley, but at the same time to reassure him. "My financial position, perhaps?" he inquired, sarcastically.

"Is it relevant?" Antony sounded surprised.

"No. No, of course it isn't."

"Then—" He shrugged and spread his hands in a gesture as expansive as any of Angelo's.

"I've gone along with you to humor Jo," said Eversley. "But it's a damned uncomfortable position, you know, once you start assuming Bromley's innocence."

"Are the emeralds insured?" Maitland wasn't quite sure how his companion would take the question.

"I don't see . . . what are you getting at?"

"A few facts, if I can."

"Motive? I see. There's nothing wrong with our financial position, you know."

"Our—?"

"The company. And as for insurance, that's Cooke's department really."

"Is he here?"

"I expect he's in his office. An industrious type," said Eversley in a languid way that no longer rang true. "Shall I—?"

Before Maitland could reply there was Angelo's voice calling, "Francesco," down the length of the studio; and at the same time a small man with dark, heavy eyebrows that gave him the look of a nervous Mephistopheles came into the studio from the passage that led to the back door. Eversley came to his feet, and Maitland followed suit more slowly, reaching up with his left hand to put his coffee cup out of harm's way on a shelf behind his chair. "Over here, Andrew," Frank Eversley called imperatively; and added as the little man came toward them, "This is Mr. Maitland; Angelo wants him to be given every facility."

"Jo said there was someone to see me."

"Well, here you are. As far as I can tell he thinks I had designs on Giuditta's emeralds." And almost before he had finished, Eversley had turned and left them, striding down the studio toward the waiting set.

"You mustn't say things like that, you know," said the little man severely.

"For the record," Antony told him, "I have an open mind. Are you Major Cooke?"

"I am."

"Antony Maitland. Did Miss Marston explain—?"

"Mr. Valenti did. Maitland? Maitland? I've heard of you," said Cooke, as if the words were an accusation.

"Can we talk here, or are they going to start shooting?" said Antony, almost as uneasily as he might have done if the cameramen had been loading their rifles. He glanced over his shoulder as he spoke, and saw that Jo had returned and was crossing the studio; she seemed in no way daunted by the noisy argument that had broken out again with Angelo as its center.

"Not for some time yet." The flicker of a smile disturbed Cooke's gravity. "At least, I doubt it. We can sit down if you like"—he made no move towards the group of chairs—"but this is a fool's errand you're on, do you realize that?"

The fact might be self-evident, but he saw no reason to agree with it. "Are you so sure of Bromley's guilt?"

"There seems no reason to doubt it."

"Except that his denials are . . . rather convincing."

"They didn't convince the jury," Cooke pointed out sharply.

"But either of the other two young men might have had an equal motive, for all we know."

"You might have had a motive; I might have had a motive," said the Major irritably. "I don't see what difference that makes."

"Tell me about Michael Ross," suggested Maitland.

"Why should you think I know anything about him?"

"Don't you?"

"He's a free-lance journalist," said Cooke, as though that should finish the matter.

"When did you meet him?"

"Couple of months ago. No, more than that, around the end of January. I ran into an old acquaintance of mine—John Drayton, fellow I was at school with—in Regent Street one afternoon. And Ross was with him."

"A casual meeting, then."

"Yes, of course."

"But you have become better acquainted with Ross since then?"

"Oh, yes."

"How was that?"

"It would have been difficult to avoid doing so, without open rudeness." Cooke seemed both puzzled and uneasy. "He was fascinated by the background of the film company—which is not, you know, Mr. Maitland, an uncommon reaction; but in his case there might be more justification for his interest."

"A journalist, you said. Was he looking for material?"

"So he said."

"Is that why he was asked to the party, to write it up?"

"It was Mr. Valenti's doing, but I believe that was in his mind."

"I see. Did you tell this to the police?"

"Nobody asked me," said Cooke simply.

"It didn't occur to you . . . no, I suppose not."

"*I* didn't think he had the faintest intention of writing about the film," said Cooke defensively. "But I did think he'd fallen for Jo Marston; I still think so."

"All the same—"

"You're determined to make trouble," the little man told him petulantly. "Anyone can say these things—"

"What things, Major?"

"That—that someone else might have stolen the emeralds. It doesn't make it true. And these further inquiries might lead to a most damaging scandal."

"Not unless Miss Marston's right about Bromley being innocent."

"Perhaps you don't quite realize our position, Mr. Maitland." Cooke was severe again. "To people in the public eye the wrong kind of publicity—"

"Unfortunately, there are two sides to the question . . . aren't there?" said Maitland, who had a good deal of sympathy with this point of view, but no intention of saying so.

"Yes, I suppose."

"Now take Ross, for instance: do you know any of his friends?"

"I can't recall—"

"A tall man, very thin," Antony began, but had no need to amplify the description.

"You've met Drayton?"

"Apparently. He didn't tell me his name."

"Well, I didn't get the impression they were close friends, you know. Rather offhand, if you know what I mean. In fact, I seem to remember Ross telling me that he only knew Drayton in the most casual way."

"Was he at the party too?"

"He may have been asked. I didn't see him there."

"What is his occupation?"

"I have no idea at all." Cooke's tone had sharpened. "I may have known him for a long time but we are by no means intimate. Nor do I see—"

"Never mind," said Antony wearily. Again he was finding himself in sympathy with the other man's reaction.

"And what was all that about suspecting Frank?"

"Not my idea."

"He said—"

"A joke, perhaps. Not a very good one." He hadn't a shred of excuse for any more personal questions, he knew, and Cooke was a touchy little man, only too ready to resent it when he stepped out of line. He felt suddenly impatient with the assignment; with Jo for asking his help when there was nothing he could do, and with himself for his rash agreement. And most of all, perhaps, with Chief Inspector Sykes, who had put ideas into his head so that now he was imagining . . . "He told me you'd know if the emeralds were insured," he said, becoming aware of the Major's speculative look.

"Well, of course they were. There's a good deal of money tied up there, Mr. Maitland," he added, suddenly—and surprisingly

—confidential. "And not so easy to get a price at a moment's notice."

"How much does the necklace weigh?"

"That has really nothing to do with it. The emeralds are unusually large, for unflawed stones, that is. But besides the intrinsic value there is the setting—a thing of real beauty. And the romantic history, of course."

"I was thinking rather what the chances were of Bromley not knowing it had been planted on him."

"Well, as to that, I have to admit it isn't *heavy*. But I really don't think—"

"No, you told me. How many ways are there in and out of the studio?"

Cooke seemed a little flustered by the abrupt change of subject. "The main door," he said. "That's at the far end, behind the set. It's locked today, or should be. The door I came in by: rather a hole-in-the-corner entrance, but useful. And the door to the dressing rooms."

"Can you get out that way; outside, I mean?"

"There's a door at the end of the corridor."

"The night of the party—"

"The main door was open, with a commissionaire on duty. The others were locked and he had the keys. I was there when the police questioned him. And if you want to complete the picture, Mr. Maitland," he added—and for some reason he sounded triumphant—"the windows of the dressing rooms are far too small for anyone to get through. Only the ventilators open, you see."

"Was there a commissionaire on the gate too?"

"Yes, but he wasn't checking up on people, just letting them through."

"And—just one other thing—where was the dancing?"

Cooke frowned. "Where the set is now; the end of the studio nearest the main door."

"Thank you," said Maitland. "That's very helpful. Now, Mr. Valenti told me I should be able to see Giuditta. Do you think—?"

"I'll show you." It might have been relief that made him so eager. He darted off towards the door that led to the dressing room corridor, with Maitland at his heels, but before they reached it Giuditta had made her entrance.

CHAPTER 5

It occurred to Antony later that each of the people he had seen that morning had come in as though on cue, and he amused himself with the thought that this wasn't merely a coincidence— or in the case of Cooke and Eversley the consequence of Jo's promptings—but that long association with the film world had given them a special instinct in the matter, so that to choose the right moment had become completely natural. But when he first saw Giuditta his only conscious thought was a vague wonderment as to why this magnificent creature should have chosen to attire herself in a sacklike dress made up in an unattractive mud-colored material; with the fact that her feet were bare and her dark hair loose on her shoulders he had no quarrel at all.

Asked to describe her he would have said—and did say later to Jenny—that she was tall and rather sturdily built, with skin as brown as though she lived in the sunshine, and warm brown eyes. Pressed for details, he might have admitted that her eyes were her only real beauty, that her mouth was too full, her face not a perfect oval; but the fact remained that she glowed like a jewel in the dusty setting of the studio, with a brilliance for which her appearance on the screen had in no way prepared him.

And, incredibly, no one else in the studio took any notice at all except Major Cooke, who was babbling an introduction. In the background Angelo's voice rose almost to a wail; Jo seemed to have joined in the discussion, and the waiting actors too; the cameramen sounded as acrimonious as ever. Giuditta looked up at him and said in a soft voice:

"Jo has spoken of you, *signore*. Here I am!" She seemed to be congratulating him, perhaps in the simple belief that it was a privilege to meet her, and Antony, bowing over her hand, abandoned himself to his own chameleon-like tendency to take color from his surroundings.

"Signorina—" (It was awkward, wasn't it, this habit of using only a Christian name?)

"But I am not a girl," she protested. "Is this to flatter me, or do you not know I am married?"

What had Jo said . . . they lived together? "Signora Valenti," he said doubtfully, and this time was answered with a ripple of laughter and a decisive shake of the head.

"I have not seen my husband for five . . . six years. He is a dull man, we will not speak of him." She paused, as though paying her defunct marriage a small tribute of silence, but when she raised her head again he saw a gleam of amusement in her dark eyes. "Life is much more amusing with Angelo," she confided. "Now you shall tell me what I can do for you."

At some time during this exchange Major Cooke had slipped away. Maitland released the brown hand that was still lying in his. "Signora Giuditta, *lei è molto gentile.*"

She drew away a little, looking up at him with an affectation of surprise. "How is this? I thought you English, yet you speak my name as it should be spoken; which is not easy, I think."

"It is itself music, *signora.*" He accompanied the words with an extravagant gesture, but rather spoiled the effect by grinning.

"Now I will tell you," said Giuditta impressively. "All these years since I come to your gray country . . . you know I am a child when I come from Italy, *signore?"*

"Certamente," said Antony, who knew nothing of the kind.

"At first I would make them—the newspapers—print always *joo*-DEET-*tah* beside my name, as the dictionary shows it; then, surely, it is not so difficult. But still there is always a hardness . . . they do not try," she complained.

"Unforgivable."

"So I think. But if we are to talk together, *signore,* we should sit down." Without waiting for a reply she turned and walked gracefully ahead of him to the corner with the group of chairs. When she had seated herself she stretched out her legs and stared pensively at her bare feet. "Angelo will be angry," she said. The idea seemed to cause her a vague feeling of regret.

"But I've talked to him already; he was very helpful." That wasn't precisely true, but at least he hadn't been obstructive.

Giuditta shook her head at him. "Not for that. It is that I have forgotten my shoes again," she explained. "Does it look so odd?"

"Uncomfortable, perhaps, on the wooden floor."

"No, I am so used, you see. Why should I not do as I like? But Angelo says it is to look as a peasant. And then for the film I must wear this dress!" Her tone was properly scornful of the unreasonableness of men. "But I do not need shoes for the scene we are to play, so perhaps he will not notice," she added, more cheerfully. "Now, *signore,* this poor little Jo—"

"Signora, you saw the man who attacked you."

She had a frown for his sudden earnestness. "For a moment only. And never his face."

"But you were able to describe him . . . his height . . . the way he moved."

"So vaguely. It could have been anyone."

"Not quite anyone," he said seriously. Giuditta found his eyes fixed intently on her face, but in an impersonal way that made her wonder if he had—incomprehensibly—forgotten who she was.

"Non capisco," she said, shaking her head at him.

"It could not have been . . . Mr. Eversley, for instance."

"I should like a light for my cigarette, *signore."* Her voice was gently plaintive. He saw now that she had pulled out a packet of Players from a pocket in the sacklike dress.

"Yes, of course." He fumbled for matches, struck one, held it for her. A deliberate evasion? He realized confusedly that he hadn't the least idea. As she leaned closer he caught the faintest breath of perfume, elusive, tantalizing.

"Grazie."

"Prego." The response was automatic; his mind was fixed on the question that hadn't been answered yet. He watched her as she leaned back again and drew on her cigarette until it was burning with an even glow. "I asked you, *signora*—"

If his persistence disappointed her she gave no sign of it. Instead she said as though she had just made a delightful discovery, "I have heard of the third degree."

"Per favore—" She laughed aloud at his downcast look. *"Signora,* you said you would help me."

"And it means so much to you?"

"If there has been an injustice—" But he stopped there because he knew he could never explain.

"You do not think that what you said to me might be . . . injustice?"

"It wasn't a statement." He was aware of being outmaneuvered, and he spoke with a sort of desperation. "Who will tell me anything, if I don't ask?"

"The man I saw was not so tall as Frank Eversley, *signore."*

"But you were not in a position to identify him as Bromley."

"The description fitted, that is all. As it fitted twenty, thirty, fifty other men who were here that night."

"How long were you in the dressing room before the thief came in?"

"One minute . . . two." Her gesture was vague enough to convince him that it would be useless to press for a more precise answer. "I sit at the dressing table, and I hear the door open but I think it is Angelo who comes. And when I look up the man is right behind me, and it is too late."

"A dreadful experience."

"Certainly it is a dreadful experience," she assured him earnestly. Perhaps his sympathy had sounded a trifle forced. "When I am not unconscious any more there is the doctor, and Angelo, who is saying, 'Tell me . . . tell me'—it is not helpful, that. And then there is the police."

"But you think it was Bromley." His tone was flat, but there was a question in his eyes.

"Why do you ask me this? You do not like the answer if I tell you, I think."

"I see."

"I am sorry, *signore*." Her tone was warm again with sympathy. "It is foolish to concern yourself unless . . . it is for Jo?"

"I think if it were," said Maitland, amused in spite of himself, "I should be content to have Bromley safely in prison."

"Yes, that is logical. But you English . . . sometimes there is a—a generosity in these matters that is admirable, perhaps, but not very sensible." He contented himself with grinning at her by way of answer. "It is not a laughing matter," she told him.

"No, indeed. Do you know Larry Truscott . . . Michael Ross?"

"The two young men who are also Jo's suitors? I know Michael, of course. Larry I have met that night."

"Could either of them be the man who hit you?" He spoke stubbornly, but with a note of apology as well.

"Neither is so tall as Frank. But why look further, when they have found my emeralds?"

This time he refused the digression. "I suppose you know nothing of Larry Truscott."

"A nice young man." A shrug dismissed him.

"And Ross?"

"Inquisitive; but that is natural."

"You know him well?"

"No, and no, *signore*." The suggestion seemed to offend her. "It is business, if he wishes to write about us, and Angelo says—"

"What did Angelo say?" Maitland prompted, after a moment's pause.

"That we cannot afford to ignore publicity." Giuditta said this with a pleased air; as though she were pulling a fast one, thought Antony sadly.

"Do you know a man called Drayton? John Drayton."

"He comes here sometimes. He is a friend of *il Maggiore*."
Something in her voice alerted him; he looked at her sharply, but maintained his casual tone.

"Do you like him?"

"*Così così.*"

"Why not?"

"I did not say—" She dropped the end of her cigarette on the floor and gave him an appealing look. "If you will tread on it, *signore*—"

He had to get up to do so. "You were hardly enthusiastic," he said dryly.

"It is just that—that he is not my kind of man."

"Do you know what his occupation is?"

"How should I, when I know him hardly at all? In fact, I have not seen him since this year began; I remember so well because there was a party for the New Year."

"One long round of pleasure," said Maitland absently.

"*Santa vacca!* And work, *signore*. Hard, hard work."

"*Come?*"

"You do not understand? It is an American expression," she said proudly, and came to her feet as she spoke.

"American?" It took him a moment to find her meaning. "Holy cow!" he drawled, and the dark eyes twinkled at him appreciatively.

"Angelo does not know the difference when an American speaks, or an Englishman. I have a better ear. And you will notice, *signore*, I do not say 'British' when I mean someone from *here*."

"I am sure you are far too perceptive to make such a mistake." It was easy to fall back into the light tone which had started their interview; at the same time he was conscious of disappointment. Because there were so many questions that needed to be asked, but he was here on sufferance only; and as far as the people at the studio were concerned the case was closed.

Giuditta was asking, "Why have we not met before?" Her bantering tone made it clear that there were to be more questions. "I find we are sympathetic."

"You are very good, *signora.*"

"There is, besides, the fact that you understand me. We can laugh together . . . men are sometimes so serious. And you have not yet asked me to sleep with you," she pointed out. He wasn't quite sure which of them she was congratulating about this.

"As we've known each other for quite twenty minutes, I suppose that must be a record," said Antony, enchanted. And allowed his mind to turn for an irreverent moment on the possibility of engineering an encounter between Giuditta and Uncle Nick.

"Now you are laughing again, and you have not told me why. But we shall be friends, shall we not? Very cool, very correct, in the English way." She put a hand on his arm, and began to move slowly towards the group at the other end of the studio. "Are you married?" she asked.

"Yes."

"What is her name?"

"Jenny."

"Jen-ny? Giovanna? Why are you smiling?"

"Because she is neither 'very cool,' nor 'very correct.' "

"A haughty English lady," said Giuditta positively. "Will you be so cruel as to destroy all my illusions?"

"Would you like to condemn me to life with an iceberg, *signora?*"

"Perhaps I would." They were very near the cameras and the arc lights now; the argument there seemed to be continuing unabated, but Angelo must have sensed their approach for he spun round and came towards them, leaving the tumult to subside behind him.

"Giuditta *mia,* we are waiting!" he told her.

"I am sorry, Angelo."

Perhaps it was the fact that she spoke in English that reminded him of Maitland's presence. "You have been talking to the *signore.* Well, I forgive you." He was all good humor again.

"You are finished, yes?" he said hopefully to Antony.

"I'm afraid I've taken up a great deal of your time."

"We are too happy." But already his attention was turning back to the waiting set. "Over there, Giuditta. You come in by the door, and there is surprise when you find that Francesco is already in the room."

Antony stood for a moment, and then turned away. They were moving away from him into the circle of lights, to be engulfed immediately into their own, unreal world. It was Jo's world too, and he had an uneasy feeling that if he talked to her now he wouldn't recognize her. As he went he heard Angelo's voice raised again in an impassioned tirade. "Giuditta, you are dressed, yes, but what of your face?" And for the first time he realized that, unlike Jo and Eversley, she had worn no makeup when she talked to him. Certainly she looked better that way . . . and, no doubt, she knew it.

CHAPTER 6

It is so easy to walk into a bank, so apparently difficult—unless you are staging a holdup—to get beyond the barrier which has been set up, ostensibly for your convenience as a customer but actually as a safeguard. And unless, of course, it happens to be one of those days when the Manager sends out a polite message that he would like a word with you . . .

But the Head Office ought to be different, and the Northumbrian and Wessex prides itself on its position as one of the big six. Maitland, extracting himself from the revolving door that had just admitted him to the most imposing building in Gracechurch Street, was disappointed to find himself in a perfectly ordinary branch office. He had to admit it was impressive; large economy size, he thought . . . not that economy seemed to have had anything to do with it. It had apparently been designed by someone with a passion for marble and mahogany, or perhaps the directors had a financial interest in these commodities. He was looking about him and vaguely considering retreat when a messenger detached himself from his position near a wicket labeled FOREIGN EXCHANGE, SECURITIES and came towards him.

"Can I help you, sir?"

Antony removed his gaze from the carving at the top of a massive pillar, thought reverently for a moment of Jerome K. Jerome, and mastered a desire to ask, "Do you sell boots?" Instead, "I seem to have got into the wrong place," he said. "I have an appointment with Mr. Warren."

"Which Mr. Warren would that be, sir?"

"Advance Department," said Antony, even more vaguely than before.

"Oh, Head Office. This is the Gracechurch Street Branch, sir; most people get in here the first time. If you go through that door at the back you needn't go into the street again."

Beyond the door the same air of quiet dignity prevailed, but the atmosphere was less obviously financial. There was a marble court with a real fountain, a few chairs in dignified disarray, and a lift shaft; nothing in the shape of an inquiry desk, but after a moment another messenger materialized—the place seemed to be crawling with them—and directed him in tones which struck a nice balance between the obsequious and the condescending.

"Advance Department? First floor, sir." He then accompanied Maitland to the lift and himself repeated his destination to the attendant, apparently under the impression that his charge was feebleminded. Which may not be so far wrong, thought Antony bitterly, as they ascended.

Upstairs it might have been any rather old-fashioned set of offices that had been maintained through the years regardless of expense. There was a wide hall with a marble floor; an archway on the right that led into a long, thickly carpeted corridor lighted by crystal chandeliers, that even at a glance showed itself to be of an almost unimaginable splendor; three steps down on the left to a spacious lobby with doors on either side, and a double door at the far end. "Through there, sir," said the lift-man obligingly.

Somehow Antony seemed to have acquired another guide— he wasn't quite sure where this one had come from—and the

odd thing was that the man seemed to know where he was
headed. Probably bank people communicated with each other
by ESP. Or radar . . . like bats. Anyway, it was all obviously
part of a softening-up process, designed to intimidate the client,
to put him in a properly humble frame of mind. The doors leading from the lobby were anonymous, but the messenger made
without hesitation for the third on the right and ushered Maitland in a few moments later with the self-satisfied air of one
who has successfully completed a delicate, and perhaps dangerous, mission.

Ever since he arrived, and earlier when he telephoned to make
the appointment, Antony had been conscious of "Grandfather's"
spirit hovering beneficently over him, an unlikely guardian angel.
He wasn't quite sure what General Managers did, but the name
of William Marston was obviously one of power. Equally obviously, he thought as the interview progressed, he'd have been
thrown out on his ear at the first awkward question if he hadn't
been sponsored, as it were, from on high.

It was a medium-sized room, paneled in mahogany and bril-
liantly lighted. Beyond the window was a gleam of pale sunlight,
completely eclipsed by the radiance within. At a wide mahogany
desk in the center of the room sat a shortish, broad-shouldered
man in his late forties, with mouse-colored hair and rather pale
gray eyes. The sort of person it would be difficult to describe,
except perhaps by saying that his features were indeterminate,
but who seemed to Antony, even at first glance, about as un-
assertive as a dynamo. He was giving his visitor the red-carpet
treatment, coming round the desk to shake his hand, hovering
solicitously until he was sure he had chosen the most comfortable chair, pushing forward a box of cigarettes. When he
was quite certain that nothing was wanting to Antony's comfort
he seated himself again, leaned forward with his hands clasped
on the desk before him, and said affably, "I'm not quite sure
what is your interest in Bromley, Mr. Maitland."

Antony was by no means sure himself. He took refuge in a
half-truth, saying casually, "I've been in touch with his solicitor.
They were given leave to appeal, you know."

"I see." For one reason or another David Warren showed no

desire to question him more closely. "How can I help you then?" His eyes dropped for a moment to the papers on his desk and the bulky files that waited for his attention, but if it was a reproach it was a very subtle one, and in no way reflected in his voice.

"I need to know something of him personally." Antony hadn't meant to sound apologetic. "It seemed to me—"

"Yes, of course. I had his file sent down. He came to the Department from Manchester Branch three years ago."

"Was his record there satisfactory?"

"Excellent."

"What was his position here?"

"When he came, what we call an I.R., which only means he kept the individual records of the customers on his section. Later he was promoted to a more senior position."

"Still in . . . 'B' Section, wasn't it?"

"Yes."

"That means at least that he gave satisfaction . . . that he was trusted."

"You may take that as a fact, Mr. Maitland. It is in its way an honor to be transferred to this Department; it meant he could be sure of sympathetic consideration when future appointments were being made."

"What did you think of him yourself?"

"I liked him as a person and was completely satisfied with his work."

"And now?"

"I have to admit I was wrong in my judgment."

"I've been wondering . . . I suppose in one way you don't have to be so careful . . . he wasn't handling cash, I mean."

"My dear Mr. Maitland, this work demands the highest degree of integrity."

"I was thinking, you see, about his deposit account."

"What about it?" (Warren was doing rather well. The slight sharpness that had crept into his voice was the first hint he had given that his patience was not inexhaustible).

"I thought he'd have had to keep it at one of your branches."

"Of course he did. There are special rates for the staff."

"Then didn't anyone think it odd when he drew out all his savings . . . something like five hundred pounds?" He saw Warren hesitate, and added quickly, "He told me that himself."

"The matter was raised, of course. He told me his aunt was ill, the lady who is shown on his application as his next of kin. He said he was sending her money, and I had no reason to doubt his word."

"No, I see." The information, which he really should have expected, did nothing to cheer him. He pulled out one of his tattered envelopes and wrote a few words, balancing it awkwardly on his knee. "How did Bromley come to be friendly with the Anglo-Italian film people?" he asked; and, looking up, saw his companion's expression change for the first time . . . anger . . . resentment? He couldn't be sure.

"That was brought out at the trial, Mr. Maitland. Don't you remember?"

"Yes, but didn't he already know them through the Bank?"

"Of course not. There was no question of his being in touch with the public."

"But he could learn of a client's affairs."

"If the account happened to be on his section. But I must remind you that such information is confidential."

"Bromley would have some knowledge of the Anglo-Italian account," Maitland insisted.

There was a pause. Warren seemed to be consulting some private deity who lived on top of the bookcase behind Antony's head; or perhaps he was merely conjuring up the spirit of William Marston for advice. He said at last, reluctantly, "He did."

"What sort of knowledge?"

"Personal details of the partners. The amount of the firm's indebtedness, of course. How the account had been conducted. The security."

"Are the partners' accounts also with your Bank?"

"Yes." From his expression he might have been wondering whether the word was too informative. "With our Cricklewood Branch," he added, as though the admission itself might somehow be incriminating.

"Mr. Valenti . . . Major Cooke—?"

"It is the Major with whom I have most to do," said Warren, seeming to find some refreshment in the thought. "Mr. Eversley is also a partner," he added, with what Antony felt was undue recklessness. "He owns about twenty percent of the stock."

"Signora Giuditta?"

"Except that she was widely advertised in the press as the owner of the emeralds that were stolen, I know nothing of the lady."

"Doesn't she own them?" But the question was too direct . . . or not direct enough? Warren sat eyeing him stonily. "Are the emeralds charged as security to the Bank?" asked Maitland bluntly.

"I cannot see—"

"I'm trying to find out the worst that can be said about Roy Bromley." And that was true, so far as it went.

"I thought you wanted to help him."

"I have to know the worst, if I'm to do anything at all."

"Very well then." It was like drawing teeth, just as painful for the victim. "They are charged to the Bank, and the information was readily available on the file. For that matter, they are generally lodged at the Branch."

"I see." If he were to approach the firm's finances at all it would have to be obliquely. "Is it an unusual arrangement for a film company to have bank borrowing?"

"My dear Mr. Maitland, it is the most natural thing in the world." Warren sounded positively enthusiastic.

"Not a sign of financial instability?"

"Certainly not. Borrowing would not be available to a firm that was financially unstable." Perhaps he had forgotten Anglo-Italian Films altogether; in any case there could be no harm in citing a purely hypothetical instance. "We generally make a fixed loan, secured, and reviewed—say—at six monthly intervals. Then, for convenience, a certain amount of in-and-out borrowing, which we can cover in Provisions."

"Is that a good thing?"

"Of course it is. We are allowed to make provision in our accounts for possible bad debts—"

"But you said——"

"The operative word is 'possible,' Mr. Maitland."

"I see. Something to do with taxation." For once he actually felt as vague as he sounded. And he supposed the information was useful, but what he really wanted to know was whether the Bank were still as confident of Anglo-Italian's stability as they had been when the loan was first made; and Warren wasn't going to tell him, he might as well make up his mind to that. "As far as you're concerned," he said slowly, "Roy Bromley has also been written off as a bad debt."

"I'm afraid that's true. A clever young man, who might have had a brilliant future if he hadn't also been foolish."

Antony was in no mood to be amused by paradoxes, though he noted with interest the note of genuine regret in Warren's voice. "A pity," he agreed. "I've been wondering: do you know Michael Ross?"

"No, I don't think so." Warren looked puzzled.

"Or a man called John Drayton?"

"I don't recall . . . should I know them?"

"I thought perhaps they might also be customers of the Bank."

"I should hardly know that. Unless they had borrowing, of course, and the accounts came up for review on one of my sections."

"No, of course. Stupid of me. Is Mr. Truscott—Larry Truscott—still with you?"

"He is."

"I suppose that means you consider him reliable."

"Are you reminding me I was wrong about Bromley?" Warren smiled as he spoke. "I'd still venture to be certain in Truscott's case. A steady young man, I might even say rather dull. He'll do well enough as Accountant in a country branch. It was a mistake to bring him here." He glanced at his watch and added, hopefully, "Would you like to see him?"

"Very much, if it won't be interrupting things too much."

"Friday afternoon," said Warren. This time his smile was a little sour. "I expect his mind has already turned to the weekend. I'll take you to him." But he hesitated before he reached the door, and turned, and asked, frowning, "Am I right in thinking it was Miss Marston who aroused your interest in Bromley's case?"

"Quite right."

"Do you think . . . but I suppose it isn't fair to ask you that."

"The answer's simple anyway. I don't yet know if anything can be done."

"It seems to me," said Warren, "that in this case you might easily do more harm than good."

This time Antony had to grope for his meaning. "You mean . . . prolong the agony?" he said.

"I mean precisely that. Marston is indulgent, but the sooner Jo starts getting over this unfortunate business the better."

"You may be right."

"I *am* right," said Warren, decisively.

CHAPTER 7

Beyond the double doors the mahogany-minded planner had allowed his passion full rein. It was a huge, lofty room, with windows running the full length on either side and the different sections separated by breast-high partitions. Until he became attuned to it, Antony found the noise—the clatter of typewriters, and an odd, clanking sound from an unidentified machine in one corner—almost insupportable. Warren, who seemed unaffected, led the way down the left-hand aisle.

"B" Section was as big as most ordinary rooms. It had a built-in desk on either side, with wooden filing drawers fitting snugly under each so that there remained just enough space for a kneehole. Along the back wall stood a row of metal cabinets, and every possible surface was heaped up with papers. To the uninstructed eye it seemed impossible that anything could ever be found; and the young man who got up from one of the desks as they went in had a worried look, as though something of the sort might have occurred to him too.

David Warren wasted no time on the introductions, nor did

he attempt to satisfy Truscott's curiosity beyond adding curtly, "Mr. Maitland has the General Managers' authority to ask you some questions." His mind, Antony thought, had already turned back to some high financial matter, but he took leave of his unwelcome visitor amiably enough.

Larry Truscott was a square-built young man with thick, sandy hair that obviously took no notice at all of any directions he gave it, mild blue eyes, several freckles, and a stubborn chin. He regarded Maitland with some misgiving, and said warily, "Questions? What sort of questions?" rather as though the word was a bomb that might be expected to explode at any moment.

"About Roy Bromley."

"Oh, I see." He sounded relieved, but he added almost immediately, "Well, as a matter of fact, I *don't,* but I expect you'll explain. Shall we sit down? It isn't exactly comfortable, I'm afraid."

"Never mind." There was only one spare chair, and it was obviously built for utility, not relaxation. Antony seated himself, and the illusion of privacy was complete; or would have been, if he could have forgotten altogether the noise that Advance Department generated as it went about its affairs.

"You see," said Truscott, "I thought perhaps someone had the idea I'd been cooking the books. Not that there's much to be done in that line here, as far as I can see. But if you aren't one of the Inspectors, what are you?"

"I'm not here professionally." (Perhaps on the whole it would simplify matters if he had a record made of the protest.)

"But—?" said Larry, and paused hopefully.

"I'm a barrister."

"Oh, *that* Maitland. Jo was talking about you."

"It's Jo Marston's fault I'm here," said Antony, allowing a certain amount of bitterness to be evident in his tone.

"And she made old W.M. vouch for you? What a girl!" said Truscott, grinning.

"Something like that."

"Yes, but . . . what about Roy? He said he was framed, but do you think that's true?"

"I'm trying to find out. What do you think about it? I may

say," he added, as Larry hesitated, "that any communication you care to make will be treated as confidential."

"Well, you know, I liked Roy all right, but when it happened . . . well, what could anyone think? And of course he'd deny it; you couldn't go on that."

"He convinced Miss Marston."

"Yes, I know." Truscott glanced at his companion uneasily. "That doesn't count really . . . do you think?"

"Did you know he was in difficulties financially?"

"I knew he was worried, but I thought it was about Jo . . . and W.M. You can't deny the situation was sticky."

"Had Bromley told you about his engagement?"

"Not exactly. It wasn't official, but I'd heard a rumor. There are always rumors, especially about something like that. Even old—even Mr. Warren had heard about it. Of course, when I saw them together it was obvious how they felt."

"That was the night of the studio party, the night the theft took place?"

"Yes. We all went in style, in W.M.'s Daimler; I was glad of the lift, but it was pretty clear I was just a sort of red herring . . . so that the chauffeur wouldn't suspect there was anything particular about her calling for Roy."

"About the party: did you see anything that would confirm Bromley's story of not leaving the studio at the relevant time?"

"If I had, I wouldn't have waited till now to say so. The trouble was, nobody was noticing. There'd been a good deal of champagne, and everyone was talking . . . not even listening, you know, just chattering. Not that I mean they were *all* tight," he added doubtfully.

Antony smiled. "You remember, at least, when you joined Bromley and Miss Marston just before the police arrived. I believe Francis Eversley was with them."

"That's right. And that fellow Ross. I was hoping to persuade Jo to have the next dance with me."

"Tell me what happened."

"She'd promised it to Roy."

"I meant, did anyone else join the group, did you all stay together, how were you standing?"

"That's a tall order."

"Take your time."

"Well—" Larry was frowning over the question. "I was danc-ing with a girl called Molly, but when the music stopped she rushed off . . . said she saw someone she knew. I think she was afraid the band might start up again; I'm not all that good. So I looked round for Jo; she joined Roy and Eversley, and I did too."

"Wait a bit. You mentioned Michael Ross a moment ago."

"He was there as well."

"Did you see him join them?"

"Now you mention it, yes."

"From the dance floor?"

"No, the other way. *Not* from the dressing rooms, if that's what you're thinking."

"How long had the dance lasted?"

Truscott looked at him without replying for a moment. "If Roy didn't do it, somebody framed him," he said at last, slowly.

"That seems a fair enough statement."

"Well, I haven't got an alibi, if that's what you mean. The dance was nearly over when I saw Molly by herself, and we'd been talking earlier, so it seemed a good idea—" He broke off there and sat looking at Maitland in rather a helpless way.

"You've every right to resent my questions," Antony told him. The odd thing was, Truscott didn't seem resentful.

"It's just . . . I was wondering . . . what Jo said to you."

"Only that she didn't believe Bromley stole the emeralds."

"I see." He was silent again for a while, and then he said, "It means so much to her."

"I'm afraid it does," Antony agreed.

"Do you think he might be innocent?"

"I think I'd like to know for sure."

"All right then. I didn't steal the emeralds, but I could have done. And I could have planted them on Roy, I suppose. If you're looking for motive I don't think I'm a very good bet; I mean, I'm hard up, of course, but so is everyone else. And it wasn't a spur-of-the-moment job, was it? It had been carefully planned."

"Anyone who knew about the d'Albret emeralds could have guessed Giuditta would be wearing them," said Maitland, in an expressionless voice.

"And I'd just as much chance as Roy to read the file. Is that it?"

"It's a point I have to consider." He smiled suddenly. "Don't make too much of it; my interests are divided."

"Ross and Eversley?" Truscott didn't seem to find the assurance particularly cheering. "I don't know how they stand on this alibi question, of course, but they were certainly both with Roy when the police arrived."

"Do you know enough about them to make a guess about motive?"

"Not really. Eversley's all right, a bit affected, that's all. And he ought to be well off—oughtn't he?—personally, I mean; he's been a star for years."

"And Ross?"

"He was making up to Jo; damned insinuating sort of fellow. Didn't seem best pleased about Roy. No telling whether he was hard up or not."

"How were you all standing when the police arrived?"

"I'll show you." His chair grated back on the wooden floor as he came quickly to his feet. "Say that's Roy"—the Stock Exchange Official List thudded to the floor—"Jo beside him, we'll use Lady Monica Trenton's file for Jo; Eversley over here, that's the AngIt file, as it happens"—it was a very fat one— "*Review* will do for Ross, he says he's a journalist; and here I am, this pile of transfers that ought to have been recorded a month ago."

The diagram tallied exactly with the one Eversley had drawn. "It doesn't really help all that much," said Antony, regarding it sadly.

"I didn't see any funny business, you know, but I couldn't swear the emeralds weren't planted on Roy," said Truscott; strangely, he seemed to be offering encouragement. "And I don't suppose either of the others could swear about me."

"No one else approached you?"

"Only Major Cooke. He came up to speak to Eversley when

the police arrived; I think he must have been asking him to do something about it, because Eversley went forward then to talk to them."

"Could Cooke—?"

"Hold on." He paused, screwing up his eyes. "No, I'm sorry," he went on, relaxing after a moment's fierce concentration. "I just don't know."

"What did you think of Cooke?"

"That was the first time I met him; of course, I've seen him here. I never could understand, as a matter of fact . . . well, I mean, he seems a shady type to me."

"Does Warren agree with you?"

"I never asked him." Truscott grinned, and then was unduly solemn again. "I grant he's better equipped to make a judgment. I say . . . it is all right to talk like this to you, is it? I mean, we take an oath, all very solemn—"

"What about?"

"Oh, not to divulge the contents of accounts. That sort of thing."

"I think I can get what I want without taking you off the strait and narrow."

"I daresay it's all right, what I said about Major Cooke. It's just opinion, and if you met him—"

"I have met him." Truscott looked at him expectantly, but he did not amplify the statement. "Do you know a chap called Drayton? John Drayton?"

"I don't think . . . should I?"

"He's a friend of Michael Ross."

"Oh, in that case . . . I thought for a moment the name seemed familiar, but I hardly know Ross, you see."

"Tell me about Bromley's work then. What did he do?"

"Well!" Larry had his worried look again. "Any account with borrowing is reported at least once a year, but mostly it's oftener than that. Roy's job would be to—to assess the position, check up to see if there'd been any changes in the security, whether the stocks were keeping their value, that kind of thing. Then he'd make his recommendations—report in six months, or whatever it might be—and draft a letter to the Branch, and the whole thing would go forward to Mr. Landor, or to Mr. Warren if the borrowing was over ten thousand pounds."

"That sounds relatively simple."

"It isn't simple at all," said Truscott indignantly. "I've sort of got landed with the whole thing at the moment, and the things I'm supposed to know don't bear thinking of." But for all that he seemed prepared to discourse on them at length. "All about the stock market, and insurance, and property values, and what balance sheets really mean; which generally isn't at all the same thing as what they say."

"And the Anglo-Italian reports would list the emeralds among the securities, and how much they were insured for, I suppose." As Maitland spoke he glanced down at the file that had been thrown on the floor to represent Frank Eversley; the top sheet was some sort of printed form, with *R.1 month* scrawled across the top in green ink. Larry was saying:

"Well, of course it would. They report on everything. I mean, if Giuditta suffered from rheumatism—which, of course, she doesn't—we'd be told about that, because she's a sort of asset and it might affect the company's earning power, you see."

"I'm beginning to get the idea."

"Or if it was a farm account, say—" Larry seemed to be warming to his theme, apparently from a sense of grievance. "The report might say he beat his wife and was kind to his cows. Then we'd know it was a safe bet if he wanted to borrow to improve his herd."

"So long as his wife didn't decide on any drastic counter-attack," Antony suggested, amused by this single-minded approach.

"Oh, we'd make sure his insurance was in order," Larry told him seriously.

"I'm sure you would." His tone was dry. Truscott looked up and caught his eye, and laughed reluctantly.

"Not my cup of tea," he said. "I could just about stand the Bank in a country branch, but—"

"I thought there was a good deal of competition for jobs in this department."

"Not by me. All I wanted was to be left peacefully alone, but the thing is, you see"—his voice sank, as though he were admitting to some nameless vice—"I play rugger."

Antony's brain was already crammed with a good deal of undigested information, but this seemed to make even less sense than what had gone before. "I don't see—"

"They're great on sports. That's why I was transferred up here, so I could play for them. And—"

"It's nice to see you holding an At Home, Truscott," said a dry voice from the passage, "but do you think your friend will excuse you long enough to find me the Wantage file?"

He was a smallish man with a bristling mustache, a heavily lined face, and—for all his dryness—a twinkling eye. Larry seemed in no way abashed by the interruption; he came to his feet, said briskly, "Mr. Maitland . . . Mr. Landor," and started to root like a terrier among the papers on his desk.

Landor gave Antony an amiable look. "Are you an American?" he inquired. And added, as Antony shook his head, "I thought perhaps you'd been trying to convert our friend here to the game of baseball." He glanced down for a moment at the arrangement of files on the floor.

"He's a friend of Mr. Marston's," said Larry, who seemed to have found what he wanted. He obviously felt no need to justify Antony's presence, he was on the easiest of terms with the newcomer; and when he added, "Mr. Warren brought him in," he was explaining only so far as politeness seemed to demand.

In an equal spirit of courtesy, Landor murmured something that sounded vaguely complimentary; but when he took the file and looked at it his whole manner underwent a change. "Grant £2000," he read in a shaking voice. "Now, how the hell does he justify that?"

"There's a guarantee by Mrs. Wantage, sir. She's good for the whole amount."

"Dammit, I know that. It's unethical, that's what it is. If I had my way—" He broke off, gave Larry a smoldering look, and added, no less explosively, "Don't say it's for the good of the Bank; making a god of it, that's what he's doing."

"It's a pity, sir," said Truscott stolidly.

But Landor had already suffered a change of mood. He

clutched his file to him with his left hand, and turned to hold out his right to Antony; an amiable grin deepened the lines about his mouth. "Glad to have met you, Mr.—er— Great country, America. Great game, baseball, I suppose . . . if you understand it." The last words drifted back to them from the passage as he disappeared toward the swinging door.

"It's none of my business," said Maitland, "but what was all that about?"

"He's the Controller on this section," said Larry, as though that explained everything.

"I guessed that much."

"Well, he can grant loans up to ten thousand pounds at his own discretion, but he can't reject tuppence ha'penny without sending it up to Mr. Warren. It's quite logical really," he added, as Antony opened his mouth to ask a further question. "We *want* people to borrow money."

This idea seemed so fantastic that Maitland took his time to think it out. "But not unless they've got some anyway," he said at last.

"That goes without saying. Well, you see, Mr. Landor thinks we've a moral duty to consider our customer's best interests, whereas Mr. Warren . . . well, I suppose he's right really," said Truscott doubtfully. "But it gets tricky sometimes." All at once he seemed in the mood for confidences. "They've had a sort of rivalry for ages, or so I've been told. Mr. Warren was Accountant at Piccadilly when Mr. Landor was doing Securities there; and in case you don't know, I can assure you, the Accountant at a branch is very well placed for getting himself disliked."

"I suppose so." He was still on his feet, and now he glanced down again at Larry's diagram. "I don't seem to have got to first base," he said, "but I ought to be going. Give you time to finish your week's work."

"I'm not all that keen." He bent to retrieve the books and files from the floor, and dropped them untidily on the desk. Then he turned back to Maitland and said with an air of resolution, "Can I ask you a question?"

"Yes, of course."

"Jo asked you to start this, I know that. But do you think
. . . I don't want her to get hurt any more."

An echo of his own thoughts, a reminder of his own uncertainty. "Do you want to see Bromley free?" he asked.

"That isn't really so easy." Larry seemed to be having some
difficulty in arranging his ideas. "Even if he is a thief, I was
never very keen on retribution. The only thing is, there's Jo.
That's what you really meant, isn't it?"

"More or less."

"I'd give a good deal for her to have what she wants, but—
perhaps I'm like Mr. Landor—not unless it's good for her." He
smiled, but his eyes were troubled. "She's a good kid, you
know," he said earnestly.

"I know." Antony moved toward the opening into the passage. "I'll try to look out for her," he promised.

But as he made his way back to the street again through the
complexities of the building he was wondering what had given
the Chief Controller the idea that Larry Truscott wasn't very
bright; because if he hadn't exactly said that, he'd certainly
implied it.

Come to think of it, Bromley had told him much the same
thing.

He went straight home from the Bank, and in retrospect the
day's adventures made quite an amusing story. But that was
really the only positive thing about the evening; that and the
message from chambers that the conference with Mr. Bellerby
and Mr. Longman had been rescheduled for the following day.
He phoned Jo, and was informed in stately tones that she was
not at home; he thought about phoning Sykes, but it didn't seem
fair to disturb him after office hours, when no one could say it
was urgent; and when he went back to Michael Ross's flat he
drew another blank. If the message had been delivered Ross had
chosen to disregard it, and the caretaker, on inquiry, rather
thought he'd seen him go out half an hour before.

"But even if I'd seen him," he told Jenny despondently when
he got back to Kempenfeldt Square, "I don't suppose it would
have done any good at all."

"Except to round things off neatly," said Jenny, who was mending. She had been looking for her scissors, but at this point despaired of finding them and bit off the thread. She knew very well that Antony was tired, and most likely his shoulder was hurting him, but she had arranged with herself years ago never to mention that.

"It would be some satisfaction at least. When I've talked to Ross, I don't see what else I can do. But it's maddening, love. I've got the strongest feeling—" He broke off there, and shrugged, and said, "Oh, well!"

Jenny was scowling at the hem she had just repaired. After a while she said in an expressionless voice, "Uncle Nick is dining with the Garfields."

"*That* won't have put him in a better mood," said Antony with a sort of gloomy satisfaction.

"No, I'm afraid . . . he says it's all very well trying to help people, but Where is it Going to Lead." (This was quite unlike anything Sir Nicholas was likely to have said, but the sentiment was recognizable enough.) "I expect," Jenny added, when Antony made no immediate reply, "he thinks you're going to get involved with the police again."

"Didn't you tell him I was cooperating with them this time?"

"I explained to him very clearly about Inspector Sykes—"

"Chief Inspector."

"Yes, I always forget. I explained very clearly, but I don't think it impressed him at all." She was watching Antony as she spoke, and the worried look left her face when he smiled at her. "But he seems to be expecting trouble," she insisted.

"Never mind. He'll calm down when nothing happens," Antony told her; and thought, at the time, that the prediction was a reasonable one. So whatever he was expecting, it wasn't that he would be aroused by the telephone bell at three o'clock the next morning, or that when he stumbled into the living room to answer it would be Jo's voice that greeted him, a little higher-pitched than he remembered it, and fairly crackling with excitement. He held the receiver away from his ear till she had finished and then said unkindly, "Take a deep breath, and start again."

"Weren't you listening?"

"I couldn't. You're squeaking like a bat, and the human ear is only capable—"

"I'm sorry you're cross, but this is serious." Something in her tone caught his attention, making him curious and at the same time unwilling to hear. . . . "I thought you ought to know at once," said Jo. "Michael Ross has been murdered."

CHAPTER 8

Surprise sharpened his tone. He said, "How do you know?" and thought immediately that there were half a dozen other questions he could more profitably have asked.

But it didn't really matter. Jo was wound up to communicate, and obviously intended to do so. "I was there. I found him." And then, more hesitantly, "At least . . . Larry and I."

"Where are you now?"

"At home. I just got in."

"The police—?"

"I made a statement." That was Jo on her dignity again, with all the excitement frozen out of her voice.

"I see. You'll have to start at the beginning, if you want me to understand. You're making my head spin," he complained.

"Well, I'd been having dinner with Angelo and Giuditta, and of course I left at ten o'clock—"

"Where do they live?"

"They have a penthouse at Montague Court."

"And why did you leave at ten o'clock, *of course?*"

"Because Angelo goes to bed then. Always, when he's at

home. And he doesn't like his people to be late, anyway, when we're working."

"Not even on Friday night?"

"We shall be shooting tomorrow. At least, we should have been."

"Right. You say Larry Truscott was with you."

"No, I didn't. He came to meet me."

"Were you expecting him?"

"Well . . . I thought he might. But he wasn't there when I left Montague Court. Do you know Harrowby Square?"

"Not intimately."

"Well, you have to go through to Somers Street to catch a bus, and there's an alleyway—quite narrow—between two of the buildings that makes a shortcut. So I went down there, and there isn't too much light so I didn't see them at first." She paused and took a deep breath, and added, picking her words, "Michael was dead, and Larry had just come up the other way and found him."

"You said Ross was murdered."

"So he was. He'd been stabbed."

"How long since it happened?"

Her eagerness had gone now; he thought at first she wasn't going to reply at all to his question, and when she did he again had the sense that she was choosing carefully the exact phrases she would use. "It couldn't have been long, I do see that. Not many people use the alley at that time of night, but it isn't deserted."

"You'd better tell me it all, Jo."

"All right then. I will. We went back to Montague Court to telephone; Larry wouldn't let me go alone. And then I stayed there and he went back to—to Michael again. And then the police came, and there was an Inspector, and when they'd finished looking at things there were a lot of questions. And that's what's worrying me, you see."

"Not yet."

"They think it's Larry. I could tell."

"Why?"

"Well, first they wanted to know what Michael was doing

there, and he *did* know I was going to see Giuditta because he
asked me to go out with him and the easiest excuse is always
to tell the truth, if you can. So they made up their minds he
was coming to meet me—at least, that Inspector did—and of
course it may have been true. And he'd been stabbed in the
back, halfway down the alley, and Larry was a bit late and had
been running, and the manager at the flats told them he'd still
been out of breath when we went in to phone. I just know they
think he did it."

"Wait a bit. What was his motive?"

"That's the awful part. Me."

"Could that be true?"

"I don't know. They've both been . . . oh, you know, at-
tentive. But Larry knew about Roy."

"What about the weapon?"

"That's what made it even more horrible: it was still in
Michael's back."

"What sort—?"

"I don't know. I don't know!"

"Did you see Larry when you turned into the alley?"

"No, I told you, it was dark."

"There'd be lights in Somers Street. Wouldn't you have seen
a silhouette, at least?"

"If he'd been standing up, but he'd found Michael already."
She sounded subdued. "That's what I wanted to ask you. Do
you think they'll arrest him?"

"They'll be making inquiries. If the weapon can be traced—"

"But it's so silly to say he'd have killed Michael; what good
would it have done?"

"I expect you're the only person who could answer that, Jo;
and the police may not believe you."

"Oh?" She thought that out for a moment, and then said
violently, "It isn't fair!"

"What did you think of Michael Ross?"

"I liked him all right, he was amusing." Her tone was re-
served; perhaps for the first time in her life she didn't expect
unquestioningly to be believed.

"And Larry?"

"He's nice. He's very nice. But he isn't Roy." This was said firmly enough, but as she went on her hesitation was very marked. "Mr. Maitland, do you think—do you think what happened has something to do with the emeralds?"

That, of course, was what she had telephoned to say, though her concern for Larry Truscott was probably genuine enough. He should be commending her single-mindedness; instead he felt a faint, a very faint disappointment. "I don't know," he said; which was true, even though it had been the first idea that came into his mind when he heard what had happened. "I don't know," he added with more energy, "but I mean to find out."

"Well, I really think you should," said Jo.

After that, it surprised neither Antony nor Jenny when their breakfast was interrupted by the information, conveyed by Gibbs on the house telephone in the frostiest of tones, that two persons had called . . . he understood they were policemen. This might mean anything from the constable on the beat to the Assistant Commissioner (Crime), but it seemed most likely the visitors were somewhere in between. Maitland grimaced at the receiver and said without enthusiasm, "What have you done with them?"

"I took the liberty of putting them in the study."

"That's all very well, but—"

"Sir Nicholas is still in the dining room," said Gibbs.

"All right, I'll come down."

He found his uncle eating toast and marmalade, with a folded copy of *The Times* propped up against the coffeepot, and reading a fascinating paragraph headed "Legitimacy and Estoppel." Sir Nicholas's expression was forbidding by the time Antony had finished a brief explanation of what had happened, but he said only, "No doubt you know your own business best."

"But, Uncle Nick—"

"I gather you propose to make it your business . . . this whole rather confusing affair," said Sir Nicholas in a dissatisfied tone.

"That's just the effect of Jenny's explanations."

"Isn't it confusing?"

"Well . . . yes. But it does seem now there might be something in Jo Marston's idea that Bromley is innocent."

"No need to sound defensive, Antony. Go and talk to your policemen. I wonder if they will agree with you. Though I think you might have guessed something like this would happen," said Sir Nicholas unfairly. "These film people are notoriously unreliable."

"The dead man had nothing to do with the films, sir."

"Hadn't he? Well, the principle is the same, I expect." His eyes were straying back to the newspaper again, but Antony was in no doubt that it had now lost its interest. He was conscious of exasperation as he crossed the hall to the study.

In anticipation of Sir Nicholas's presence, the fire there was glowing already, and the two men who awaited him were standing well within the range of its warmth; understandably, because it was much colder today. Neither of them was in uniform. The younger of the pair was shock-haired, heavily built, and in repose his face had a sullen look. But at the time Antony hardly noticed him, he was too taken up with the other; because he hadn't expected Scotland Yard to be on the job quite so quickly, and if he had he wouldn't—being by nature an optimist—have considered the possibility of Detective Inspector Conway being assigned to the case.

Conway was a thin-faced man with a pugnacious jaw and an acid look of displeasure. The last time they had met . . . but that was beside the point now, and the detective's greeting was courteous enough, though not entirely hiding his animosity. "Well, Mr. Maitland. So we meet again."

"Good morning, Inspector. We do keep—er—running into each other, don't we?"

"This is Sergeant Mayhew." Conway indicated his silent companion. Antony gave him a grin, but his attention was all for the Inspector. "It seems a pity to disturb you so early," Conway went on, "but there are a few questions—"

"There always are," said Antony, resigned. "You'd better sit down." He walked toward the fire as he spoke, so that they had very little choice but to take the easy chairs that stood on either side of the hearth. When they were settled he took up his own favorite position, back to the grate, with one shoulder leaning against the high mantel, and wondered how long it would be before Conway's disapproval spilled over into open antagonism. Not that there was any real cause . . . "You're wondering why I wanted so see Michael Ross last night," he said.

"Then you were expecting our visit." Conway's look was sharply suspicious. "How did you know——?"

"I know Ross is dead; Miss Marston phoned me. And I left my name with the caretaker when I found he was out."

"Why did Miss Marston inform you?"

"She thought I'd be interested," said Antony, and saw Conway's lips tighten. "No, really, Inspector, that's perfectly true. I'd been wanting to talk to him about the theft of the d'Albret emeralds."

"Emeralds?" Conway was momentarily out of his depth, and he reacted almost automatically. "What nonsense is all this, Mr. Maitland?" he asked.

"You wrong me, Inspector. I'm trying to help you."

"Are you, indeed?" The detective had recovered from his annoyance; his tone was precise, sarcastic. "What do you know of Michael Ross?"

"Nothing, except what other people have told me. He was a journalist—I've never heard of him, by the way—and he was one of the two or three people who could have stolen the emeralds at the Anglo-Italian film studio and palmed them off on Bromley before they were searched."

"This has nothing to do——"

"You've heard about the emeralds, haven't you?"

"Yes, of course. Not a very interesting case, Mr. Maitland. An amateur job, and the thief didn't get away with it."

"Doesn't this make you wonder at all?"

"I don't understand you," said Conway flatly.

"Whether the right man got the blame, I mean."

"There can be no connection."

"The same people are involved," Antony pointed out. "Some of the same people," he corrected himself.

"I might have known," said the detective bitterly, "that you would do your best to complicate what is a very simple affair."

"Simple, Inspector? Are you telling me you know who killed Ross?"

But Conway was not to be lured into so glaring an indiscretion. "I have no intention of giving you any information at all," he said; and stiffened when he saw Maitland's grin. "I asked you a straightforward question: why you wanted to see this man."

"I think I've answered that, haven't I?"

"You're asking me to believe that you're investigating a case that is closed."

"I hardly think you can call it that, Inspector. Not now."

Conway ignored the provocation, but his voice was more waspish than ever. "You never met Michael Ross? You know nothing of his movements last night?"

"The caretaker said he was out. That was at nine-thirty, more or less."

"Nine-thirty-seven," snapped Conway, and came to his feet, stiff as a ramrod. Sergeant Mayhew got up more slowly, and Maitland detached his shoulder from the mantelpiece.

"I was rather surprised, because I left a message for him the evening before, but I don't know if he got it, of course."

"Indeed?"

"A friend of his was at the flat when I called. He didn't give his name."

"That was on Thursday evening?"

"It was." He paused, as an idea struck him. "I wrote my name and telephone number on a pad on the desk. Was the note still there?"

Conway shook his head. "Not there, or anywhere else in the flat," he said, brusquely. "Should it have been? There was plenty of time to read it and throw it away."

"I was wondering if he ever saw it. It would have been so easy to put me off, if the time I suggested wasn't convenient."

"And just as easy to forget the whole thing."

"Yes, I suppose. It's so nice to meet for once on an uncontroversial occasion," he added, as Conway made an impatient movement. "Must you really go, Inspector?"

"We're doing no good here." The detective spoke harshly, so that Antony's voice, by contrast, sounded abnormally mild.

"Ross had a friend called Drayton," he remarked, thoughtfully.

"What of it?"

"His name cropped up. I'm curious, that's all."

"I've told you, Mr. Maitland, I'm not interested in the theft of the emeralds, if that's what you're talking about. The case is closed."

"What will you bet?" He grinned as Conway's expression became even more rigid, and added apologetically, "No, of course, you're not a betting man. But can't I interest you in Drayton, Inspector?"

"I see no reason—"

"Then tell me one thing before we part. Where did Ross work?"

"At home, I suppose."

"Yes, I've been told far too often that he was a free-lance journalist, but—"

"He was so described in his passport."

"Well, did you see any signs of his profession? There was no typewriter on the desk, for instance; I'd have thought he'd find writing everything in longhand intolerably slow."

"I daresay he did," said Conway shortly; but for a brief, unguarded moment there was a doubtful look in his eyes. "And as you're so curious—that was your own word, wasn't it, Mr. Maitland?—there was writing paper in one of the drawers."

"But what was he working on? Don't tell me he'd completed one assignment and not commenced another."

"Why not?"

"No reference books. Nothing in the wastepaper basket. None of the clutter the simplest piece of composition seems to engender."

"May I remind you, Mr. Maitland, it is Ross who has been murdered. We don't suspect him of anything."

"I do," said Antony, with a simplicity that the detective obviously didn't find at all disarming.

"I must warn you—"

"Yes, Inspector?" Something in the quiet tone stopped Conway in midsentence, and his next words came with an effect of anticlimax.

"One day you'll meddle in my affairs, and end by being sorry for it."

"If our problems overlap—" Maitland spread his hands in a gesture that disclaimed responsibility. Conway gave an impatient exclamation and marched stiff-backed towards the door; and it was at this precise moment that Gibbs pushed it open, and announced with a tactlessness that Antony could only consider diabolically inspired:

"Mr. Truscott is here to see you, sir."

CHAPTER 9

Another couple of minutes and he'd have been rid of Conway's presence; now there wasn't even time to put Larry off. He came into the room on the butler's heels, saying urgently, "I hope you don't mind, Mr. Maitland. I thought you could tell me—" at which point he caught sight of Conway and stopped in a hurry.

The Inspector had whirled round to favor Antony with one of his more suspicious glares. Antony, who saw nothing funny in the situation, smiled at him. Sergeant Mayhew continued to look stolid and uncomprehending.

Larry had halted a few paces inside the room. He gave a start when Gibbs retired and closed the door gently behind him, then his eyes turned to Antony and he said at random, "I'm sorry. I didn't know—"

"Inspector Conway is just leaving," said Maitland hopefully. Sergeant Mayhew stirred, and coughed, for all the world like a grandfather clock getting ready to strike.

"You were wanting to see Mr. Truscott, sir," he remarked heavily.

"Yes," said Conway. His hesitation could not have underlined more clearly his reluctance to leave the two men alone together. After a moment he turned to Maitland and added curtly, "Are you representing him?"

"Does he need legal advice, Inspector?"

Conway compressed his lips. Larry glanced from one to the other of them, obviously puzzled. "He said last night I should see my solicitor, only I don't have one. That's why I thought—" The sentence trailed away uneasily, and indeed it would have been difficult to be unaware of the undercurrent of tension in the quiet room.

Maitland was looking at the detective with the glimmer of a smile. "You warned me not to interfere, Inspector," he said.

"You know very well what I meant. I've nothing against the —the proper discharge of your professional duties."

"But your notions of propriety are much more strict than mine," Antony pointed out. "How urgent is your desire to talk to Mr. Truscott?"

"I must insist—"

"Not before he's consulted his solicitor, Inspector." The reproachful tone was willfully provocative. "If you went back to the Yard now, I'm sure he'd be willing to see you there once the matter has been arranged."

"After you've had the chance to prime him," said Conway hotly, and broke off when he saw his tormentor's grin.

"Difficult, isn't it?" said Antony, with sympathy. "However, Mr. Truscott's a friend of mine; he might be willing to waive the formalities and answer your questions here and now. Provided, of course, you've no objection to my being present."

"I've told them everything already," said Larry resentfully. "In fact, I've told them twice."

"The third time they may believe you. Shall we try, Inspector?"

Sergeant Mayhew gave another of his premonitory rumbles and said portentously, "I wouldn't be surprised if that was the best thing we could do."

"Oh, very well!" Conway's tone was uncharacteristically pettish.

Maitland looked at Larry. "What about it?" he asked.

"Whatever you say." He moved forward a few steps, stiffly. His eyes were fixed anxiously on Antony's face. "Jo told me—"

"Never mind that!" Antony spoke more sharply than he intended, and when he turned to take his place on the hearthrug again he met Sergeant Mayhew's eye for a moment, and would have sworn that there was some amusement there. Well, the bargain he had made pleased neither him nor Conway, but he didn't see what else he could have done. The Inspector was quite capable of working himself up into a state of sufficient moral indignation to make an arrest forthwith, even if he hadn't planned it that way. He wondered if it was his own discomfiture that pleased the sergeant, or that of Mayhew's superior officer. "Hadn't we better all sit down?" he said.

Conway took charge then, directing Truscott to the chair the sergeant had previously occupied, while Mayhew retired a little so that he could rest his notebook on a corner of the desk. The detective then resumed his former position, but did not seem in any hurry to begin.

"All right then," said Maitland, as the silence lengthened. "You've made rather a production of this, Inspector. Are you cautioning us?"

"No!" The word was snapped out, and Antony's eyebrows went up. Sergeant Mayhew coughed and said gruffly:

"Mr. Truscott has made a statement. We merely require his corroboration on certain points."

"Then all that about consulting our solicitor—"

"In his own interests," said Conway. His eye was bleak, but he seemed to have his temper in control again. "Now, Mr. Truscott, you say you went to Somers Street by bus yesterday evening."

"Yes, I did." Larry had a bewildered air about him, as though he couldn't quite understand how the present situation had arisen.

"Why did you do that?"

"It seemed a good idea to see Miss Marston home." He glanced up at Maitland and cleared his throat and added with a touch of defiance in his voice, "I don't know when I got off the bus exactly, but I meant to be at Montague Court at ten o'clock and I was a bit late."

"How had you spent the earlier part of the evening?"

"I had a meal, and then went to a cinema."

"Where was that?"

"The Strand Corner House. Then I went to the Empire in Leicester Square." From his resigned tone it was obvious that all these questions had been asked and answered before.

"Where you were so engrossed by the film that you forgot to leave time enough to get across town in time for your appointment," said Conway sarcastically. Maitland clicked his tongue disapprovingly, but made no more overt attempt to interrupt. Larry looked from one of them to the other with a sort of despair and said:

"It wasn't exactly an appointment. I just thought I'd meet her. And there should have been plenty of time if the bus hadn't—"

"Ah, yes. It took half an hour to get along Piccadilly," said Conway. "That was what you told me, wasn't it?"

"Something like that."

"Try to be a little more precise."

"How can I? I didn't notice the time."

"Why not leave it there?" Maitland seemed to throw out the suggestion casually, and when Conway looked up at him in irritation he appeared to have withdrawn his attention and be absorbed in watching Sergeant Mayhew's hieroglyphics. But then he looked down directly at the Inspector and added in the same light tone, "I doubt if you can disprove our statement on the point, but we can't prove it either. Be content with that."

"So when you got off the bus, at some time unspecified—"

"I think it was about two or three minutes past ten," Larry volunteered with the air of one making a discovery.

"What then?"

"I walked along to the alley that leads to Harrowby Square, I don't know its name. When I turned into it there was no one about and I was hurrying. I nearly tripped over Ross's body."

"There was no one else in the alley?"

"I saw no one. I heard no one." He seemed to be making a violent effort to visualize the scene. "I suppose a man could have moved along stealthily in the shadows . . . there's a lamp halfway down, but the main thing would be to avoid being seen against the light at either end, and if he was wearing rubber soles—"

"Even so, do you really think someone could have been there without your seeing him?"

"If I'd killed a man I'd take precautions, and if someone came along—"

"Just a minute," Maitland interrupted him. "I think we'll just stick to the facts . . . don't you agree, Inspector."

"That would suit me very well," said Conway dryly. Antony grinned, and glanced at Larry Truscott.

"I asked for that," he admitted.

"And when you saw Ross?" Conway's tone was dry still, and no more friendly than before.

"I didn't know who it was, of course. I thought it was someone ill, or drunk. So I turned him a little, tugging at his shoulder, and saw his face in the light of the street lamp before I felt the knife jar against the cobbles. I knew then what had happened, and I let him fall back on his face again."

"Do you think he was dead?"

"I thought so then, and now I know I was right. I heard the doctor tell you—no, it was the Divisional Inspector he was talking to—that Ross must have died instantly."

"Luck, or judgment?" said Antony, his eyes on Conway's face. The detective gave him an inimical look, and answered curtly:

"How should I know?"

"Never mind." His tone was resigned, but there was a speculative gleam in his eye.

"What then?" said Conway, turning back to Truscott. "You knelt by the corpse—"

"I was on one knee, as far as I remember; and I didn't hear Jo—Miss Marston—coming, or I'd have stopped her, of course.

When I did see her I got up, and took her arm, and pushed her a little way down the alley. And then I told her who it was."

"What was her reaction?"

"She said—"

"You don't have to answer that," said Maitland casually, his eyes on Mayhew's pencil again.

"Oh?" said Larry blankly.

"Then perhaps I may be permitted to ask why you didn't stay with the body, while Miss Marston went to phone?" Conway was heavily sarcastic.

"You may ask anything you like," Antony told him cordially, "but it doesn't follow you'll get a reply."

Truscott had a doubtful look. "It's very simple really," he began. But added more confidently, when Maitland remained silent, "I couldn't let her go alone, and perhaps meet the murderer."

"Returning to the scene of his crime, no doubt."

"It may not have been very sensible, but you'd have done the same thing."

"You mustn't credit the Inspector with human feelings, Larry; he doesn't approve of them," said Maitland. Conway ignored the comment and said harshly:

"You both went back to Montague Court. You, Mr. Truscott, were breathless when you arrived there; there was blood on your hands, on your cuffs, and on the front of your jacket."

"Not really surprising, Inspector. And as easily explained by his innocence as by his guilt," said Antony, as though the matter was hardly worth his concern.

"Perhaps *he* would like to give me the explanation," suggested Conway pointedly.

"I'd been hurrying, but I don't think it was that," said Larry. "I think it was more excitement, and being worried about Jo . . . you know, how much she'd seen. And the blood . . . well, of course, I touched him before I knew."

"And when you were shown the weapon," snapped Conway, suddenly losing patience, "you said you had never seen it before. Do you still say that?"

"It's still true."

"Very well! Just one more question, Mr. Truscott. What are your relations with Miss Marston?"

Antony opened his mouth to protest but closed it again when Larry said quietly, "She is a friend whom I've known for two months, just about."

"You say you first met at the studio party on the tenth of February. But you have seen a good deal of her since then."

"In the circumstances—"

"What was so special about the circumstances?"

"I think you know very well. When Bromley was arrested—"

"That gave you a chance to pursue the . . . friendship."

"—she was upset, of course." For all the emotion he showed, Truscott might not have heard the interruption. "It seemed up to his friends to rally round."

"An agreeable duty, no doubt. Was Ross one of these friends?"

"He knew Bromley. I don't know how well."

"But, like you, he was solicitous for Miss Marston's welfare."

"I don't know anything about that."

"Why do you think he was near Montague Court last night?"

"Facts, Inspector," said Maitland. This time he was looking at Conway, and just for a moment his casual air had deserted him. Conway returned the look with one of tight-lipped displeasure, and Antony added gently, "Don't you think?"

"I think perhaps we have all the facts we need." Conway came to his feet as he spoke.

"What about the weapon?"

"I have no information to give you, Mr. Maitland."

"I see." Antony appeared rather pleased than otherwise with what sounded like a snub, and Larry looked at him curiously. Conway nodded curtly by way of valediction, and made for the door; Sergeant Mayhew pocketed his notebook and ambled after him. Antony followed them into the hall.

"I hope you're satisfied, Inspector."

Conway gave him a look; a very expressive one that really left no need for words. He shrugged into his overcoat, ignoring Gibbs, who had materialized in his own uncanny way. "I wonder, Mr. Maitland, if you would be so interested in Mr.

Truscott's affairs if you didn't feel some benefit might accrue to Roy Bromley from the murder."

"Truscott asked my help," said Antony amiably.

"So I heard." He paused a moment to glare at his unfortunate sergeant, who appeared unmoved, and then walked towards the door, saying as he went, "I think in this case, Mr. Maitland, it will take more than your ingenuity to confuse the issue."

"And the trouble is," said Antony to his uncle, when he made his apologies at lunchtime for having monopolized the study for so long, "he really does think it's all perfectly straightforward."

"Isn't it?" asked Sir Nicholas disagreeably.

But that was later. Now Antony went back to the study and found Larry Truscott standing on the hearthrug and staring gloomily down at the fire, as though something he saw there confirmed his worst suspicions. He looked up and grinned at Maitland in a tentative way. "It's an awful bore," he said, "but I don't think that went too badly, do you?"

"As well as could be expected. All the same, there's this question of a solicitor."

"Do you really think I need one?"

"For heaven's sake . . . of course you do!" said Maitland forcefully.

"I thought perhaps . . . I mean, it all seems so unlikely. Shall I be arrested?"

"Probably. Unless something crops up to distract the police."

"I see. That's quite a thought, isn't it?" He hesitated, and then said self-consciously, "You asked him about the weapon, and you almost seemed pleased when he wouldn't tell you."

"That's the cause of the delay. They're still trying to trace it."

"Well, it isn't mine. They can't connect it with me."

"What did it look like?"

"Typical sort of scout knife," said Larry vaguely. "Nothing special about it at all."

"That doesn't sound very hopeful. The thing is, you see, they'll want to trace it first; after all, something might crop up in the course of their investigations to clear you. But if there's nothing to show the weapon couldn't have been in your possession—"

"I didn't quite understand that, I'm afraid," said Larry slowly. "It takes a bit of getting used to."

"Were you ever in the service?"

"N-no." The question seemed to puzzle him, but then he grinned. "Cadet Corps at school," he volunteered, "but the training didn't happen to include a course in stabbing people in the back."

"They never teach you anything worth knowing at school," Antony grumbled. "However, in this case perhaps it's just as well. Does Conway know you're left-handed?"

"No one asked me. I expect he noticed."

"He may not have done. You weren't smoking."

"No, but I'd like to," said Larry, and produced a packet with an air of relief when Antony said impatiently:

"Why don't you then?" and went to get the cigarette box from his uncle's desk. "We might be able to spring it on the prosecution in court," he said, restoring the box to its place when he saw his guest was already lighting up. "That is, if the medical evidence seems to favor a right-handed blow." And he gave his companion a long, considering look.

"I didn't kill Ross, if that's what you're wondering," said Truscott uncomfortably.

It was exactly what Antony had been wondering, and he thought again that Mr. Warren had been a good deal wide of the mark in considering his subordinate dull—unless indeed he equated everything with Suitability for a Career in Banking, in which case his remarks had, perhaps, some justification. But Larry was beginning to fidget under this prolonged scrutiny, so Antony said "Good!" heartily. And then, "Geoffrey Horton's a friend of mine, but he's good at his job, and accustomed to criminal cases. Would you like me to get in touch with him?"

"If . . . if you think . . . if you don't mind." The idea seemed to make Truscott nervous; perhaps he had a superstitious feeling that consulting a solicitor somehow brought his need of one nearer. "You're very kind," he added, suddenly formal.

Antony smiled at him. "Inspector Conway would tell you I'm furthering my own ends," he said; and watched with interest while the other man grappled with the implications of this remark. "He thinks I'm interested in Ross's death because it provides a possibility of clearing Bromley on the theft charge."

"And are you?"

"Of course. You've only to add that Geoffrey is one of the few people who will tolerate my meddling."

"But if the theft and the murder are connected . . . if you can prove that—"

"It might not necessarily prove your innocence," Maitland warned him.

"What I was thinking . . . at least they couldn't say it was because of Jo," said Truscott. He seemed to have recovered his equanimity and returned Antony's puzzled look calmly.

"Does that mean so much to you?" Maitland sounded angry.

"Yes, of course."

"Look here then, what did you mean when you said it wasn't *exactly* an appointment?"

"Just that . . . well, Jo said she wasn't expecting me," said Larry uncomfortably. "I didn't want to contradict her."

"It wasn't true?"

"I didn't mean she was lying, unless perhaps she thought it would help me. More likely it's just a misunderstanding; my landlady isn't very good at the telephone."

"You'd better tell me."

"She said there was a message from Miss Marston to say she'd be leaving Montague Court at ten o'clock. I knew that already, as a matter of fact; but it did sound—didn't it?—as if she wanted me to meet her." He paused, and then added doubtfully, "You didn't want me to tell Inspector Conway—"

"No, but there'll be no avoiding the question if the matter comes to trial. What will you say, Truscott—you'll be on oath, remember—when the Crown Counsel asks you how you really feel about Jo?"

"I'm not frightfully keen on perjury," said Larry. "Would it help if I said I wasn't in love with her?"

"I very much doubt it." His expression relaxed; if he had been angry, the anger had died. "Have you told her?" he asked.

"Of course not." Larry was emphatic. Maitland eyed him for

a moment before he strolled across to pick up the telephone from the desk.

"At least, we've got *something* to be thankful for," he remarked.

CHAPTER 10

He got to chambers with about two minutes to spare before Mr. Bellerby and his client were due; and found himself wondering as their talk progressed whether Inspector Conway would have called Mr. Longman's affairs straightforward too. Probably he would, on the grounds that black was black, and any attempt to argue that it was really a nice shade of gray must necessarily be disingenuous. And in this case he might well be right. Antony went home to luncheon in a depressed state of mind, and found the message that awaited him—that Mr. William Marston would be grateful if Mr. Maitland could spare the time to visit him that afternoon—distracting, but not particularly cheering.

He incurred Sir Nicholas's further displeasure by eating hurriedly and in an absentminded way, and then excusing himself from coffee on the grounds that he had to telephone Sykes. He found the Chief Inspector at home, and apologized for disturbing him, but even to his own ears the words sounded insincere.

"Think nothing of it." Sykes was as placid as ever. "I was rather expecting to hear from you, Mr. Maitland."

"Because this chap Ross has got himself killed?" Sykes gave a grunt that was probably affirmative. "Well then, what do you make of it?"

"It isn't my case, you know."

"I know," agreed Antony ruefully. "But Conway made it quite clear he doesn't think it's connected with the emeralds, so there's no harm in our discussing *that*."

"Have you something to tell me?"

"Nothing but questions, I'm afraid."

"What are they?"

"You already told me you know nothing of Michael Ross. Have you ever heard of a chap called Drayton?"

"There's a Sergeant Drayton in Records." Sykes sounded amused.

"John Drayton," said Antony carefully.

There was a moment's silence. "What do you know of him, Mr. Maitland?" the detective inquired at last.

"I'm asking you," Antony pointed out. And added, when there was no immediate reply, "I met him at Ross's flat . . . at least, I think I did."

"Surely you know."

"He didn't introduce himself. Ross wasn't there. But later Drayton was described to me and I think—"

"Did you tell Inspector Conway this?"

"He wasn't interested," said Antony virtuously. "You know, I don't want to run down one of your colleagues, but I've only to make a suggestion—"

"Are you sure that's altogether Conway's fault?" asked Sykes dryly. "If you'd ever tried to resist the temptation to pull his leg—"

"I must try it sometime. What about Drayton, Chief Inspector? Is he known to the police?"

"At one time, very well." There was another pause, longer than before, and it was all Antony could do not to break in with an impatient question. "Up to about five or six years ago he was believed to be one of the most successful jewel thieves in the business. I can't say more than that; we never got our hands on him, not in my time. I believe he was careless once, when he was younger. Spent part of the war years inside, or so I heard."

"Did he retire?"

"So we suppose."

"Well, what does he do now?" Even when Sykes was in communicative vein there was always the feeling of trying to get blood out of a stone.

"I'd very much like to be able to answer that question." There was a note in the detective's voice that was almost wistful. "He definitely stopped operating, and after a while he just naturally dropped out of sight."

"How did you know?"

"Well, of course . . . oh, I see. No more jobs with his signature. And I'd have been glad to get my hands on him," he added, more forcefully than usual. "He had a nasty mind."

"What exactly—?"

"He was mean," said Sykes thoughtfully. "It's one thing for a chap to hit out in a panic; all wrong, of course, but understandable. But with Drayton it was violence for its own sake, or so I always thought."

"A pleasant type."

"Well, I tell you straight, Mr. Maitland, he's the sort you want to watch out for."

"Could he have changed his angle, perhaps? Gone over to administration, for instance."

"You're thinking of that business I was telling you about."

"The Association. Yes."

"Well, he could," said Sykes doubtfully, "but it doesn't feel right somehow." He paused, considering. "He was an artist in his way, not a businessman."

"Could he be operating for them?"

"Well, if he is I'll retire tomorrow on half pay, and I can't say fairer than that."

"If he'd changed his ways? You spoke about his 'signature.' "

"He couldn't have done it, not so drastically. It isn't in his nature." Sykes was positive.

"I see. You say it's five years since he pulled a job."

This time there was a noticeable silence before the detective replied. "At least five years," he said at last. "And I'll grant you, Mr. Maitland, it was after that we first got wind of the Association. But if you're thinking he might be the chief buyer, I doubt if he'd have the necessary connections."

"Now, how can you possibly know that?"

"He's an insular type." Sykes was unperturbed by the note of incredulity. "Now, the chap I'm interested in—"

"But Drayton's mixed up with Ross."

"Do you know anything to connect either of them with the theft of the emeralds?"

Antony laughed, not very happily. "Don't be so damned reasonable."

"Well, do you?" Sykes persisted.

"Not a thing. Except Ross's presence at the film studio. What I think is another matter."

"Now, you know as well as I do, Mr. Maitland—"

"I know you have an odd weakness for seeing things proved."

"And how do you connect the two men?"

"It was Drayton who introduced Ross to the film people . . . to Major Cooke, to be exact."

"If there's one thing that convinces me Ross wasn't involved in the theft—"

"You mean they'd have been more cautious. Yes, I suppose . . . but Ross has been murdered, don't forget that."

"What are you suggesting?"

"I don't quite know." He sounded restless now, and his tone was discontented. "I'd like to know more of Ross's affairs. So easy to say you're a writer."

"It may even be true," Sykes suggested.

"So it may." He thought about that for a moment, and then added, "Drayton knew my name."

"Well, but—"

"Don't tell me 'More people know Tom Fool,' " said Maitland, suddenly amused again. "Because it wouldn't be polite."

"I suppose not," Sykes agreed; but when he put down the phone five minutes later, Antony was unable to persuade himself that the detective was in any way impressed by his arguments. Well, to be honest, even to his own ears they had a specious sound.

He reached Motcombe Crescent at about three o'clock, and found William Marston's house without difficulty, even though it had dispensed at some time with the convenient anonymity of a number and called itself Motcombe Chambers. Beside the front door six neatly framed visiting cards identified an equal number of bell pushes, but the front room on the first floor to which he was presently ushered had an air of permanency about it, as though the bookshelves, the heavy walnut desk, and the deep leather chairs had been in their respective places for a very long time indeed.

And inevitably, of course, his expectations were confounded. The man who rose to greet him—Jo's grandfather presumably— was nothing like the patriarchal figure his imagination had conjured up. He was a spare, rather dapper little man, youthful looking in spite of graying hair, with an easy manner and a compelling eye. His greeting was pleasant but a good deal short of the effusive. "I believe you've already met David Warren," he added.

"Mr. Warren was kind enough to see me yesterday." Maitland was at his quietest, most diffident; Warren's greeting was equally conventional, but he gave the newcomer a hard look. Outside his own setting he looked shorter than Antony had remembered, but with his stocky build he would have made two of William Marston.

It was a cold afternoon, and the warmth of the fire was welcome. "I asked you to come here," said Marston, who had wasted very little time on the preliminary courtesies, "because in the circumstances I felt it would be helpful to have your opinion."

It would be more helpful, Antony thought, if I'd formed one. "On what particular point, sir?" he asked warily. And then, "I hope Miss Marston explained my position."

"Oddly enough, I believe she explained quite clearly." Marston paused a moment, smiling, before he added, more seriously, "I was surprised, I admit, that you were willing to

take so much trouble on her behalf; but now it seems I may
have cause to be grateful to you. If I have been mistaken—"

"About Bromley?"

"Yes, of course." There was a touch of impatience in his
voice, but he added surprisingly, "I may have been overready
to believe in his guilt. It isn't, I admit, the match I want for
my granddaughter, but perhaps I should have had more faith
in her judgment."

"If you were mistaken, you weren't the only one." He glanced
at Warren, and then back at his host again. "What exactly is in
your mind?"

"This man who was killed—another friend of my granddaughter, it seems—"

"And the fact that the police seem to suspect young Truscott," Warren put in, as the older man seemed to hesitate.

"They do not, however, think that the theft and the murder
are in any way connected," said Antony, not committing himself.

"But surely—"

"Too much of a coincidence? You may be right."

"You're being rather evasive, Mr. Maitland." Even here,
where he seemed to be making some effort to subdue his per-
sonality, Warren's energy and forcefulness were very apparent.
"We want to know if you've reached a decision as to Bromley's
guilt or innocence."

"I think—but unfortunately my opinion doesn't matter—I
think he was genuinely indignant about being framed."

"Then he didn't steal the emeralds? Who do you think did?"

"You're going too fast for me, Mr. Warren. And if I knew it
wouldn't help, unless I could prove it."

"You talked to Truscott yesterday."

"I did. I also heard your opinion of him." He smiled as he
spoke, but there was no answering amusement in Warren's eyes.

"And formed your own?"

"Of course. I've been wrong too often to be sure it was the
right one."

"You may as well put our problem bluntly, David. If Truscott killed this man Ross, why did he do it?"

"The idea seems to be that they were both in love with Miss Marston."

"That is what my granddaughter told me."

"And what I inferred from a rather cryptic conversation this morning with the detective in charge of the case," Warren put in.

"But surely it is more likely to have been something to do with the theft," Marston protested. "If Truscott stabbed him—"

"You're assuming rather a lot, sir. I can appreciate that your main concern is for Miss Marston; but we don't know that Truscott is guilty."

"He told me he was going to see you," said Warren. In an odd way the words sounded like an accusation.

"So he did."

"I have the impression that the case against him is a strong one."

"It is also circumstantial."

"Isn't that always true in a case of murder?"

"Mostly, I admit. But you're getting me confused," Maitland complained. His eyes moved slowly from one to the other of his companions. "Are you more concerned with seeing justice done to Bromley, or with Miss Marston's good name?"

Warren met his look unmoved. William Marston made a quick, involuntary gesture, as though by way of protest. "With justice," he said.

"But you won't be sorry if my—er—pursuit of justice shows that the motive for Ross's murder had nothing to do with Miss Marston."

"Naturally, I shall be very relieved." He spoke levelly, but he couldn't quite hide his resentment. "I don't find your way of putting it altogether palatable, Mr. Maitland," he said.

"You'll forgive me, sir, if I say that doesn't worry me overmuch." He smiled disarmingly as he spoke, and Marston's manner softened a little and he nodded his head as though acknowledging that a point had been made.

"That is reasonable," he admitted. "But I have to admit the prospect of scandal appalls me. If I could take Jo right away—"

"If you're thinking of Saint-Tropez, sir," said Warren bluntly, "the police won't allow you to take her abroad." His manner towards the older man was an odd mixture of deference and firmness.

"I suppose not. In any case, she has never cared for the villa," said Marston, almost fretfully.

"And apart from the question of her evidence, there is her contract with Anglo-Italian Films," Antony pointed out. William Marston nodded his head in a discouraged way.

"It's a pity she was ever allowed to get mixed up with them," said Warren briskly. "But the contract needn't worry us. I think I may say I have a certain amount of influence." He looked challengingly at Maitland, daring him to disagree.

"Now, you know, David, while Jo is in her present mood—"

"I'm not quite a fool," Warren assured him. "But she'll get over all this nonsense."

Marston had a doubtful look for that. "I'm not at all sure she will, while she looks on Bromley as a martyr," he said. "But I'm more concerned about the murder; can her name be kept out of it, Mr. Maitland?"

"Not if Truscott is arrested . . . unless the police change their mind about his motive."

"I see." In an odd way the bluntness seemed to have a reviving effect on his spirits. "I know you think it's all my fault, David," he added in a sharper tone, "but I really don't see what I could have done about it."

"When she wanted you to agree to the contract? Called her bluff," said Warren bracingly. "The trouble is, you don't understand her, W.M." He smiled as he spoke. Maitland said into the silence that followed:

"May I ask you one thing? In the interests of justice, of course."

"Certainly."

"Well, perhaps the question should more properly be addressed to Mr. Warren." He turned his head a little to meet the banker's eye, and added in an offhand way, "What does 'R.1 month' mean?"

Warren frowned. "I don't see what that can have to do with Ross's murder," he protested.

"Neither do I, but I hope you'll answer."

"Well, then, it's an abbreviation we use in Advance Department to indicate to the typist that the Branch should be instructed to report on an account in one month's time. As you might have guessed," he added, with a tinge of sarcasm in his tone.

"I did. I also guessed that an account under such frequent report was perhaps giving the Bank some little concern."

Warren glanced quickly at William Marston. "In general, that would be true," he said shortly.

"And in the case of the Anglo-Italian Film Company—?"

"Truscott had no right to give you any such information."

"He didn't. The file was on his desk, and I've rather good eyesight. I'm quite prepared to treat the matter as confidential."

"Until it suits you to do otherwise, no doubt," said Warren, unappeased.

"Just what I was about to add," Antony agreed cordially. "It would explain, too, why you feel you might have some influence—"

"That is an extremely improper suggestion." Warren's color heightened to an alarming degree.

"I'm sorry. The niceties of the financial world escape me."

"What do you mean?"

"In my ignorance I imagined—you must forgive me if I am wrong—that you were proposing to bring some sort of pressure to bear on Signor Valenti, if at any time it seemed expedient to break Miss Marston's contract." His tone was almost apologetic, and surprisingly Warren threw back his head and laughed.

"Financial pressure. Do you know of any better kind?" he said. "It's done every day, but we don't talk about it. And if it were to Jo's advantage—" He seemed to have talked himself back into good humor again.

William Marston had been silent for a time, but obviously not uninterested. He said now, reprovingly, "There is no question of anything *dishonest*, Mr. Maitland."

"Of course not."

"But I should like to know what was in your mind when you raised the question of the film company's standing."

"I'm trying to consider every possibility."

"An insurance swindle?" said Warren alertly. "Now you *do* interest me. The insurance moneys, of course, would come to the Bank, but I imagine the person who held the d'Albret emeralds could be assured of their fetching a reasonable sum."

"There are difficulties about the theory." Marston spoke slowly, thinking it out.

"It has its attractions too," Warren told him.

"On that basis," said Marston, "why did Michael Ross die?"

"Because he saw the thief in the act of planting the emeralds on Roy Bromley." Warren swung round to face Maitland again. "That's what you're thinking, isn't it?" he demanded. "Blackmail."

"Among a dozen other, equally unlikely, theories," said Antony gently, and watched the excitement fade from the other man's eyes.

"Yes, well, I suppose I got carried away rather. I admit"—his manner had stiffened now—"I'd like to see a solution that exonerated both Truscott and Bromley."

"And that left Jo out of the reckoning," said Antony, his eyes on Marston's face; and when the older man turned to meet his look he smiled at him. "If I can be said to have a 'client' in this business, it's your granddaughter," he added. "You may be sure I shall do my best to protect her interests. But I can't twist the facts, you know."

"I thought that was what lawyers were for," said Warren sardonically. But William Marston raised a hand to silence him.

"I'm grateful for that assurance," he said quietly. "It's as much . . . more . . . than I have a right to expect."

There was really nothing to be said after that, and he made no demur when Maitland got up to go. Antony was surprised, and not altogether pleased, when Warren expressed his intention of accompanying him. But most likely Jo was out; it seemed improbable that her grandfather could have kept her bottled up during the period of his visit if she had been anywhere on the premises.

He was making for the tube station, and Warren fell into step beside him without any immediate attempt to break the silence. It was still cold, too cold perhaps for the rain that had seemed to threaten; Antony turned up the collar of his raincoat, but it was an unconscious gesture; he was thinking of the events of the past half hour, and wondering a little uneasily if it had been quite wise . . .

But gradually he became aware of a sort of smoldering anger in his companion, and straight away he was unable to understand why he hadn't noticed it before. Warren was staring straight ahead, and he still hadn't spoken, but the inference was as inescapable as if he had shouted his displeasure aloud. After a moment he turned and, finding Maitland's eyes fixed meditatively on his face, laughed shortly and said:

"I wonder how long it will take W.M. to realize you didn't tell him a thing."

"About as long as it takes to dawn on him that there was no reassurance I could give him," said Antony mildly. As there was no reply to this, he went on after a brief pause, "Now, speaking as an outsider, I'd have said you had an ax to grind yourself."

"No!" Warren's mouth closed with a snap on the word, as though he were determined neither to amplify it nor to explain more fully what he meant.

"I thought you rather took to the 'insurance' theory."

"Too convenient, I'm afraid. I've never really doubted Bromley's guilt, and now if young Truscott's been getting himself into trouble—"

"Your own reading of his character notwithstanding?"

"Yes, I know." He brushed the reminder aside. "Any man can go to pieces over a woman."

"Don't you think it's rather a coincidence if the theft and the murder are unconnected?"

"W.M. would like to think so," said Warren dryly. "He's always been soft with Jo. Letting her dine with the Valentis, for instance . . . as if working with them wasn't enough. I told him there was no need for that. Now there'll be a scandal, and he knows well enough he's only himself to blame."

"An uncomfortable state of mind." Maitland had slipped back into his casual manner.

"And you don't think there's anything to be done to prevent

it?" Warren glanced at his companion as he spoke, and added awkwardly as he caught Antony's eye, "As a friend of the family . . . well, I'm interested, you see."

"That's very natural."

"W.M.'s got it into his head you can do something . . . find out the truth . . . keep Jo out of the picture." He was earnest suddenly, his anger forgotten. "I don't see it myself, but then I've no background in this kind of thing. What may be obvious to the trained mind—"

"I'm a lawyer, you know, not a b-blooming bloodhound," said Antony, hiding his annoyance well enough. "I thought Jo had explained."

"Yes. Yes, of course," Warren told him hastily. "But I've read about you—haven't I?—from time to time."

"H-have you indeed?" This time there could be no doubt at all that he didn't like the way the conversation was going.

"A very impressive record of success in court." Warren nodded. And again there was the sidelong, speculative glance. "But I was thinking rather of your earlier connection with Intelligence—"

"You didn't read about *that* in the papers," said Maitland flatly.

"Someone spoke of it. W.M., I think." (Of course, he'd check up when he knew Jo had been to see me, Maitland thought.)

"I'm afraid he would be disappointed." The flat tone should have discouraged any further questions. "There's very little glamour—"

"I thought . . . I couldn't help noticing you've got a stiff arm. Wasn't that the war?"

"More or l-less." He couldn't altogether hide his furious resentment at his companion's persistence; and, as always, the reaction—involuntary as it was—angered him still further. Twenty years was long enough to forget . . .

"Bad luck," said Warren. He seemed to realize at last that his remarks were unwelcome. "I was in the Army myself," he said, probably by way of an oblique apology. "Saw the whole thing from Dunkirk on, and never a scratch even though I got myself mixed up in that bloody business at Arnhem."

His voice ran on, smoothing over any awkwardness that Maitland's touchiness had caused. But Antony was in no doubt at all that the earlier clumsiness had been deliberate, an attempt to weigh him up; and probably Marston's idea in the first place. He was conscious of a certain wry amusement as he wondered what Warren—who had apparently enjoyed *his* war—had made of his own instinctive recoil from the subject; but he had no intention at all of becoming involved in an exchange of reminiscence, no matter how amusingly the other man dangled the bait of his own experiences. And he was a good *raconteur,* it was churlish not to respond; Antony was saved from embarrassment only by his exasperation. Who did Marston think he was—or Warren himself for that matter—that they should be trying to assess in him abilities which he had never claimed?

"It isn't a bit of use," he said, interrupting again to speak his thought aloud. "I've no intention of offering Mr. Marston my references." And watched, with a return of amusement, the almost ludicrous look of consternation that spread itself across David Warren's features.

"My dear fellow, what must you think of us?" That was the Bank man again, afraid of offending a favored customer; but his quick comprehension showed Maitland that his guess hadn't been so far astray.

"I just thought it might be as well to get that clear. My only responsibility—if I have one—" he added reflectively, and Warren broke in in his eager way.

"To Jo . . . I realize that. But you can understand W.M.'s anxiety."

"On the whole, I'd rather it had been expressed to me."

"Of course." Warren smiled suddenly. "He didn't want to seem to be cross-examining you, he said. And I admit I didn't think you'd be so tough a nut to crack," he added ruefully.

The last of Maitland's irritation vanished. After all, they had their point of view. "Forget it," he said.

"I suppose I should thank you." Warren was himself again, the alien note of apology gone from his tone. "As for Jo—"

"What about her?"

"I don't know that I agree with W.M. . . . not altogether. A little adversity might do her all the good in the world. Bring her to her senses," he explained, and turned his head to smile at Maitland as though confident of his understanding.

"Well, it might." Antony sounded doubtful. "Who lives may learn," he added equably, and quickened his pace as he saw the entrance to the underground only a little way ahead.

CHAPTER 11

If he had been at all concerned about where Jo had got to, the problem was solved when he got back at Kempenfeldt Square. He thought he recognized the beige coat that was thrown across a chair in the upstairs hall, and when he strolled across to push open the door of the living room the clear tones of her voice were unmistakable.

When he went in she surprised him by getting up, and coming across the room to give him her hand. Over her head his eyes met Jenny's for an instant, then he looked down at Jo and said lightly, "You don't seem any the worse for your adventure."

She did not attempt to answer that, or even to match his tone. "You've been to see Grandfather," she said seriously.

"Yes," he agreed; and waited for her to ask him why. But she wasn't in any doubt about that.

"Now he wants Roy to be innocent," she said, and he thought it was indignation that lent a quiver to her voice. "I think it's beastly of him."

The hand that lay in his was very cold. "You'd better come back to the fire," he told her. "How long have you been here?"

He crossed the room to push one of the wing chairs a token two inches nearer the hearth.

"I oughtn't to stay," said Jo, hesitating. "I don't want to be a nuisance."

"Too late to worry about *that*," said Antony, without sympathy. It was probably his bracing tone, rather than Jenny's reassuring, "Of course you'll stay," that brought Jo sweeping across the room to seat herself regally in the high-backed chair. "Now what are you complaining about?" he asked her. "I thought that was what you wanted, to convince your grandfather—"

"He doesn't really believe it," said Jo. "It's just—it's just expediency. But that doesn't matter really. I wanted to make sure . . . you won't stop trying, will you?"

Again his eyes met Jenny's. He said ruefully, "I won't stop trying."

"But do you think . . . does this make any difference?"

"I don't know. I don't know yet."

"You see, it's dreadfully important."

"Yes, you told me that."

She sighed. "And now there's Larry. He wouldn't kill anybody, you know. Well, he wouldn't," she insisted, when he did not immediately reply. "I know—I couldn't help knowing Michael Ross was making up to me; and Larry is always kind. But that could be all it is . . . just kindness."

"Is that what you told the police?"

"Of course it is. It's true."

"I'm glad to hear it. Tell me, Jo, what was Ross like?"

She frowned a little over the question. "About the same height as Larry, more slightly built, much more—much more address. Good company, a very good dancer. He liked music too, but he was a bit highbrow about it."

"Did he talk about his job?"

"Not much. I hadn't really thought about that before. Only if you seemed to think he was asking too many questions. He wanted to write about the film, you know . . . about Angelo, and Giuditta, and everyone."

"Have you been seeing much of him?"

"I've been out with him . . . now and then."

"Did your grandfather approve?"

"Not really," said Jo, and gave a sudden, gurgling laugh. "He said he wasn't a gentleman."

"You said he 'made up to you,'" Antony reminded her.

"I could handle that," she assured him airily. Then she looked at Jenny and added confidingly, "I thought perhaps it might reconcile Grandfather to my marrying Roy, if he saw what *might* happen."

"I'd have done exactly the same thing myself," said Jenny seriously.

"Minx," said Antony, without rancor; dividing the criticism, it seemed, indiscriminately between them. Jenny grinned at him.

"Did it work?" she asked.

"Well, I think it might have done, in time. But there's no denying Grandfather's very stubborn about what he wants," said Jo regretfully. And then, "Oh, dear, I keep forgetting Michael's dead."

"Did he ever talk to you about his friends, or introduce you to any of them?"

"I certainly never met any, and I don't really remember if he mentioned people he knew."

"A chap called Drayton, for instance. John Drayton." She shook her head. "Oh, well, tell me about last night instead."

She stiffened. "I told you."

"Yes, I know you don't want to think about it, and you needn't now. I meant the earlier part of the evening."

"What about it?"

"You had dinner with Angelo and Giuditta. Were there any other guests?"

"Just Frank Eversley."

"And he left when you did, at ten o'clock?"

"No, he went earlier. About a quarter to, I should think."

"Do you know why?"

"Giuditta asked him that, she said he should take me home; but I didn't encourage that idea, of course, because I did wonder if Larry might be waiting for me. And Frank just said, 'Let's say I have my reasons'"—the words were drawled in a very fair mimicry of Eversley's tone—"and you could tell he wasn't very pleased to be asked."

"What did you think the reasons were?"

"I wasn't very interested. Giuditta said when he had gone, 'It is that redheaded *bambola*,' and Angelo said, 'No harm in that,' and Giuditta pulled a face—a doubtful sort of face—and said, 'No harm, but she is very expensive.' " So far she had been taken up with her narrative, but now she gave him a frightened look and said uneasily, "I don't know why you should be interested in that."

"Don't be silly, Jo," said Antony irritably. "Of course you know."

"Because he was one of the people who could have planted the emeralds on Roy? But so could Larry, and you don't think he killed Michael."

"I don't think he killed him because of you," Antony told her, and sat back to watch her work that out.

She flushed, and twisted her fingers together, and said, not looking at him, "That isn't a very nice thing to say."

"I'm not trying to be nice."

She raised her eyes to meet his for a moment, and then fell to studying her hands again. "I see."

"Did you know Ross would be waiting for you last night?"

"I told you I thought perhaps Larry . . . I wouldn't have let them both come."

"Why not? Did you think they'd quarrel?"

"That isn't what I meant at all."

"But Ross was there to meet you, don't you think? Whether you expected him or not."

"Oh, yes, I suppose so."

"Had he ever done that before?"

"No, but I can't think of any other reason." She paused, and added in a small voice, "He knew I should be at Angelo's, and I'm sure he'd heard about the ten o'clock rule."

"You've said several times you thought Truscott *might* meet you—"

"Yes, he told me about the message he got; it was really very silly of him not to realize I wouldn't drag him half across town

to walk to the bus stop with me. I expect it was just his landlady muddling things; we met her one day and she's one of
those benevolent types," said Jo scornfully.

"I see." There might be something there for Geoffrey, or
there might not; more likely someone was lying, and even a
lie might start out with innocent intent. "Now, when you turned
into the alley—"

"You said I needn't think about that."

"That was five minutes ago," Antony pointed out.

"Oh, very well!"

"Bear with me, Jo. This is important. When did you first
realize what had happened?"

"I just thought someone was ill. Then Larry told me—"

"What did you think? What did you say?"

"I think I said, 'Oh, *Larry!*' "

"Charmingly noncommittal," snapped Antony, suddenly losing patience again. This time when she looked up at him her
eyes were steady.

"I was shocked," she said, "and frightened. I didn't say it
reproachfully, as if I thought he'd killed Michael. I never
thought that . . . not for an instant."

"Sure about that?" He turned to look at Jenny and said as
though in answer to a spoken protest, "It's a question that's
going to be asked."

"Don't worry, darling. Jo is much more single-minded than
you give her credit for."

"That's what I'm afraid of," said Antony obscurely, and
watched his wife's serious look dissolve into a smile.

"You needn't be," she asserted.

Jo seemed to be considering whether to embark on a protest
of her own, but perhaps she found Jenny's smile reassuring. She
said firmly, "I'm quite, quite sure," and folded her hands on
her lap and looked up at Antony with the eyes of a martyr.

"Yes, I suppose it would be an error to underestimate you,"
he remarked grimly. "All right then, we'll leave it there."

"And I'll make some tea," said Jenny.

In the end they all went into the kitchen to wait for the kettle
to boil, and carried what they needed back piecemeal into the

living room in a thoroughly disorganized way. Antony was silent, thinking over what Jo had told him; but presently his mind returned to the question of the financial status of Anglo-Italian Films, which he found intriguing, and he thought he might as well ask her. . . .

"A sort of patchwork affair," Jo was saying, and it took him a moment to realize that Jenny must have asked her about the film. "Several stories in one, really. My bit's about my first love . . . it's all very sweet and tender, and I shouldn't think anyone will believe a word of it." She paused, considering this statement, and then shook her head. "I don't know, though; Angelo has the most frostbitten ideas, but somehow they always seem to add up."

"Even at the box office?" said Antony.

"I suppose so." But for some reason the question seemed to trouble her. "I don't know much about that, really. Angelo only talks about artistic merit, and Giuditta says she knows nothing about money, and Frank is inclined to be—to be cynical. I mean, if he says we're having a crisis I don't know whether to believe him or not."

"What does Major Cooke have to say?"

"Well, nothing to me, of course. Giuditta says he's always preaching death and destruction, but she seems to think there's nothing in it."

Antony passed his cup for a refill. "Mr. Warren was with your grandfather when I saw him." The remark seemed to him to follow naturally on what they had been saying.

"Was he? I suppose . . . what did he say about Larry?"

"He seemed concerned—" Her wide-eyed stare was disconcerting, but he didn't feel he could explain. It seemed, however, that he might just as well have spoken bluntly.

"Not for Larry, I expect."

"Well—" he said. Suddenly, unexpectedly, her smile was impish.

"Larry says David makes him tired, he's so—so dynamic."

"That sounds more like your grandfather's opinion. His phraseology, at any rate."

"Perhaps that isn't exactly what Larry said. Grandfather

thinks the world of David, you know." In some way she contrived to make this rather unoriginal statement sound like an opinion arrived at only after the deepest consideration. She was so serious that Antony smiled and asked idly:

"Don't you agree?"

"I'm sorry for him, of course," said Jo. "I mean, I expect it's because his wife died that he throws himself into his work with such—such dedication. Only I can't help feeling sometimes that perhaps she wouldn't have died at all if he hadn't worn her out." She paused, and then grinned again. "I'm a cat," she said. "Grandfather says his devotion to his job is wholly admirable, and he'll end up one of the General Managers."

"The height of all ambition," said Antony absently. "Not the sort of person, then, to make a mistake about a firm's standing?"

"Oh, I shouldn't think so." She sounded horrified; blasphemy against one of Grandfather's canons was evidently a deadly sin . . . and Jo herself not so unimpressed as she would like to appear by his opinions.

"Larry said the Bank wants to lend money," Maitland said. Obscurely, this was an explanation of his train of thought, but the idea still appeared to him to be unreasonable.

"Why, yes, of course."

"It's just a vague sort of idea I had." Not very helpful, because the whole situation could easily have changed since the original loan was made. And Angelo might not worry if the company's finances were shaky, but the other partners were unlikely to be quite so lighthearted about it. But how did that fit in with the fact that Ross had been murdered?

On the whole, the enigmatic Mr. Drayton was still more interesting than any of them. And if another figure stood in the shadows behind him, as Sykes had hinted, it was too early yet to worry about that.

CHAPTER 12

It didn't seem a good idea to seek out Angelo and Giuditta too early next morning; they might be sleeping, or they might be at church, there was no telling. Antony phoned Major Cooke instead, at about ten o'clock, and that wasn't a very popular move either. First there was a good deal of skirmishing with a series of youthful voices whose reluctance he put down uncharitably, and probably correctly, to a feeling that the instrument was for their exclusive use, rather than to any consideration for "Daddy." Finally there was Cooke himself, very irascible, and he couldn't flatter himself that the announcement of his identity had a noticeably mellowing effect. For whatever reason, the Major was less nervous this morning than when last they had talked, and a request for Drayton's address was received with something like a snarl.

"He isn't in the phone book," said Antony patiently.

"No, but I can't see any reason—"

"I want to know more of Ross, and Drayton knew him."

He felt on edge himself this morning, and it wasn't too

easy to suppress his inclination to reply in kind.

"I thought your interest was confined to the theft of the emeralds," said Cooke unpleasantly. But he added grudgingly, when no comment was forthcoming, "Last I heard he was living at Thames Ditton, but that was a couple of years back."

"Do you think he may still be there?"

"How should I know? Houseboat moored at Latimer Reach, perfectly bloody idea," said Cooke; and slammed down the receiver in the midst of Maitland's gratitude.

There seemed nothing for it but to go down to Thames Ditton and see for himself. At worst, there was a chance of getting a line on Drayton's present address. If Sykes had known about *that* setup, he'd have surely mentioned it; in fact, he'd probably be interested, but tomorrow was also a good day.

After last night's downpour the morning had a clear, rain-washed look. Jenny said, "It'll be a nice run," and bundled the breakfast things into the sink. Later, when they were on their way and for a moment the road was clear in front of them, she said casually, "This man Drayton—"

"What about him, love?"

"When you saw him before you weren't altogether happy about him."

He glanced at her then, but her eyes were intent on the road-way. There was nothing unusual in her attitude; as always when she was driving it was at once relaxed and utterly absorbed. "I didn't like him," he said. "But I'm still not sure it was Drayton I saw at Ross's flat."

She brushed that aside, the gesture scarcely more than the loosening of her left hand on the steering wheel, but its meaning unmistakable. "What are you going to ask him?"

The truthful answer would have been: I shall leave that to the inspiration of the moment. "About Ross," he said. "That's reasonable, as they were friends."

"He may not be a reasonable person."

"I shouldn't be surprised. But I think he'll be at pains to seem so."

"Why should he? I mean, a lot of people don't like answering questions."

"No," said Antony thoughtfully, and gave her a grin. "Anything personal in that remark?" he asked.

"Oh, well!" said Jenny. And then, "You won't forget about Roy Bromley, will you? It's terribly important to Jo."

"My dearest love, that's the whole purpose of the exercise."

"There's Inspector Sykes's gang," she pointed out. "And one thing does seem to be leading to another . . . don't you think?"

Latimer Reach proved easy enough to find. Jenny was able to park where she could look across the river, and settled herself with a book. Antony walked along the towing path until he came to a group of small boats that had a lived-in air. And sure enough, as he passed the third in line a girl came on deck with an armful of washing, and he was able to ask her, "Does John Drayton still live here?"

"Drayton . . . I don't think—" She frowned over the query for a moment, and then turned to call, "Harry!" over her shoulder. A tousled head appeared. "Do you know a man called Drayton?"

"Not to say know." Harry jerked his head. *"Gaiety Sal,* about a hundred yards further on. Keeps to himself, Mr. Drayton does."

Gaiety Sal belied her name, a depressing-looking craft on whose outward appearance neither love nor labor had been expended. But unlike the others he had passed, she seemed to be intended exclusively as a residence, a converted barge, Maitland thought, but it was obviously many years since she had moved from her mooring; and her size seemed to offer a possibility of comfort that the smaller boats had lacked. He was considering the etiquette demanded of a caller—should he stand on the path and yell, or step aboard and knock decorously on the nearest door—when he became aware that the galley door was in fact open; and through it there came, before he had time for further debate, the tall man he had seen at Ross's flat. He had an iron pan in his hand, and the fragrance of frying bacon surrounded him like an aura. And even here, in slacks and a high-necked pullover, he contrived to retain his look of elegance.

Antony said, "We haven't been introduced, but I think you must be John Drayton."

"If it's of any interest to you, I am." Neither words nor tone was cordial.

"My name—"

"Yes, I remember your name, Mr. Maitland. You came to Michael's flat."

"You know what's happened?"

"We are not quite out of the world here." The idea seemed to amuse him.

"He was a friend of yours. I'm sorry." Drayton made no reply to this, but his lips tightened a little. "Your breakfast's getting cold," Antony pointed out.

"It will wait. Did you see Michael the day he died?"

"No. I kept the evening appointment, but he wasn't at home."

"I see." There was still the abruptness, but a degree of calculation had crept into his manner now. "He said he'd let you know—"

"That he'd be out that evening?"

"If he had to go out. But you can't have gone to the trouble of seeking me out here, Mr. Maitland, just to find out if I delivered your message."

"I didn't, of course." As they talked he had strolled up to the strip of planking that ran between the barge and the shore; Drayton made no gesture of invitation, but neither did he try to bar the way when Antony stepped across onto the deck. "Do you mind," he said, having done so, "if I come aboard?"

Drayton's thin lips twisted into a sneer. "Don't hesitate to make yourself at home." His eyes were cold, and hard as glass. "How did you know where to find me?" he added.

"Major Cooke—"

"And why did you want to? You're meddling in things that don't concern you, Mr. Maitland." There was a stillness about him now; he seemed quite unaware that he was still holding the heavy pan.

"Am I?"

"First the d'Albert emeralds. But they were recovered, weren't they? The thief was caught."

"That's what I'm trying to find out."

"I'm afraid I don't understand you."

"Whether the right man was convicted. You know the Anglo-Italian film people, don't you?"

"Some of them, in a casual sort of way. I haven't seen any of them for some time."

"Not since the New Year," Antony agreed.

"You seem remarkably well informed of my movements," said Drayton sharply. "Now why should that interest you, I wonder."

Maitland shrugged. "Things come up," he said vaguely. "I expect Ross told you what happened at the party on Shrove Tuesday."

"He mentioned it. I wasn't particularly interested, especially after Bromley's arrest."

"Do you know Bromley?"

"What makes you think that?" The cold eyes were unfriendly.

"Nothing, I suppose." Maitland smiled. "Except perhaps *now;* because your answer was rather evasive."

"If you can give me one good reason why I should be putting up with all this—"

"Your innate goodness of heart," said Antony, still gently.

"Insufficient, I'm afraid." He looked down, as though surprised, at the congealing contents of the pan and twisted so that he could put it down somewhere inside the galley. Then he said slowly, "Why should you be interested in this man?"

"In Bromley? I don't think I am, particularly. But at the risk of sounding smug, I am interested in justice."

For the first time Drayton laughed; Antony thought it an unpleasant sound. "A pretty word!"

"Yes, isn't it?" He sounded pleased to have found a point of agreement.

"And now you're extending your interest to cover Michael's death." There was a spark of anger in the pale eyes. "Aren't you afraid, Mr. Maitland, that your activities might be resented?"

"Is that a threat?" Antony wondered.

"A warning merely."

"Based on logic, I suppose, not on knowledge." He sounded depressed.

"It isn't always . . . wise to know too much."

It occurred to Antony that, if that were true, he ought to be as safe as any man in London. He'd even been wrong when he told Jenny that Drayton would be at pains to appear reasonable. "Why do you think Ross was killed?" he said, and saw the other man's quick frown.

"Perhaps the police could tell you that, Mr. Maitland. I don't feel competent to make a guess."

"Love, or money?" said Antony vaguely. "Or was it, perhaps, some other reason?" And this time Drayton's flash of expression was one of naked viciousness. He said, tight-lipped:

"You'd better go."

"Yes, I've disturbed you long enough. You've been very patient with me." The conventional words fell oddly between them. He crossed to the shore and then turned to add, by way of valediction, "I'm grateful for your help."

He was to remember later, without pleasure, the look in Drayton's eyes as he stood in silence, waiting for his unwelcome visitor to leave.

After lunch, a telephone call revealed a surprising enthusiasm on Angelo's part for his suggested visit. "We shall be so glad, *signore*," said Angelo in his ear, too loudly for comfort. *"Venga quando vuole."*

"In about an hour's time," said Maitland. And scowled at the telephone, after he had replaced the receiver, until Jenny broke the silence by asking:

"Was he rude to you?"

"On the contrary, love."

"Then—"

"I'm wondering why he wasn't," he explained.

He went on foot to Montague Court, which seemed as good a way as any of ensuring that he did not arrive too soon. There were puddles in the park, but the sun was still shining and the daffodils had a cheerful look. There was the feel of spring, and —even here in town—the smell of spring. He thought again of Roy Bromley, and of Jo saying, "It isn't nice, being in prison"; and he took a moment to wonder whether she realized—with all her sympathy—what a massive understatement that was. And clearer still there was Jenny's voice, "It's terribly important," and he remembered for the first time that he had no idea what she and Jo had had to say to one another.

It was at this point that he realized he was being followed.

He couldn't have told what instinct first alerted him; once the idea occurred to him he had no difficulty in spotting the man in the brown overcoat. A plump little man, inconspicuous enough in the ordinary way, but not, he thought, particularly expert at the job he had undertaken. Antony loitered, crossing the road, and the other man was equally hesitant; when he lengthened his stride, his shadow was almost running. Easy enough to shake him, but did it really matter, after all? The exercise would do him good.

The odd thing was that the development didn't surprise him. If anything, he was gratified, because it tended to confirm an idea that had somehow got into his head. But even now it was the wildest guess. . . .

If it was spring in the streets, it was spring too in the penthouse apartment. Angelo himself let him in, and led the way to a large untidy room that seemed full of reflected sunshine. There were flowers everywhere; too many flowers, thrust indiscriminately into vases with no apparent attempt at arrangement, and then set down in the first available space. For some reason the effect, which should have been overwhelming, was altogether charming.

And in the midst of all this there was Giuditta, rising with casual grace from a deep sofa and holding out her hand with a soft murmur of greeting. Her hair was swept up today into an elaborate erection (perhaps it was the influence of the season that made Antony think, irreverently, of a bird's nest), she was carefully made up, her slippers were on her feet, and she wore a wonderful gown of crimson and gold brocade. " 'More than oriental splendor,' " he murmured, bowing over her hand.

"Come?"

"I was quoting, *signora*. A reprehensible habit. And I'm afraid my command of your language is insufficient for translation."

"No matter. We are so pleased to see you." She sank down

on the sofa again, and gestured invitingly, so that he should sit beside her. "You shall tell us, Antonio, what this policeman is thinking; and what it means, this sad affair of Michael's death."

"I suppose you mean Inspector Conway," said Maitland cautiously; and turned to look at Angelo, who was on his feet still and regarding them benevolently. In shirt sleeves and with his collar unbuttoned, the little man looked by no means a match for Giuditta's magnificence, but his high spirits were infectious and his buoyancy undiminished.

"The severe Inspector Conway," he agreed, nodding in a pleased way, as though over some unexpected display of intelligence. "But first I shall give you a drink." He glanced at the clock, though it could hardly have been informative because of the spray of mimosa that drooped across its face, and added suspiciously, "You will not ask for tea."

Maitland assured him that he would not.

"Then I give you wine. Not Chianti . . . which to your restaurants is the only wine from Italy; this is from Piedmont, a superb wine, mellow."

Antony accepted a glass meekly, though it wasn't exactly his idea of a suitable tipple for three-thirty in the afternoon. Angelo filled Giuditta's glass and his own, and came back to smile at him encouragingly. *"Alla sua salute!"* he said. And then, "To come back to this Inspector—"

"I saw him yesterday." It seemed more like a month ago.

"Giuseppina has told me."

"Well, he didn't tell me what he was thinking, of course."

But for the moment he had only to go with the tide. "He came here," said Angelo, "on Friday night. Very late, after we had retired. When did Giuseppina leave us? he wanted to know. Is it reasonable that we should know this precisely?"

"At two minutes past ten o'clock," said Giuditta. Angelo gave her a hurt look, and flung himself down in a low chair opposite the sofa.

"I am an old man," he said with considerable pathos, "and I cannot change my ways. And to ask me about this Lorenzo— the little Giuseppina tells me this is incorrect, but no matter, his

other name is barbarous, even for an Englishman. How can I
tell what he thinks, what he feels, what he does?"

"No doubt the Inspector thought that your work must give
you an insight into human behavior," Maitland suggested. The
wine was sparkling, and oversweet; perhaps it would serve to
mellow his tongue.

"That is true, of course," said Angelo, becoming more cheerful. "The young man is in love, that is evident, but for the rest
. . . how can I, who have the soul of an artist, understand one
who is a banker?"

"I don't think he's a very good one," Antony pointed out.
He glanced at Giuditta, and thought there was a faint amusement in her eyes; but her voice was serious as she spoke.

"It will not be good publicity if he is arrested."

That was an angle that hadn't struck him, and even now he
was more taken up with the thought that they seemed well
enough informed without asking for his opinion. He said, frowning, "I don't quite see—"

"Giuseppina," Angelo told him, as though that made everything clear. Perhaps it was Maitland's puzzled look that
prompted the further flow of explanation. "For two films now
I have built up the image of a fresh, innocent young girl; and
do not doubt me, *signore,* there is a future for innocence." He
paused, apparently to contemplate with pleasure the picture
he had drawn; but then his expression changed, his shoulders
drooped, he was a man overcome by care. "If now she is to
be dragged through your police courts—"

"No one's thinking of arresting Jo," said Antony, startled.

"What difference? Here are two young men at odds over
her—"

"A good deal of difference, I should have thought, from her
point of view," said Maitland; but Angelo's gesture consigned
the objection to the oblivion it deserved.

"For Giuditta, that is different." He looked at her com-
placently. "Always there are men in an agony of devotion! A
suicide . . . a murder, even . . . no one will think anything
of it, except perhaps to say, 'Let us see for ourselves how

beautiful she is.' " He broke off, and added in a completely different tone, "For myself I do not believe it."

"What don't you believe?"

"That an Englishman will kill his rival for love."

"Was Ross his rival?"

"This—this Larry may have thought so."

"*Signore.*" He turned sharply at the sound of Giuditta's voice. "Do not misunderstand, we are concerned for Jo herself, not just for our silly films. But I am not in agreement with Angelo; I think perhaps, even in England, a man might kill for love."

He smiled at her anxious look. "Such a thing has been known."

"Jo is *una bellissima ragazza.*" Only a woman as beautiful as Giuditta, he thought, could have spoken so simply, with such a complete lack of envy. "I think perhaps you do not realize, Antonio, how very attractive she is. And it is not only the young men. So I think, if a quarrel sprang up—" She broke off, watching his expression. "You do not believe it," she said.

"Could you explain how Larry Truscott came to be carrying a knife?"

"The police must think they can explain it, if Jo is right and they are thinking of an arrest."

"Oh, in court!" He sounded rueful. "I could make the jury believe it myself, if I appeared for the Crown. But here and now . . . we've all met him and talked to him; wouldn't premeditation be rather hard to swallow? And harder still in view of Jo's feelings for Roy Bromley."

"He is in prison for three years."

"*La donna è mobile,*" he said, laughing at her and making the words a question.

"No. Oh, no! But she is only eighteen." She looked at Angelo. "You are both of you against me," she told him. "So it is decided then between you, Larry is not an assassin."

"I only meant to imply," said Maitland, "that I thought the motive for Ross's murder must have something to do with the theft—the attempted theft—of your emeralds, *signora.*"

Her hand flew to her throat, as though she were wearing the

necklace and would find its touch reassuring. "I do not understand you."

"If you are right, then it does not concern us," said Angelo, as though the matter were settled. "We will have some more wine." He bounced up, collected the glasses, and hurried across the room.

"Antonio." He turned his head and found Giuditta's eyes fixed on him imploringly. "You think perhaps Michael saw the thief . . . knew who it was?"

"It's possible . . . don't you think?"

"She is as clever as she is beautiful," said Angelo, rejoining them with three full glasses on a small tray, which he offered with a flourish. Perhaps he didn't recognize drama unless he himself engendered or directed it; his tone now was cheerfully matter-of-fact. "No doubt that is what happened, for he was a blackmailer, we know."

"Angelo!"

"But you knew this, *carissima*. And for his murder I have an alibi, so why should I fear to admit a motive? Besides, I did not listen to his threats, so there was no reason—"

"You're saying Ross tried to *blackmail* you?" said Antony, almost as explosively as Angelo himself might have done. The Italian's eyes opened wide as though in surprise at the violence of this reaction.

"I do not myself find it strange," he said. "He thought I was a soft touch—do you say?—and he admitted to me that he was in need of money."

"Will you tell me?"

"But why?" Giuditta protested. "When it can have no bearing—"

"It might help me to understand what Ross was like, *signora*."

"I shall tell you," Angelo declared. He seemed strangely insensitive to her distress; there was even something admonitory in the look he gave her. "It is merely that he thought I had stolen the emeralds, and would be willing to pay for his silence."

"But you couldn't—"

"At the end of the war, *signore*, when first they came into my possession."

"I see," said Antony doubtfully.

"But there could be no doubt about my ownership, for the man who sold them to me was dead."

Maitland relaxed suddenly and grinned at him. "How did he die?"

"In the bombing, *signore;* he and all his family. And the *palazzo* in ruins." He spread his hands to convey the extent of the desolation. "As a patriot, I am with the Resistance, of course." He returned Antony's smile, twinkling at him. "Signor Ross was 'trying it on,' " he asserted. "And perhaps if my conscience had not been perfectly clear—"

"That is always an advantage," Maitland agreed.

"So we understand one another." Angelo beamed at him.

"When did you have this discussion with Michael Ross?"

"Before the party. A week before, perhaps."

"But still he was invited—"

"I did not wish to make an unpleasantness." He succeeded in sounding as though this were the most reasonable thing in the world. "There was, besides, the article he was to write . . . the romance of the emeralds . . . of Giuditta's beauty . . . of my own genius."

"Do you think he would have done this?"

"He said so, *signore.*"

"And it never occurred to you, when the emeralds were stolen, that the police might be interested in what you knew of him."

"But why?" Faced with the question, and with the bewilderment implicit in Angelo's wide-flung hands, Antony could only shake his head. "Perhaps if the thief had not been caught . . . but he was caught, *signore.*"

"Yes, I see." A moment ago he had thought himself on Angelo's wavelength; now it seemed they had no mental contact at all. He picked up his glass, and glanced sideways at Giuditta, who said promptly:

"I did not know then what Michael had tried to do. Only later Angelo told me."

"How much later?"

Her eyebrows went up a little, a mild rebuke for the unexpected roughness of his tone. "Yesterday, as was natural. After we heard of his death."

Maitland drank and put down the glass again. There was a small glow of warmth from the wine, but it didn't really touch the sudden chill he felt. "Do you know John Drayton, Signor Valenti?" he asked.

"No, I . . . why, yes, of course, it is the friend of *il Maggiore*."

"Ross's friend also."

"Is that true? But we have not seen him for so long. And then, so small an acquaintance—"

"Why does this man interest you?" asked Giuditta softly.

"I don't think I can answer that." He turned to look at her. "He keeps cropping up, that's all."

"Well, one thing I can tell you: he has not been to the studio since Michael first came there."

"Was there anyone he was particularly friendly with?"

"With Cooke, of course," said Angelo. "Perhaps also with Francesco."

"I do not think so at all," said Giuditta flatly.

"But I assure you, it is true."

"Mr. Eversley was here on Friday night, wasn't he? As well as Jo."

"They both came to dine."

"I've been wondering why they didn't leave together."

"But why should it matter?" Angelo sounded revolted by the unreasonableness of the question.

"I don't suppose it does. All the same—"

"It was Jo that was being tactful, Antonio." He must be in favor again, he thought, noting the use of his name. "He had an engagement, perhaps."

"So he left at nine forty-five, and she waited until ten o'clock?"

"Yes."

"Did she say anything to make you think that either of these young men—Truscott or Ross—might be coming to meet her?"

"Nothing," said Angelo. Giuditta hesitated, and when she spoke she sounded far less positive.

"I do not think she would be surprised to find one of them there."

"Did you ever observe any signs of ill feeling between them?"

"We have not seen them together since the night of the studio party."

"But you've seen both of them with Jo?"

"Oh, yes."

"And if Bromley is innocent, you think Ross might perhaps have been blackmailing the real thief?"

This time Angelo nodded energetically, but Giuditta was silent and looked down at her hands. "But come, *carissima*," he said encouragingly, "this was your own idea."

"It was a foolish thing to say," said Giuditta briefly. She raised her head, and met Maitland's eyes, and said on a note of entreaty, "You will agree, Antonio. It was just . . . something to say."

"Was it, *signora*?" But it was difficult to disregard the appeal. "I must go," he said, and got to his feet, and saw her look of relief, quickly disguised. But a moment later she was echoing, with apparent sincerity, Angelo's invitation.

"Spero che ritornerà presto."

Downstairs there was still the problem of the man in the brown overcoat, and it was odd that Maitland was more urgently concerned to wonder what had gone wrong with the recent interview, after it had started out so well. He walked to Somers Street through the alley where Michael Ross had died, pacing the distance absentmindedly and noting the placing of the single, old-fashioned lamp; but there was no answer there to his questions. When he went to the bus stop the plump man lingered indecisively a few yards away; make it easy for him, then, by going upstairs and leaving him to take a seat where he could watch the platform. Halfway along he changed his mind about playing tag where the traffic was heavier, and losing his shadow that way. He stayed with the bus to the nearest point to Kempenfeldt Square, and walked the rest of the way home at a leisurely pace.

When he got in he used the phone in the study. There was a sabbath hush on the room, an odd feeling of detachment that communicated itself as he sat listening to the shrilling of the bell. He'd no reason, after all, to expect that Sykes would be at home awaiting his convenience. But just as he was about to replace the receiver he heard the click that told him the connection had been made, and then the detective's placid greeting.

"Asleep, Chief Inspector?"

"To be precise, Mr. Maitland, I was digging."

"You and me both," said Antony, and sighed. "But that wasn't why I disturbed you."

"I hoped perhaps you had something positive to tell me."

"Well, I have, in a way. I'm being followed."

The pause while Sykes weighed this statement was of the briefest. "Where are you?" he asked.

"At home. There's a chap outside in the square who's just been with me to Montague Court and back. Not police, unless he's been told to be clumsy."

"At the moment there seems to be no reason—"

"No. Precisely. But I'm not imagining things, Chief Inspector."

"I'll get someone onto it."

"Thank you. About five foot five, I should say, inclined to stoutness. Round, pink face, clean-shaven. Brown overcoat and a bowler—"

"Are you sure he wasn't trying to sell you insurance?" asked Sykes dryly.

"Quite sure. You don't seem to me to be taking this seriously," Antony complained.

"Well now, Mr. Maitland—"

"Never mind. There's just one other thing while we're talking . . . would you like Drayton's address?"

Again the faint hesitation. "I'd be interested," Sykes told him.

"Latimer Reach, Thames Ditton. A houseboat called *Gaiety Sal*. At least," he added doubtfully, "he was there this morning."

"You saw him?"

"Yes. Nothing for you, I'm afraid, nothing *positive*." He echoed Sykes's word with a hint of malice, but then, suddenly, he was urgent to be gone. "I'll be at home all the evening, if you want me. And I'm sorry, really I am, if I've spoiled your day."

"It's always a pleasure to hear from you, Mr. Maitland," said Sykes in his precise way, and with no more than an undertone of amusement in his voice.

"Oh, go to the devil!" said Antony, exasperated.

CHAPTER 13

Upstairs, as he had expected, Sir Nicholas was having tea with Jenny. "This will probably save my life," said Antony, accepting a cup and placing it in a convenient position on the mantelpiece. "Angelo stayed me with flagons—*Asti spumante,* if I'm not mistaken." Sir Nicholas grimaced. "Precisely, sir. A trifle cloying. Now, if those are cucumber sandwiches, love—"

"You'd better take the plate," said Jenny, resigned.

"It would be interesting to know," Sir Nicholas remarked, helping himself in a casual way to what remained of the buttered toast, "how much longer you are going to devote to this affair, and just what you think you are accomplishing."

Antony, who had taken his stance on the hearthrug, looked down questioningly at his wife. "Geoffrey was on the phone about half an hour ago," she told him.

"Oh, I see." That explained at least the coldness of his uncle's tone. "Is he still fed up with me?"

"I'm afraid he is, rather." She glanced at Sir Nicholas as she spoke, and he took up the complaint with energy.

"He wants to know what you're trying to do: clear Bromley,

or persuade the police they haven't got a case against Truscott?"

"I told you Inspector Conway was in charge, Uncle Nick."

"Yes, I know he's no friend of yours. But you might try answering the question, Antony."

"Well, I don't know. Both, I suppose."

"I realize that, as far as Bromley is concerned, your sympathies were aroused; but I am not quite clear," said Sir Nicholas meditatively, "on what you base this touching belief in Truscott's innocence."

Maitland turned to retrieve his cup, and abandoned his place on the hearthrug in favor of one of the chairs. "I don't suppose I'd believe him if I wasn't sure the theft and the murder were connected," he said.

"Would that necessarily clear Truscott?"

"Oh, no. Not if he stole the emeralds and Ross was blackmailing him. But I don't think he was the thief."

"Guessing again, Antony?"

"If you like, sir."

"I don't like," Sir Nicholas grumbled. "I thought I'd made that clear. And now I suppose you'll tell me it's none of my affair."

"He was much too nicely brought up, Uncle Nick," said Jenny. Sir Nicholas darted a scandalized look at her. Antony laughed suddenly, and said:

"If you can bear with me, I'd like to tell you my ideas."

"I don't see how I can stop you," said Sir Nicholas disagreeably.

Jenny was engaged, with the utmost concentration, in squeezing the last drops from the teapot. "I should like to hear," she said; it struck him suddenly that she was uneasy . . . a reflection, perhaps, of his own mood? Or was there something more? "From what Jo told me, I don't think Larry Truscott would be the kind of man to kill anyone." She put down the pot and looked from one to the other of her companions. "Too correct," she said.

"It isn't really safe to say that about anyone, love," Antony told her. "Warren said, 'Any man may go to pieces over a woman,' and he's not so far off, at that."

"But you said—" Jenny's protest was cut short by Sir Nicholas, who asked in a bored tone:

"Who is Warren?"

"One of the Chief Controllers in the Advance Department of the Northumbrian and Wessex Bank," said Antony with precision. And then, more humanly, "I say, Uncle Nick, did you know that banks *like* lending money?"

"I think I am conversant with the more elementary rules of commerce," said Sir Nicholas, deflating him neatly. Maitland grinned.

"Well, Warren only comes into the picture because he looks after the Anglo-Italian account; and if the company are in a bad way financially—as I think they are—the theft might have been intended as an insurance swindle. The insurance on the emeralds is in order, that's one thing I'm sure about. That was my first idea, and that would make Eversley the thief."

"With or without his partners' knowledge?"

"Without, I think. Cooke is a testy little man, when he's sure enough of his ground, but I don't think he has anything on his conscience. And Angelo . . . it isn't Angelo's kind of fiddle, too devious. Besides, I'd be very much surprised if he'd consent to any scheme which might harm Giuditta. And before you start getting sentimental over that, Jenny, I may as well add that she's what the Bank romantically call a business asset."

"But she's beautiful," Jenny protested. "Isn't he in love with her?"

"Oh, I think so. But he's probably the only person in the world who isn't at all awed by her beauty," said Antony slowly; probably the explanation was as much for his own information as hers.

"But Eversley would have had to tell them if he meant to sell the emeralds to boost the company's finances."

"Oh, if the plan had succeeded, that would have been a different matter. Even Angelo—"

"No doubt these speculations are of interest," said Sir Nicholas, "but you said, your *first* idea."

"Yes, I discarded it pretty early on. Look, we've got to start from the fact of Bromley's innocence."

"Is that a fair assumption?"

"For the purposes of argument, Uncle Nick."

"Very well." He leaned back in his chair and folded his hands across his stomach. "Expound," he invited.

"Well, the theft itself poses certain problems. I mean, no one in his senses would want to hang round indefinitely with the emeralds in his pocket. If there had been an accomplice they could have been tossed to him through one of the dressing room windows; there was no check on people coming into the perimeter area, only when they were actually going into the studio. So I think we can take it the thief worked alone.

"I began by eliminating Bromley, but Eversley can be eliminated too, by the same argument. Either of them would have been missed if he left the party early, or even if he went out for long enough to dispose of the emeralds safely. Truscott I also eliminated, though more tentatively, because it was the first time he had been to the studio; he'd had no chance to lay any plans. He might have given way to a sudden temptation, but once I'd seen him I was pretty sure that whatever had happened it wasn't that."

"Too correct," said Jenny stubbornly. Antony ignored her.

"So that left Michael Ross," he said.

"Yes, we are capable of so elementary a sum," said Sir Nicholas, rousing himself.

"Well, take a look at him for a moment. I've no idea what he lived on, but I'm pretty sure it wasn't journalism. As far as the party was concerned, he could expect much greater freedom of action than the others. He wasn't a well-known film star, he wasn't escorting anybody, and he knew the terrain . . . he'd made it his business to know it. From a chance meeting with Cooke he deliberately cultivated the film people—"

"People are curious about the films," said Jenny. "And then there was Jo."

"I'm in no danger of forgetting Jo."

Sir Nicholas opened his eyes again. "An attractive young lady," he remarked judicially. "If you're right about this man Ross, Antony, what went wrong with his plan? Surely he would have left the studio immediately."

"I expect that's what he meant to do. But the door at the end of the dressing room corridor was locked, he probably didn't expect that; no one could get out of the windows, only the transoms open; and the small door at the far end of the studio was locked too. That only left the main entrance, with the commissionaire on duty; I can understand him fighting shy of that."

"Not to the extent of staying in the studio, surely, when the other possibilities were exhausted."

"No, of course not. But at that point, you see, Eversley called to him. He wouldn't want to attract attention by ignoring him, but I should think he meant to get away as quickly as he decently could. And that's another thing, as I told you: he had a hole in his trouser pocket."

"He was a bachelor, wasn't he?" said Jenny.

"I was just thinking that would have been a convenient place to carry the sandbag. After he'd disposed of it by leaving it in the passage he could easily have forgotten about the hole."

"Not the most efficient of thieves," Sir Nicholas pointed out gently. "I take it that you are about to postulate a connection between Ross and this—er—Association that Chief Inspector Sykes so unwisely mentioned to you."

"Well, sir . . . yes, I am. But first let's consider his acquaintance with a man called Drayton, who has—shall we say?—suspicious antecedents."

"Nicely phrased." Sir Nicholas nodded his approval. "By all means let us consider it."

"I wondered if Drayton might be the head of the Association. Sykes didn't agree; I told you his reasons. All the same, Drayton has been living for five or six years since he 'retired'—like Ross, with no visible means of support. So I'm going to make another assumption: that he's something to do with them."

"Unwarranted."

"You know, sir, he could be useful; I mean, he'd know the underworld and could act as a sort of go-between—"

"I have always flattered myself," said Sir Nicholas pensively, "that you took after your father's side of the family. But he was a silent man."

"I'll be through much quicker if you'll grant me this further assumption."

"Guesswork." The thought seemed to depress him. "Well, go on."

"As far as the Association is concerned, Sykes spoke of the Chief Buyer, a chap with the ability to organize and the knowledge to market the proceeds lucratively. I'm putting Drayton into the hierarchy as a sort of middleman, between him and the fellows who actually do the dirty work."

"I see." No one could have regarded the comment as enthusiastic. "Granted the original premise that the Association exists at all, that seems reasonable," Sir Nicholas went on sadly. "Are you now going to explain why Ross should have been killed?"

"I was coming to that. He'd failed, you see, and I don't suppose that made him very popular. It was all right as long as Bromley was quietly in prison, but then the case was reopened and I went to Ross's flat and Drayton saw me there. And quite obviously he recognized my name."

"I have always deplored the amount of publicity that your activities have attracted from time to time," said Sir Nicholas, but there was a gleam in his eye that Antony chose to construe as an awakening interest. "So you think Ross was killed—by this man Drayton, presumably—to prevent him from talking to you. Isn't that a little drastic?"

"It is, of course, but it all fits in. Drayton was keen on making a definite appointment for me, though until he knew who I was he'd been about as unhelpful as could be; but that isn't to say he passed the message on. It was the one way—don't you see?—he could be sure I shouldn't talk to Ross before he had time to lay his plans. If Ross hadn't told him he was going out on Friday evening he'd have thought up some reason to get him away from the flat. As it was, all he had to do was follow him and take the first chance—"

"Ugh!" said Jenny.

"I'm glad you have so much proper feeling, my dear," said Sir Nicholas, smiling at her.

"Well, I didn't say I approved of it, but I bet that's what happened," Antony protested. "And as for its being drastic, the

Association may already have decided to dispose of Ross if it became expedient, once they felt he couldn't be trusted to carry out orders. There's another thing, too, that I haven't had a chance to tell you about yet: he'd been trying a little blackmail as a sideline, almost certainly unauthorized. So what with one thing and another—"

"There's no proof at all that they would be prepared to go to those lengths."

"No. N-no. But another thing Sykes said was that Drayton . . . I think how he put it was that he enjoyed violence." He paused, frowning. Somehow he found this all too easy to believe. "And I can't forget that Jim Arnold was afraid of what would happen if he talked out of turn."

"It's all very well, my dear boy, but I don't think Horton will like it," said Sir Nicholas, with deceptive cordiality.

"No proof? He can't expect everything at once."

"Are you seriously suggesting—?"

"If we could identify the chap Sykes calls the Chief Buyer we'd be getting somewhere."

"I'll allow his existence, if you like. The Chief Inspector is not an imaginative man. But even if he is connected with . . . all this in some way," said Sir Nicholas, with a gesture that conveyed, as clearly as his tone, his distaste for the conclusion, "he might be anyone at all, so far as I can see. Someone you've never heard of," he added, rubbing it in.

"Don't be such a ray of sunshine, Uncle Nick. There's one lead . . . Drayton."

"If he is, as you suggest, an intermediary, I imagine his meetings with his principal are few, and those carefully arranged."

"Yes, I should think so too. All the same—"

"All the same Antony, you'll leave it to the police."

"In which case, damn-all will be done." He got up as he spoke and moved restlessly to the window. "Sykes doesn't like guesses any more than you do, sir."

"If I thought there was a chance of your getting anywhere . . . but do you seriously think you can?"

There was nothing to be seen of the man in the brown coat,

but that wasn't to say he'd gone. "I know—all right, Uncle Nick, I think I know—that the Chief Buyer is someone I've met and talked to during the last few days," Maitland said, his eyes intent on the shadows that lay alongside the dusty garden in the center of the square.

"What makes you say that?"

"I expect Jenny told you I went to see Drayton this morning." He dropped the curtain and turned back to the room again. "He knew altogether too much about my activities. Someone had told him—"

"Major Cooke . . . *was* he regular Army, by the way?"

"I haven't the faintest idea. But not him; he wasn't even certain where Drayton was living now."

"Come now!" Sir Nicholas moved a little, not altogether abandoning his lounging position but contriving nevertheless to convey a sharper interest. "He told you that . . . were you constrained to believe him?"

Antony gave him a grin. "Unless he's the Chief Buyer he'd no reason to lie to me. If he is he'd be the last person to put me in touch with Drayton; so easy to say he didn't know his address."

Sir Nicholas considered this. "You may be right," he said grudgingly. "Who else have you seen who knew what you were about?"

"Jo, first of all; I think we must absolve Jo. And Roy Bromley, who would certainly not be languishing in prison if he were the head of a criminal organization. Then on Friday I went to the film studio and saw Angelo, Eversley, Cooke, and Giuditta."

"You absolved Eversley too, just now."

"As the thief, sir. Not from the—the more important role."

"Angelo, then. Has he no other name?" added Sir Nicholas impatiently.

"Valenti. I suppose Giuditta has too, but I don't know it."

"Having seen her at the cinema I find it difficult to believe—"

Antony found the idea amusing. "Not in character," he agreed. "But I didn't know you were a fan of hers. Besides, she thinks Eversley stole her emeralds, and unless that was a double bluff it ought to let her out. There's one thing about Angelo, though: he made a point of telling me that Ross had tried to blackmail him. And if I'm sure of anything it's that he had some reason for doing so."

"But, darling—" said Jenny, and subsided again as Sir Nicholas turned his eyes on her.

"If Ross saw the emeralds placed in Bromley's pocket, and later tried to blackmail the thief—"

"I discarded that idea when I decided Ross stole them himself," Maitland told him. "Angelo might have been trying to be genuinely helpful, though I doubt it. Or he might have been trying to take the heat off the Association, of course."

"I wish you'd confine yourself to the Queen's English," remarked Sir Nicholas plaintively. "In any event, your reasoning is vague and probably invalid."

"I'm just thinking aloud, sir."

"So much is obvious. But since the whole idea is most likely based on a fallacy it seems uncommonly like a waste of time," he added, glowering at his nephew as though daring him to contradict. When he was satisfied that no retort was intended he went on, still repressively, "From your interviews on Friday morning, then, we have obtained the two names: Signor Valenti, and Francis Eversley."

"And in the afternoon I talked to Warren at the Bank, and to Larry Truscott. There was a chap called Landor too, but unless Larry told him why I was there—"

"And on Saturday," said Jenny, raising her head but avoiding Sir Nicholas's eye, "you went to see Jo's grandfather." Antony stiffened, and his eyes were intent again.

"What made you think of him, love?"

"It's just that, if he happened to be the Chief Buyer—" She broke off and looked at Sir Nicholas, and then at her husband again. "Well, *if* he was, it would have been so easy for him to arrange for Roy Bromley to be framed."

"You mean, to rid Jo of an unwelcome suitor?"

"Yes . . . don't you see? It would be practically foolproof. I think he had his own ideas about who she ought to marry."

"Then what about the murder?"

"Perhaps Ross was blackmailing him. Everything you said about the Association could be true, Antony; but if Michael Ross was the real thief he was the one person who could queer Grandfather's pitch . . . with Jo, for instance."

Maitland took a deep breath and looked at his uncle. "She's got a point," he said. Sir Nicholas abandoned his indolent pose and sat up straight in his chair the better to emphasize his protest.

"I have lost all hope," he said, in measured tones as though he were pronouncing an anathema, "of finding the least semblance of good sense in either of you. After this flight of imagination—couched, moreover, in the most vile of colloquial terms—I can only say—"

"You needn't, darling, I'm sorry. It must . . . it must be contagious," said Jenny penitently. But Antony ignored both protest and apology and said with some force:

"Don't discourage her, Uncle Nick. It makes a good deal of sense to me. What about David Warren, Jenny? What's the case against him?"

"I don't know him," she protested.

"You don't know Marston either."

"No, but . . . Jo talked about him, you see. And I couldn't help seeing then how convenient it was for him that Roy went to prison."

"And now Larry Truscott is suspected of Ross's murder. He's in love with Jo too; at least everyone says so."

"I hadn't actually got that far." Jenny looked startled. "Oh, dear, it's quite true, isn't it?"

"Don't worry, love. It isn't proof."

"No, and you don't really have to find extra reasons, do you?" She seemed eager now to discount what she had been saying. "I mean, a man's a criminal because he wants money, I suppose; he doesn't need any other motive. And that would go for Mr. Warren, or Francis Eversley, or Angelo, or anyone else you can think of."

"I can't think of anybody else, but that's enough to be going on with."

"More than enough!" said Sir Nicholas, at his most repressive.

But Antony was deep in his argument, and took no notice.

"As far as having 'connections abroad,'" he said, "which is a thing Sykes insists on, so far as I can see any one of the four might do. Angelo, certainly; Mr. Marston . . . now I come to think of it, he spoke of taking Jo abroad and I gathered he had a villa somewhere or other; Warren survived Arnhem . . . queer chap, he sounded as though he'd enjoyed it; and I don't know about Eversley, but—"

"He was in the Fleet Air Arm during the war," said Jenny. "I read that somewhere. Anyway, film people are always going abroad. On location," she added kindly, in an aside to Sir Nicholas, who was looking outraged.

"I hope that neither of you will hesitate for a moment to slander anyone who comes into your mind," he said, and set himself, a trifle grimly, to demolish his nephew's arguments. In fact, he stayed to supper, so far as Jenny could see for the sole purpose of doing justice to the theme, and Antony sacrificed a bottle of Château Margaux—which he had been saving for a more auspicious occasion—in the vain hope of sweetening his uncle's mood.

CHAPTER 14

It wasn't to be expected, of course, that Sir Nicholas had finished with the subject even then, and as they made their way to chambers the following morning he treated Antony to a further lecture on the folly of the course he was pursuing, as exemplified by Michael Ross's death. Antony said mildly, "I'll take care, sir," and refrained from pointing out that they were being followed by the same stout little man who had dogged his footsteps the day before.

He had not heard from the police on Sunday evening, so presumably there had been nothing to report. As he went up the stairs in his uncle's wake he determined to have another go at Sykes at the first opportunity, but old Mr. Mallory was waiting to pounce on him, and it soon became obvious that it was going to be one of those days.

When Maitland had left the junior bar some two years before, it had not been without some qualms as to the wisdom of what he was doing; now he found himself as busy as ever, which at once relieved and, very slightly, disappointed him. The falling off in paper work ought to have lessened the pressure; at the same time, a serious crisis on the financial front might easily have ensued. Mallory continued to produce each set of papers with a deepening air of gloom, as though he expected it to be the last, but there didn't seem to be too much to worry about on that score. Now, after greeting Sir Nicholas, the clerk bustled after Antony into his own, smaller room. "If I'm not much mistaken, you'll be in court with Mr. Enderby tomorrow. And there's Mr. Horton been asking for you already, and that policeman you're so friendly with—"

Antony looked up and smiled at him. If he had ever had any idea that his uncle's clerk would one day accord him some sort of deference, the hope had withered long since. "Chief Inspector Sykes?" he asked.

"That's what he *said*." Mallory's doubtful tone seemed to be carrying caution altogether too far, but if his attitude had been queried he would certainly have affirmed that you couldn't take anything for granted. "And now there's a set of papers from Watterson's, and Mr. Rogers's clerk was telling me they'd be wanting you in that libel business—"

"For the newspaper?"

"No, Mr. Maitland, for the plaintiff."

"Well, that's good, isn't it? We don't want to starve."

The slightest twitching of Mr. Mallory's lips acknowledged that this was a pleasantry. "I don't see how we can do both, Mr. Maitland, really I don't, and I wouldn't want to disoblige Mr. Watterson—"

"He'll live," said Antony callously, his attention already taken by the papers on his desk. It wasn't as if it were the slightest use his voicing an opinion. "You'll do what you think best," he added; which had the advantage of being true. Mr. Mallory always did. He went away now, unsatisfied, to wrestle with the problem of placing Sir Nicholas in two courts at once, which was going to be necessary, he could feel it in his bones, about two weeks from now.

When he was alone, Maitland looked at the documents Mr. Enderby had sent round some three weeks before, and wondered how much he could remember of the rather tenuous line of argument he had at that time evolved. It only needed them to bring the Longman business forward, and they'd really be in trouble; but that, he rather thought, was before Alwyn, who wasn't likely to get through his list with any undue speed. A little comforted, he pulled the telephone towards him. "Get me Mr. Horton, will you, Hill?" and counted to ten slowly while he waited for the connection to be made, because he rather thought he'd need to exercise patience before they were through.

Geoffrey was inclined to be querulous, but he kept it short; which probably only meant he had a client waiting. The phone rang again as soon as Antony replaced the receiver, and when he picked it up there was Sykes's voice, faintly reproachful. "Did you get my message, Mr. Maitland?"

"I was just going to call you."

"Oh, well then, I've saved you the trouble. This man now, that you say was following you—"

"He's wearing a Burberry this morning," said Antony helpfully, "and a soft hat."

"There was no sign of anyone loitering in Kempenfeldt Square yesterday evening," said Sykes positively.

"No perseverance; he'd probably gone home to tea. So you think I was pulling your leg?"

"I didn't say that, Mr. Maitland."

"No, but I'm very sensitive to innuendo. On the other hand, I've been wondering . . . it wasn't Inspector Conway's idea of a joke?"

"Why on earth should he do a thing like that?" Sykes wondered.

"*Joie de vivre.* Youthful high spirits. I expect you know him better than I do."

"You can put that right out of your head, Mr. Maitland. You say the man's there again?"

"He is."

"Is he worrying you in any way?"

"Not at all. A very peaceful chap; I'm getting quite fond of him. And if you send round again he'll only do another disappearing act."

"I shouldn't be surprised."

"Do I detect a note of irony? Don't worry, I'll deal with the matter myself tonight."

"Now, Mr. Maitland—"

"What's worrying you? If he's really a figment of my imagination—"

"I didn't say that!" It was very rarely that Sykes raised his voice, but this time the words were nearly a shout. Antony held the receiver at arm's length, and rubbed his ear.

"All right. Forget it. Tell me about the medical evidence instead."

"Medical evidence?" Sykes's caution had reasserted itself, and he sounded as though he had never heard the words before.

"Michael Ross's murder. And don't tell me it isn't your case—"

"Well, it isn't."

"—because I'm sure you're interested enough to have found out whatever there is to know."

"He was stabbed," said Sykes, making a concession.

"Come now, that's something! What about the weapon?"

"A long-bladed sheath knife, the kind you can buy in any store that sells camping goods." The detective's voice was completely expressionless. "Made by a firm in Sheffield, and so far as Conway could gather over the phone there'd been no change in either design or material for years."

"Any hope of tracing it?"

"All things are possible."

"I suppose that means no. Do you think . . . it doesn't sound the sort of thing a man could prove he didn't own," said Antony, and heard Sykes chuckle.

"Not quite so lucid as usual, Mr. Maitland. But you're right, it doesn't look like being useful either to defense or prosecution."

"I see. No fingerprints, I suppose."

"Every amateur," said Sykes a little tartly, "knows enough these days to wear gloves."

"Did Ross die immediately?"

"Very near." He paused, perhaps weighing the advantages

and disadvantages of discretion. "If you want it all, it looks as if the murderer came up behind him, hooked an arm round his neck, and pulled him straight back onto the dagger."

"*Straight* back?"

"Yes, I thought that was what you were fishing for. No one could swear whether it was a right-handed or a left-handed blow."

"Conway noticed that, did he?"

"That your friend Truscott is left-handed? Of course he did. Though I don't really see why it should worry you; I've heard you argue black was white in court."

"Is that nice?" said Antony reproachfully. And then, misleadingly diffident, "We're getting to that stage, are we?"

"Does it surprise you?"

"No. No, not really." He abandoned the query regretfully. "Do you know any more about Ross?"

"Not much. About Drayton, though—"

"Well?"

"He wasn't at home last night. Of course, he may have come back late."

"You went down to Thames Ditton?"

"It was a nice evening," said Sykes, almost defensively.

"So you're not such a doubting Thomas, after all!"

"Well now, I just don't like to leave anything to chance, him living on a houseboat and all."

"I thought that would interest you," Antony told him with satisfaction. "Look here . . . I was talking to him yesterday, and he knew what I was after before I told him."

"Ross could have mentioned your inquiry."

"He was the first person I tried to see . . . remember? And I never had the chance to tell him what it was about. Besides, Drayton knew I was interested in the murder, and Ross is the one person who couldn't have told him that."

"What exactly are you trying to tell me, Mr. Maitland?"

"That I really do think Drayton might lead you to your Chief Buyer."

"So if you haven't scared him away," said Sykes unkindly, "I might be able to get a line on his associates?" It wasn't until the conversation concluded that Antony thought of the very reasonable retort that if Sykes had listened to him in the first place . . . Now he remembered his argument with Sir Nicholas, and his mind recoiled from the idea of making his points again to an equally skeptical audience. He said wearily, "That's one way of doing it."

"Well, what would you suggest?"

"That you pay particular attention . . ." He enumerated his ideas doggedly, and heard at the end Sykes's deep chuckle.

"As good as a novel," the detective told him appreciatively.

"I thought I ought to tell you—"

"Always listen to the call of duty," said Sykes with approval. "Wakefield'll be reet chuff with the idea of that Signor Valenti as a mastermind."

"It would be very easy to underestimate Angelo."

"I'm glad you warned me about that," said Sykes. "I'll let you know," he added, "when I'm ready with a warrant for the Joint General Managers of the Northumbrian and Wessex," and smiled to himself as he heard the clatter of Maitland's receiver being slammed back into place.

After his indignation had cooled, Antony worked steadily until lunchtime, when he was still so engrossed that he sent Willett out for sandwiches and coffee. He grunted and went on writing when these provisions were placed on his desk, but after a moment he became aware that the clerk was hovering in the doorway, and when he looked up Willett gave him a friendly grin and came back into the room. "I thought you'd like to know we've taken the libel case, Mr. Maitland. Watterson's were quite happy when we suggested they should get Mr. Halloran."

"So I should hope." Antony sat back and stretched his cramped fingers. "How did you manage it?" he asked, and pulled the coffee cup towards him.

Willett looked gratified at this evidence of discernment. "Same as usual," he said. "I let on I thought it would be better to take the other brief."

"Someday," said Antony, "you'll get us both into trouble." He inspected his sandwich for mustard and decided that it was

probably edible as it was. "By the way, you've just been out."
Willett looked puzzled, and gestured silently towards the sup-
plies he had brought. "Did you see anyone hanging about outside?"

"There was a young man and a girl seemed to be watching
the door of this building, waiting to have lunch with someone,
I expect. They were still there when I got back."

"No one else?"

"There were a few people about. I didn't notice." Maitland
had become abstracted again, and Willett began to move towards the door. "A pretty, fair girl," he added, as though hoping to provide an alternative focus for the other man's interest.
Antony damned all blondes with a freedom he seldom allowed
himself, but still in an absentminded way; then his chair
scraped back as a thought struck him, and he made for the
window.

By craning his neck a little he could see down into the court.
Sure enough, the girl was Jo Marston, and Larry Truscott with
her. "Ask them both to come up for a minute, there's a good
chap," he said, and was still at the window when Willett appeared below and went across to speak to them. Then he returned to the desk and began to eat his sandwich. The stout
little man had not been in sight, but that wasn't to say he
wasn't lurking somewhere.

"We're very sorry," said Jo, "we thought we could catch you
when you went out to lunch." She stood in the middle of the
room for an instant, looking about her with an interest that was
quite unself-conscious; then her eyes came to rest on the desk
and she added contritely, "You *are* busy. I'd no idea." He
wasn't sure if it was the spread of papers that impressed her,
or the empty cup and plate.

Willett was placing a chair. He gave Maitland what was obviously intended to be a speaking glance before he went out,
but Antony ignored it, having no idea what it meant. When his
visitors were seated he sat down again himself, and looked at
Truscott and then at Jo. "Why aren't you both at work?" he
said.

"I've been to Cricklewood," said Jo virtuously. "I only just got back. Giuditta had to go to the dentist, and Angelo went mad and said he could do nothing . . . nothing! And so we all came home. And Larry——"

"Warren told me to take a day or two off." Truscott had obviously no intention of letting her speak his lines: "I suppose it would be embarrassing if they came to the Bank to arrest me," he added, trying to be fair.

"Have you seen the police again?"

"Not since Saturday. The inquest is tomorrow, you know. Mr. Horton said he'd go with me."

"That's all right, then." He thought perhaps this was the cause of Conway's delay; he'd wait till the inquest was safely behind him, and then make his move. "What did you want with me . . . both of you?" He wasn't too pleased to see them together, but it was a little late to protest about that now.

"Just to know if anything had happened." Jo wore her youthful assurance with an air, but beneath it was a greater tension than he had observed before. "You might have heard something more about Michael's death, you see."

"The police don't confide in me, I'm afraid." That was true enough about Conway, anyway; what Sykes had to tell him was between the two of them.

"I told you, Jo——" Larry began.

"Yes, I know. But I can ask, can't I?" She was sitting very straight, her hands clasped on her lap, and her eyes were fixed on Maitland's face, direct and questioning.

"If I could help——" he said. But there didn't seem to be any good way of ending that sentence. "As long as you're here, there's one question I'd like to ask you."

"What is it?"

"Tell me, Jo, when you told your grandfather you'd been to see me——" But it wasn't so easy, after all; he was glad when she interrupted him.

"He was angrier than I'd ever seen him. He isn't often really angry with me. But then, after Michael was killed, he said perhaps it was a good thing after all."

Antony turned his head, and met a frowning look from Larry Truscott. "What shoes were you wearing on Friday evening?"

"Shoes?" Whatever his thoughts had been, the question diverted him. "Brown walking shoes; I'd changed into slacks and a sports jacket after I left the Bank."

"It's the soles I'm really interested in."

"I see. Some sort of composition; I could have walked up behind Ross quite quietly."

"Larry!" Jo sounded horrified, but she was looking at Maitland and her eyes were indignant.

"That's what you wanted to know, isn't it?" said Larry doggedly.

"Yes, of course." He smiled at Jo. "You understood well enough the first time we talked that I couldn't help you unless I knew the worst."

"That was different." She sounded confused and uncertain. "This is murder."

"Is that all?" asked Larry abruptly.

"That's all I wanted to know. And there's nothing I can tell you, I'm afraid."

"Then we mustn't interrupt you any longer." The words were formal, but Antony was aware suddenly of a queer sort of loneliness about his visitors, so that the phrase "displaced persons" came into his mind, and in his turn he spoke abruptly, almost angrily.

"Where are you going?"

"I don't quite know." Larry turned his head. "Any ideas, Jo? I suppose we might go to the pictures."

"I suppose we might," echoed Jo, without enthusiasm. "There really doesn't seem to be anything else."

"If you're at a loose end you could go and see Jenny," Antony suggested.

"Could we do that? Could we really?" He was surprised at the eagerness in her tone.

"Why not?"

"I haven't met Mrs. Maitland. I really can't impose on her kindness," Truscott protested. Jo turned on him almost crossly.

"Don't be so stuffy, Larry. We can, can't we?" she appealed again to Antony. "You see, it would be awfully dull for Larry to go back to his digs, and I can't very well take him home with me. So if Mrs. Maitland wouldn't mind—"

"You know your way, both of you. I'll call her and tell her you're coming."

"We'd better get lunch first," Jo decided. "Tell her, about an hour."

They went then, but she turned for a moment in the doorway. "You are remembering Roy, aren't you?" she asked.

"I know . . . it's very important. I shan't forget," he assured her. But he sat frowning at the door for quite a time after it had closed behind her.

"How very sensible of you, darling," said Jenny's voice in his ear a few minutes later. "I've always wanted to start a kindergarten," she added, and laughed.

"That's just it." Her tone, rather than her words, reassured him. "They stood here looking at me like the Babes in the Wood—"

"Don't worry, Antony. I'll cope."

"All right, love, I'll leave you to it. I don't think I shall be late."

In spite of the people around them, Jo and Larry still had the illusion of being very much alone when they left the Temple and turned down the Strand. "You're in a very decisive mood today," said Larry resentfully; Jo was forging ahead at a good pace, but he found his way barred by two stout women who seemed rapt in contemplation of some very unsuitable underwear in a shop window. He slipped between them, and caught up with her, and said as he had done before, "I don't know Mrs. Maitland."

"You'll like her," Jo told him. "She's—she's real."

"And you, I suppose, are nothing but a mirage."

"N-no." She turned her head and gave him a quick, rather tremulous smile. "It's a good idea, really, Larry; unless you'd rather spend the afternoon in the National Gallery, or at Madame Tussaud's."

"I could take you home."

"And then go off by yourself; I'm not a traitor, and we said we'd stick together."

"Because you're grateful!" he said scornfully.

"Well, I don't see why I shouldn't be. You backed me up about Roy when nobody else would listen, and I don't think you even believed him . . . then."

"This is different. I may be arrested."

"Yes." This time the sidelong glance held no amusement. "Do you think I'm a sort of—of evil genius, Larry? I seem to bring my friends nothing but trouble."

"Nothing that has happened has anything to do with you," he said rather fiercely, and caught her arm as the opposing tide of pedestrians seemed to be about to sweep them apart again. "We may as well cross here."

"All right." There was a sort of docility about her as she went with him that at once pleased and angered him.

"I've no right to expect the Maitlands to treat me as a friend," he said.

"Well, neither have I. I just—just threw myself at him," said Jo, and grinned as though the memory amused her. "But I think—don't you, Larry?—that if anyone can find out the truth—" Her eyes were anxious again.

"I'm sure he'll try." He thought the words sounded grudging, and added hastily, "You can trust him, Jo."

"And I do think now," she went on, pursuing her own train of thought, "that perhaps there's a chance of proving that Roy didn't steal the emeralds." She caught at his arm suddenly, and held it as they moved, more slowly now, down the busy pavement. "When that happens it will be all right, won't it? Everything will be all right?"

He hadn't time to assess his own emotions. The blue eyes that looked up into his were the scared eyes of a child badly in need of reassurance. Not just her hand on his arm, but her whole body was trembling. "Everything will be all right, Jo," he told her. "Of course it will!"

CHAPTER 15

Antony had finished his lunch and gone back to Mr. Enderby's brief. If they were really to be in court tomorrow he'd need a word with Derek Stringer, who was also in Sir Nicholas's chambers, and who would be acting as his junior; so presently —with the argument reasonably clear in his head and a medley of indecipherable notes scribbled on the back of an old envelope in his pocket—he strolled down the corridor and found his friend alone.

An hour later, coming back to his own room, which led off the hall, he became aware that something had happened to disturb the usual serenity. Willett shot out of the clerks' office, obviously with news to impart; saw the open door of his employer's room in time and contented himself with a gesture in its direction and a hideous grimace; and disappeared again like a rabbit into its hole as Sir Nicholas came on the scene.

It was at once obvious that he was laboring under some deep emotion, and the very mildness of his greeting was sufficient cause for alarm in one who knew him well. "So there you are!" he said.

"Did you want me, sir?"

"There is a lady here who is waiting to see you."

"I was with Derek; didn't Mallory know?" He came up to his uncle's side, and through the open door saw Giuditta enthroned in one of the big leather chairs near the fireplace. "Sorry, Uncle Nick. I'll take her to my own room, shall I?"

"I should not dream of inconveniencing the lady." It seemed safe to infer from Sir Nicholas's tone that he had noted the slight twitching of Antony's lips. "Pray make yourself at home, my dear boy, make yourself at home!" he added with patent insincerity. "Here is my nephew at last, *signora*. I will leave you to your affairs."

"But no, Monsignor Nicola, we shall not turn you from your own room," she protested.

"It is my pleasure." In spite of its smoothness there was a finality in his tone; his eyes met Antony's for a moment, then he went out, and the door closed gently behind him.

Giuditta's hair was dressed more simply today, her makeup delicately applied. She wore a brown dress, which in his ignorance Maitland categorized as "simple," a fur cape had slipped back from her shoulders, and she had kicked off her shoes; but in spite of the quietness of her attire there was a sort of unconscious arrogance in her bearing, and her beauty was very apparent. Antony pushed aside some papers, and seated himself on a corner of the desk.

"You need not accord my uncle so much respect, *signora*."

"How then? Is he not a nobleman?"

"A baronet only. Very nearly the lowest form of life."

Her quick frown surprised him. "Today I do not wish to laugh."

"We will be as serious as you please," he assured her.

"I should not have come? But I needed to see you."

"How can I serve you?"

Perhaps his tone reassured her. For a moment longer she eyed him anxiously, then she relaxed again and said more naturally, "I have been to the dentist, because this I tell Angelo, and I do not lie to him. So now I am here, and he does not know. You will be discreet, Antonio *mio*. I can rely on you?"

"I won't tell him," he promised.

"He does not understand, you see. He does not believe there can be any harm in your inquiries . . . for us."

Now, if ever a man were thoroughly alive to the situation . . . "You do not agree with him, *signora?*"

"It is because I think you suspect something that is not true."

"I don't know the truth," he said soberly. "As for the rest, I should have said it was you who suspected—"

"I know nothing," said Giuditta hastily. "Nothing at all!"

"But you think—don't you?—that it was Frank Eversley who struck you . . . who took your emeralds."

"No!"

"Then why are you here?"

"I did not expect that you would be so unkind," she said, wilting gracefully.

"Never mind my unkindness." His control of the situation was slipping, so that it was rapidly degenerating, he felt, into something very like a nursery brawl. "I could have asked you outright yesterday—"

"Yes, and I am grateful, Antonio. It would not be good to talk of this with my dear Angelo."

"Well then!" When she did not immediately respond he added impatiently, "You have always thought that Eversley was the thief, and now you are afraid that Michael Ross knew it."

"How can I make you believe me? When I have told you so many times, and now I come here to tell you again, that the masked man was not so tall as Frank."

"Then you have some other reason . . . you know, perhaps, that he is in need of money?"

"That does not make him a thief."

"But it's true, isn't it? And he couldn't draw from the firm because the Bank were being awkward about further lending; they wanted to see some reduction in the overdraft, not watch it creep up and up—"

"You are unkind, Antonio," she said again, but now she was leaning forward, very much in earnest, and her whole body

was tense; as though, he thought, she could force my belief by
will power and nothing else.

"It's true, isn't it? Are you going to deny—?"

"Oh, no . . . no! I deny nothing. Only that Frank had
anything to do with these dreadful things." Her eyes were intent now; he thought for the first time that she had forgotten
herself completely, that she was no longer aware of him as a
person. "I can prove this to you," she said.

"You will tell me, perhaps, that it is not in his nature to have
murdered Ross."

"Well, I do not think it is, but how should I know, after
all? But to strike me . . . never, do you hear, Antonio? He
could never have done that."

"You spoke of proof, *signora.*"

"Yes, and now I wonder . . . will you understand?" She
paused, trying to read his expression; her eyes met his can-
didly, almost guilelessly. "I am his *amante,* I must tell you, and
never, never would he do anything to hurt me."

He got up suddenly, and went and stood near the hearth,
looking down at her. "You really believe that, don't you?" he
asked.

"Yes . . . yes . . . yes! You must see it is not reasonable.
If you and I, Antonio . . . would you *then* put on a mask and
hit me over the head?"

He turned his eyes on the fire, which was burning sulkily,
and hoped she hadn't noticed his smile. "Angelo doesn't
know?"

"He must never know!" Her sincerity was apparent; at the
same time he was aware that the scene was now going to her
liking. Pathos followed drama. "He is so jealous, Antonio. Not
that men admire me, this he expects. But he wishes that I
should love . . . only him."

"I'm not altogether surprised." Something in his tone made
her look up at him quickly. The words were gently mocking,
but his face was alight with laughter.

"Now I think perhaps you believe me," she said.

"My poor Giuditta! Not for what you have told me."

"It was true, every word."

"I should have said poor Angelo instead."

"But why?" she protested. "I love him, I do not wish to change. The other is different . . . just for a little while."

"Does Eversley know you came here?"

"Madre mia! No!"

He put out a hand to pull her to her feet. "We must let my uncle have his room back, *signora*."

"Yes, that is very well." She bent to retrieve her shoes. "But you will not forget what I have told you?"

"How could I forget?" This time she laughed back at him, but he wondered if she was really reassured.

As ill luck would have it, Sir Nicholas had just come out of the clerks' office when they went into the hall. *"Sono molto riconoscente,"* Giuditta told him in her most caressing voice. Her glance at Antony left him in no doubt of her mischievous intent. *"Arrivederla, Tio Nicola."*

"Il piacere e tutto mio," said Sir Nicholas, a trifle ambiguously, Antony thought. No one else could have made the formal phrase sound so stilted. Over his uncle's shoulder he could see old Mr. Mallory, his expression primly disapproving; all things considered, he was glad enough of the excuse to accompany the visitor until he could find her a taxi.

When he returned, Sir Nicholas was perusing a complicated statement, made by an apparently feebleminded juror, concerning alleged embracery, and his expression was austere. "She came to spin me a yarn," said Antony, half in apology. "I don't know how much of it was true."

"Very little, I dare say." His tone was crushing, but then surprisingly he smiled. "How rarely it is, Antonio *mio,* that one sees a really beautiful woman."

By the time he went home that evening Maitland was thoroughly sick of the whole affair, which seemed to have been weaving itself all day in and out of his more pressing duties. Not that Jo's troubles weren't pressing enough, in themselves, but he couldn't see his way and that in itself was annoying. In this mood, the unexpected absence of his shadow ought to have been a relief; instead it made him uneasy.

Perhaps because he was tired he decided, perversely, to walk home. So it was about six-fifteen when he crossed Kempenfeldt Square and saw a car parked outside number five, and wondered vaguely whether it belonged to Larry Truscott. But as he reached the pavement a man got out, and he recognized Frank Eversley . . . with a little difficulty, because it was the first time he had seen him without makeup.

The actor was as elegant as ever, but either the makeup or the studio lights had been kind to him. He had a haggard look, Antony thought; and then wondered if the word was an exaggeration. Perhaps loving Giuditta wasn't all beer and skittles, especially with so tempestuous a rival as Angelo in the background; but he remembered too that he hadn't been at all sure that she was telling him the truth.

"Can I have a word with you, Maitland?" Eversley's voice, at least, was well under control, as smooth as ever. "I've been waiting—"

"Not too long, I hope."

"No . . . no. I won't keep you a moment. Shall we walk round the square?"

"If you like." He fell into step with Eversley, and tried to forget that his shoulder was aching abominably.

"Giuditta's been talking to you," said the actor, still in that even tone.

"Yes." He still wasn't sure . . .

"I mean today," Frank Eversley told him. "I made her tell me."

The choice of words was not enlightening. "This afternoon," said Maitland noncommittally. "She told me you couldn't possibly have stolen her emeralds."

"But why?" said Eversley; and now his voice was alive with emotion. "I can't see why she should ever have thought such a bloody silly thing; and if she did—" He broke off there and looked questioningly at his companion.

"It isn't the theft that's worrying her now, though I think

she was always alive to the possibility of scandal; she's worried about the murder, of course."

"I see." He was quieter now. "It's this theory of Angelo's that Ross was blackmailing the thief—"

"She seemed to have an idea that absolution for one crime would cover both," said Antony apologetically. Eversley gave a sudden, explosive laugh.

"If I murdered anyone it would probably be Giuditta." He glanced at Maitland and added, "The police don't believe that . . . Angelo's theory, I mean. Do you?"

"As it happens, no."

"That's a relief, anyway. Now, if I can persuade my charming but boneheaded colleague that I don't need defending . . . or isn't it quite as simple as that?"

"Not altogether."

"And you don't, Giuditta tells me, believe that Jo's latest conquest . . . just where does that leave us, I wonder?"

"As far as I'm concerned, tired of the whole business," said Antony despondently. Eversley laughed again, uneasily this time, as though he wasn't quite sure how seriously to take the remark.

"I don't want you to misunderstand," he said. "You see, Giuditta . . . she gets ideas in her head." They walked in silence for a few minutes before he went on, "There's more behind all this, isn't there?" pushing out the suggestion tentatively as though it were a pawn he didn't particularly want to hazard.

"More than what?" asked Maitland unhelpfully, and lengthened his stride a little as they turned the corner that brought them back to the north side of the square. "Nothing's what it seems," he added, "I'll give you that."

They halted a moment as they came to Avery Street, while a Morris 1000 with "L" plates turned into the square with exaggerated caution and a grinding of gears. Eversley's face was even more haggard now; his whole attitude seemed to proclaim an indecision as marked as that of the little car's driver. He said, "It never is," and turned to meet his companion's eyes with a look that was oddly like despair.

Antony said vaguely, "In the film business, do you mean?" but Eversley brushed the interruption aside.

"She told you, didn't she? Giuditta told you."

"I don't—" Maitland began. He had no objection to discussing Eversley's love life if it would help in any way, but at the moment it seemed to him irrelevant. They had crossed the road now, and were abreast of number seven when the thought struck him and he swung round and added, no longer casual, "Ross was blackmailing you."

Eversley halted too. The shreds of his normal assurance clung to him, so that his reply sounded oddly fatalistic. "Somehow I didn't think I could rely on her discretion."

"Tell me one thing: when did it start?"

"Not long after Cooke first brought him to the studio. He must have spied on us deliberately." He seemed to be finding a bitter pleasure now in the revelation. "I couldn't even throw the little blighter out," he added. "Anything else, I could have told Angelo. Not that."

"No," said Antony. He sounded thoughtful; perhaps he was wondering how far he could push his questions. "Did he . . . were his demands exorbitant?"

"He asked me for a thousand pounds; it wouldn't have been the end, of course. I raised it somehow; my living's tied up with Anglo-Italian and I couldn't do anything else." He paused, and then went on hopelessly, "I expect you're thinking: except what was done at last."

"Something like that," Maitland agreed. And this time his tone seemed to sting Eversley to anger.

"Well?" he said. "Are you going to tell the police?"

"I can't make any promises. I don't think so," he added. "Not unless it's relevant."

"Should I thank you for your magnanimity?" Eversley demanded, dramatically enough to remind Antony for the first time of his profession.

"I hope you won't," he said tartly, and turned away. But as he reached the steps of number five a thought struck him and he looked back and smiled. "If you really want to show your gratitude," he said, "try and keep from murdering Giuditta."

For a moment Eversley eyed him doubtfully, and when he spoke it was with a return—an almost miraculous return—to his own negligent, faintly satirical manner. "I really don't feel, my dear fellow, that I can enter into any definite commitment about that."

Maitland was still smiling when he let himself into the house, but the smile faded as he went slowly up the stairs, and was replaced by a frown that wasn't altogether due to the pain in his shoulder.

When he pushed open the living room door Jenny was already halfway across the room to meet him, and over her shoulder he could see Larry Truscott get up more slowly from the chair at the left of the hearth. The fire was glowing, and one lamp was turned on in the corner. He said, "It's going to rain again, I think." And then, still casually, "Where's Jo?"

"You haven't seen her, Antony? I thought perhaps—"

"No, of course I haven't."

"I expect she remembered something she had to do." It seemed to Antony the words were addressed to Larry rather than to him, a sort of reassurance. And it was Truscott who answered, saying slowly:

"It isn't like her, Mrs. Maitland. She'd have waited to see you, or left a note."

"I expect she had some very good reason, if we only knew." Jenny turned back to her husband and gave him a considering look as though she were wondering how much he had understood of this exchange. "The thing is, darling, I hadn't any potatoes."

"You mean, she's gone shopping. Isn't it too late?"

"No, I went." She was suddenly voluble; it was clear to Antony that, while Larry seemed to be worried, Jenny was, quite simply, embarrassed. "About four o'clock. And Larry came to carry the bag, because it was too late to get them delivered, but Jo said she wouldn't because she was listening to *Iolanthe,* and she thought it was rather sweet."

"Well?"

"Well . . . when we got back she'd gone."

"It isn't *like* her," said Larry, half apologetic.

"No, but I expect there's some perfectly simple reason. Have you tried phoning her at home?"

"Larry seemed to think—"

"Try now, love. Do you mind?" Jenny gave him a doubtful look, but crossed to the desk without argument. Antony went over to the fire. "Sit down, Larry. There's really nothing to get in a fuss about."

"Don't you think so?" said Truscott bluntly.

"If you can give me one good reason—"

"I can't, of course." He sat down again and felt for his cigarette case. "But I don't seem to be able to take anything for granted, not since Friday. After all, someone killed Ross."

"If a squad of murderers called here, Gibbs would pretty soon damp their pretensions," said Antony positively. "I don't think you need worry about that."

"I didn't say I was being reasonable," said Larry, rather crossly. "Anyway, her coat's gone and she took her gloves and handbag, so obviously she left the house of her own accord. Mrs. Maitland asked the butler, and he said—" He broke off as Jenny turned and held out the receiver.

"It's Mr. Marston," she said. "He'd like to speak to you, Antony."

Maitland went across the room to her side, and she shook her head in answer to his questioning look. A moment later he heard Marston's voice, precise, authoritative. "I'm expecting her very shortly, Mr. Maitland. Shall I ask her to call you?"

"If you would be so kind."

"I wondered, you see, when Mrs. Maitland gave me her name, if perhaps there was any news."

"I'm afraid not, sir."

"Then I must be patient. Josephine should be home at any moment now. Unless, of course"—there was a trace of uncertainty in his tone—"she had an engagement of which she hadn't informed me."

"Do you think that might have happened?"

"Very easily, if she was meeting someone of whom I didn't approve. That young man Truscott, for instance. I expressly forbade her—"

"I don't think she's with Truscott, sir. You can't suggest anyone else—?"

"You seem very anxious to get in touch with her, Mr. Maitland, and yet you say—" No uncertainty now; a touch of steel beneath the surface amiability.

"I've no information, I'm sorry. Just a question I want to ask."

"I see. I shall certainly give her the message." A pause, perhaps in expectation of enlightenment. "Good night, Mr. Maitland," he added when Antony was silent, and replaced the receiver firmly.

Larry asked, "Did he know she'd been with me?" He sounded puzzled and Jenny said hastily:

"He didn't know she hadn't been at the studio. At least . . . is that what you thought, Antony?"

"It is, but it doesn't matter. Larry was telling me what Gibbs had to say."

"Oh, well, he saw her go about half an hour after we did. She ran downstairs and out of the front door without seeing him; you know how he hovers, darling. And a moment later a car started up outside, so he thought, of course, she had a taxi waiting."

"I expect she had."

"Yes, perhaps. Is there anywhere else I should try?" she added, turning to Larry.

"Well . . . Giuditta?"

This time they waited in silence while the call was made, obviously without success. Jenny came back to the fire, and sat down on the arm of the sofa. "I did wonder, Larry . . . you didn't seem quite at ease together. I did wonder if she just wanted to be by herself."

Truscott looked back at her steadily. He was a little flushed, but he answered quietly enough, "I hadn't said anything to upset her."

"Perhaps that was just the trouble," said Jenny, flaring up without warning. Antony thought she had something more to add, but before she could do so the phone rang.

Just for a moment they all sat and looked at it; a moment

of tension that to Antony, at least, was inexplicable, because he took it for granted that the caller was Jo. He said, "All right, I'll get it," and crossed to the desk and said tersely, "Maitland here."

"Ah-h." It was no more than a drawn-out sigh, but unmistakably an expression of pleasure. "Just the man I wanted."

Not Jo after all, but a voice he knew, a voice he had heard recently. Cold and without question malevolent, in spite of the trite friendliness of the words. "Drayton!" he said, and saw Truscott frown as though he were puzzled. "What do you want?"

"To set your mind at rest, an act of kindness really." There was a pause, as though the man at the other end of the wire was savoring the moment, unwilling to let it pass. "I was afraid you might be getting anxious . . . about your wife."

"Jenny—" he said, and stopped. Across the room his eyes met hers with a startled look.

"Is that her name? I don't know that I altogether—"

"Damn you! What are you trying to tell me?"

"That she's quite safe . . . for the moment. But you wouldn't want anything to happen to her, would you now?"

Even with Jenny sitting there the words shocked him momentarily into speechlessness. Afterwards he thought that his realization of what had happened had been instantaneous, but in fact several perfectly blank seconds elapsed before the thought flashed into his mind: not Jenny . . . Jo! It must have been his expression that brought Jenny across the room to his side, an anxious question in her eyes. He put his left arm round her shoulders and pulled her close to him, as though it was the only way he could convince himself of her safety.

Drayton said, "Maitland?" sharply; the silence must have been longer than he knew. And suddenly he was angry.

"W-where is she?" he said, and heard Drayton laugh.

"I warned you—didn't I?—that it might not be wise to interfere."

"If you h-harm her, D-drayton—"

"Gently, my friend, gently. Don't waste my time with heroics."

"Where is she?" said Antony again, this time more steadily.

"Do you really expect me to tell you?" The cold voice was mocking. "Now, I'm not going to make any threats. I don't think I need to. But just imagine . . . just imagine all the things that might happen, if you don't obey my instructions."

"What must I do, then?" He had a rein on his temper now, and the angry, betraying stammer was under control.

"Why, nothing. Nothing at all."

"And if I do as you say?"

"I think you'd better," snapped Drayton, and now there was no mistaking the underlying viciousness of his tone. Antony's grip tightened involuntarily on Jenny's shoulder.

"How long—?"

"That's all I have to tell you now. You'll be hearing from me again. Until then, forget about the emeralds and that unfortunate fellow Bromley; forget about Ross's murder; and *don't go near the police.* Even if they found me—I don't think they could, but *if* they did—do you really imagine they'd find your wife alive?" He paused, and the note of enjoyment in his voice was quite unmistakable. "You know how they'd set about it, something like the siege of Sidney Street. That sort of thing takes time, and do you think I'd be idle?"

"What do you mean?"

"Must I really spell it out for you? There are ways and ways of dying. And if they got me in the end—I ask you this as a humane man, Maitland—would that really be much consolation?" He broke off there, and Antony was conscious suddenly of the stillness of the room, as though the world had come to an end while he listened and the silence could never be broken. But then Drayton added softly, "Can I rely on you?" and life was going on again and he had to reply.

"You don't leave me much choice," he said.

"If you feel your resolution weakening, go to the newspaper files. November, three years ago, so far as I remember. Moira Venner. She was only a child, of course, thirteen or fourteen, something like that. But her father was indiscreet."

"What happened to her?"

"She died." The words had a finality more menacing than

any open threat. There was a sharp click, as the connection was broken. Maitland became aware of Larry Truscott's presence, which for the moment he had forgotten; he put down the telephone slowly.

CHAPTER 16

Jenny said in a shaken voice, "You're hurting me," and he released her without apology.

"Could you hear?"

"I couldn't," said Truscott. "Except your side of it." Then, "Is it Jo?" His voice quivered a little on the words.

"I'm sorry," Antony told him. He was feeling sick and very much afraid, and the calmness of his own voice surprised him. He looked at Jenny. "I don't know how he worked it, love. He thought he was kidnapping you."

Jenny said, "But Jo—" and broke off, looking at him with horrified eyes. At the same moment Larry said:

"Who?"

"A man called Drayton."

"What does he want?"

"To put a stop to my activities."

"Does he know Jo?"

Antony shook his head. "I don't think so. He may have seen her at the studio."

"He's bound to guess," said Jenny. "She's much too young."

"It doesn't really make any difference." His eyes met hers for an instant, and they both knew he was lying. But the next thing was true . . . too true. "She'll be as safe as you would be, Jenny; no more, no less. In a way, she's just as good a hostage."

"What does he want you to do?"

"Nothing. Nothing at all." The words echoed in his mind in Drayton's mocking tone.

"But—" Larry broke off and then added with quiet desperation, "Where is the swine?"

"If I knew that I wouldn't be standing here. No . . . be quiet a minute. I want to think." He put up a hand to cover his eyes, blotting out the familiar room, and Jenny's anxious silence, and Truscott's pallor and angry, unnatural composure. There must be something . . . "He knows more than he should about what I've been doing," he said, and lowered his hand again.

"Does that help?" Larry snapped at him.

"Not at the moment. No."

"But, Antony, he must be mad. You know who he is."

"But not where he is. And if I ask the police to find him— even if I thought they could—" He paused and glanced at Larry, and then back at Jenny again. "He said he wouldn't waste my time with threats."

"But afterwards—"

"I don't know, love. I don't know." The trouble was, he was still too scared to think clearly. "He'd know he couldn't silence me indefinitely, so I think he means to disappear."

Jenny moved a little, closer to his side. She was very pale, with no trace of her usual serenity. "Antony . . . what can you do?" And just for a moment his smile was affectionate and mocking, and she stiffened slightly and said in a hurt tone, "You know I'd say that anyway. Even if it wasn't Jo . . . instead of me."

"I know it very well. As for your question, love, there's just one thing we can try. Jim Arnold's wife."

"You think she might know where Drayton is?"

"It's a chance. I can't see any other." Her eyes were questioning, and he shook his head. "Of course we must call the police, but not yet. The thing is, I"—he glanced at Larry and corrected himself—"we must get there first."

"Of course," she agreed, not altogether understanding.

"Larry, I'll need your help."

Truscott's expression had hardened. "I'm not at all sure—" he began doubtfully, and was surprised by the violence of Maitland's reaction.

"I haven't t-time to argue." He glanced at his watch, and then turned to the telephone again. "I'll get R-roger," he said over his shoulder to Jenny. "I can t-trust him."

Larry moved almost as quickly as he did, making a clumsy grab for the receiver. "You'll tell me first," he said imperatively. "Would you be doing this if it was Jenny?"

Maitland's hand dropped. "I don't know," he said. "How can I know?"

"You're risking Jo's life."

"It's a greater risk to do nothing." He was speaking quietly now. "You've got to face the fact that he's killed before."

"Ross?"

"Ross, for one."

"I see."

Jenny said into the silence, "Roger's at Grunning's Hole for the weekend. He won't be back until tomorrow."

"No. I forgot." Anger and urgency alike were banished from his voice. "I can't promise anything, Larry; I can't even give you an honest answer to your question, and certainly no guarantee of Jo's safety. All the same—"

"You'd better tell me what you want me to do." Larry's voice was steady enough, and his eyes were steady too. "I'm trusting you," he said.

If Antony was relieved he didn't show it, except, perhaps, in a sudden, uncharacteristic decisiveness. "Jenny, phone Geoffrey and see if he remembers Arnold's address; somewhere in Fulham, I think. He's to go back to the office to get it if necessary. Your job, Larry, is to make sure I'm not followed when I leave here; if I am you'll distract the chap accidental-like, while I pick up a cab. Understand?"

"Leave it to me."

He sounded determined enough to bring a flash of amusement to Maitland's eyes. "I said by accident," he repeated. "Not a rugby tackle."

"And I said I understood."

"So you did." He didn't like the tightness about Truscott's mouth, or the strained look in his eyes. "Then come back here and await instructions. No, I know you don't like the idea, but you'll do as I say. Can you drive?"

"Yes. That is . . . yes."

"Here you are," said Jenny. She finished writing, and tore the sheet from the memo pad. "He's not absolutely sure of the number—seventy-five or fifty-seven—but he remembers the street all right, because he's been there a couple of times."

"Near enough." He stared at the paper for a moment, and then crumpled it and tossed it onto the fire.

"Shall I get the car?" Jenny asked him.

"You, my love, are staying here till I get back. In fact, I think I'll just tell Uncle Nick—"

"He's out."

"Do you know where?"

"Yes, but . . . you know if you tell him, Antony, he'll insist on calling the police right away. If you don't think that's the best thing—"

He could hear Drayton's voice: . . . *something like the siege of Sidney Street . . . plenty of time for what I want to do . . . there are ways and ways of dying.* Larry was staring at him. What had he said? . . . *I'm trusting you.* "Not yet, Jenny. Not until we've tried."

"That's what I thought," she agreed. And added, inconsequently, "Did you know Uncle Nick had got himself a revolver?"

"I didn't know you knew. An automatic pistol, if you want to be accurate. Heaven forbid he should ever have cause to fire it."

"But I expect it's loaded."

"I'll take it," he assured her. "But, Jenny—" All at once

his tone was urgent. "I've got to go. I've got to know you're safe."

"I'll stay here, Antony. *I'll* be safe enough."

Mrs. James Arnold was a bustling little woman, about ten years younger than her husband, with a clean, scrubbed look, a rosy cheek, and a merry eye. The terrace house, with its shabby, smoked-brick exterior, was spotless within, but comfortable and not overtidy. She looked doubtful when she found Maitland on her doorstep, but her face cleared when he gave her his name. "Well now, that's nice," she said; and held the door wide for him to enter. She paused a moment halfway down the narrow hall, probably considering the propriety of taking him into the parlor; then to his relief she went straight on to the kitchen, which was cheerful and old-fashioned and cluttered with drying linen. In spite of his anxiety and the cold anger which had taken hold of him, he couldn't help thinking for a moment what a fool Jim Arnold was.

Mrs. Arnold swept up a pile of sheets from a chair near the open range. "Only just got them in before the rain," she said. "Sit there, Mr. Maitland; that's where Jim always likes to sit." She paused, her eyes bright and curious. "Was it something about Jim?" she asked.

"Not exactly." Now that he was here he could see it was going to be extraordinarily difficult to explain. "I've no right to ask you," he said, "but you might be able to help me."

She beamed at him. "Well now!" she said. And then, as though to explain her obvious gratification, "Thinks a lot of you, Jim does."

It wouldn't do to rush things. "How is he?"

"Oh, he's well. Looking forward to being home again. Not much more than two years now." She was confident of his interest, and quite unembarrassed.

"And the children?"

"Young Jimmy's at the Tech." Her pride was apparent. "He's a clever boy, Mr. Maitland, and going a long way, I shouldn't wonder. Doris, she's at the pictures with a girl friend tonight. Not that she hasn't got a boy—and her only sixteen—but he has to work late Mondays. And she has a good job at Marks and Spencers; likes it ever so much, she does."

Her tone was so matter-of-fact that the sheer fantasy of the situation almost overwhelmed him. And yet . . . "Jim always said he'd trust you with anything," he said with seeming irrelevance.

"What if he did? That's natural, isn't it?" Her tone had sharpened a little, a very little; he thought there was a wariness in her eyes.

"You know he was associated with a man called Drayton." Her expression was quite blank now, and she started to shake her head. "In the way of business," he persisted.

"I never knew nothing of his business."

"May I explain?"

"If you like." She looked at him almost regretfully. "It won't help none."

"First I should tell you, no one knows I'm here, and I took steps to ensure I wasn't followed. You could talk to me quite safely, if you would." Her eyes were fixed on his face, serious now, unwinking. "The other thing is it's a matter of life and death. A young girl has been kidnapped—"

"How old is she?"

"Eighteen."

"Doris will be eighteen when her dad comes home," she said inconsequently.

"I tell you, there's no danger to you or your family."

"How do you know what's dangerous?"

"Nobody saw me come."

"I'm to take your word for that, am I?" She sounded angry, but he thought he detected too the first, faint hesitation in her voice. "Jim knew better than to talk."

"But that was different, don't you see? The Association—"

"What do you know about the Association, Mr. Maitland?"

"Quite a lot." He tried to sound confident, and perhaps he succeeded too well.

"Then you don't need my help," she asserted flatly.

"I don't know where to find Drayton," he said.

"Don't try! This girl you spoke of—"

"You don't understand," he told her, and now he sounded desperate.

"She'll be home all right, if her folks play ball." She sat a moment, watching him, and her expression softened. "Leave it be," she said. "It's safest that way."

"There was a girl called Moira Venner. What happened to her?"

She shivered suddenly. "He was a double-crosser, Venner was. That's what Jim said. And he said not to worry; our kids would be safe enough, and he knew which side his bread was buttered."

"I wonder—" He spoke slowly, and broke off, looking at her with something like sympathy.

"What do you mean?" Her tone was sharp again. "You said yourself I could talk to you and no one the wiser."

"You could be a lot more frank with me, Mrs. Arnold, and still be safe. But when Jim comes home—"

"Well, what?"

"He told me he was going to retire."

"And so he is!"

"Do you think they'll let him, knowing what he does?" Just for a moment, as she looked at him, he saw the look of terror unmistakably in her eyes; and set himself deliberately to play on it. "Drayton's only safe as long as he has a hold over the men who work for him; as long as he can send them down for a stretch, or threaten their families because they don't dare go to the police. Jim has about as much hope of breaking free—"

"But he promised, Mr. Maitland. He promised."

"He'll break that promise, if he doesn't want to end up dead," said Antony brutally. "Or with Doris missing, more like."

"He wouldn't . . . he wouldn't!" She was almost frantic now. "He's a devil, Drayton is," she said, "but he wouldn't do that." It was obvious that her denials gave her no confidence at all. Maitland got up suddenly, and began to stride up and down the narrow room: past the table, with its covering of red chenille, as far as the painted dresser; and then back to the hearth again. Her eyes followed him with a sort of hopeless appeal.

"Tell me exactly why you're so afraid," he flung at her over his shoulder. And stopped at last, looking down at her, waiting. "Trust me," he said.

She shook her head mournfully; he thought her fear had come to a pitch where it had to find expression. "That can't hurt, I suppose," she said, "seeing as how you know so much. It was all talk, really; I'd have taken no notice, but I knew Jim was scared."

"What was the talk?"

"There was a child found dead, eight years old she was. Her dad had been arrested ten days before, and after that the police had some awkward questions. Seemed like he'd talked."

"But surely . . . I mean, didn't the police connect the two things?"

"Why should they? It was like you said, her ma didn't dare report her missing; that's what Jim said. And when she was found, down Hampshire way that was, no one thought anything but that it was one of these maniacs. These things happen," she told him, accepting the fact with a resignation that terrified him.

"And you think that Drayton—" He found his hands were clenched, and relaxed them slowly, deliberately.

"I'm telling you the talk, that's all." She looked up at him and added, oddly as though she was sorry for him, "You don't like it, do you? But perhaps you see now why I was afraid."

His expression must have been answer enough. After a moment he asked, "When did this happen?" and his voice rasped on the words, as though his throat was dry.

She considered the question for a little. "Four years ago, I'd say. Not long before that other kid you mentioned. The same story, that was; some kind person gave her a ride in his car. Well, it was obvious, wasn't it?"

"And you thought . . . you found no difficulty in accepting . . . that in cold blood—?" He broke off, and started walking up and down the room again; Mrs. Arnold made no attempt to reply to his incoherence, but her head turned slightly, following his movements. After a while she said again, heavily:

"These things happen."

He stopped his pacing, and came and stood near the fire as though conscious for the first time that the evening had grown chilly. "If you're right about the motive, was it always children?"

"There was a woman disappeared, after her man was arrested; but that might have been just that she didn't want no questions. She was home again all right, later on. It's best to have everything tied up legal, isn't it?" she added thoughtfully. "You'd understand that, I daresay, Mr. Maitland."

"Yes. Yes, of course. But—"

"Then there was a single chap killed himself. That's what the inquest said, but the word went round . . . well, we couldn't help wondering. And nothing recent; stands to reason no one would risk it. But it was just talk, you know. That's all it may have been, just talk."

Stands to reason no one would risk it. And he'd gone in blindly, only half believing Sykes's story, certainly with no thought of danger. And now there was Jo . . . and it might have been Jenny. "Mrs. Arnold, have you any idea at all where Drayton might be?"

She was instantly suspicious. "You said you knew about him."

"I know his place in the Association. I know where he lives, but that's the last place to find him now. And I know Jim must have had occasion to meet him from time to time. The thing is . . . where?"

"I'm not telling you that."

"But you know?"

"I'm not telling you." She began to rub her hands together. "This girl you're so worried about," she said. "If you'll just leave things alone—"

"This time it's different."

"It always is." There was something almost humorous in her

look, but the nervous movement of her hands continued. "You take my advice, Mr. Maitland, and don't go stirring up trouble."

"You don't understand!" He heard the desperation that sounded through the words, and set himself deliberately to overcome it. "There's no question at all of the girl being returned unharmed, even if I—if her family do everything he says. She may be dead now, but there's just a chance—"

"It don't sound reasonable to me."

"I think he's mad," said Antony, echoing Jenny's words; and with a sudden, nightmare feeling that they might be literally true. But. Mrs. Arnold was shaking her head.

"Malicious, more like. He's that sort, Jim always said." Her hands were still now; she was looking up at him searchingly. He mastered the impulse to plead with her, and met her eyes steadily. "Was it true what you said about no one knowing you'd come here?"

"My wife knows. No one else." For the moment he had honestly forgotten about Larry, and only remembered that he hadn't shown him the paper with the full address.

"And if you find him?"

"That's the end of Mr. Drayton . . . one way or another!" He saw her expression change, and laughed suddenly. "No, I don't mean to kill him, unless I must. But I think the police—"

"There's bail, and that. I wouldn't want him to know—" But she was hesitating now; he saw it and leaned forward eagerly.

"I'll swear on anything you like I'll never tell a soul where I got the information."

"Not the bogeys, nor nobody?"

"Certainly not the bogeys," he assured her.

"I don't know what Jim would say, I'm sure. No hope of a payoff when he comes out, if Drayton's inside."

"I'm afraid, no hope at all," he agreed, and wondered as he spoke what scruple kept him from lying to her. But strangely enough, it was his admission that seemed to decide the matter.

"Still and all, he wouldn't like murder," she said. "I can't tell you about where they met; a different place each time, I reckon. But there's one place Jim knew about, a permanent place. He said he'd like something like that himself one day, right on the river . . . and that's why he told me, you see, it was a sort of dream we had."

"Please, Mrs. Arnold—"

"Now wait a bit, I've got to think, haven't I? There's a boathouse, see, at Sunbury, with a loft over; only the loft has been made into a sort of apartment."

"A motorboat?" said Antony, momentarily diverted. That made sense, at least.

"I daresay," she agreed indifferently. "Jim went there once, I don't know why, and he said it was beautiful, what they'd done. A bathroom, and a kitchen, and all."

"Mrs. Arnold! Where—"

"He had to go to Clapton Road, a house called River View. Only the house wasn't near the river at all; there's a sort of side gate and a long path that leads down to the boathouse."

He was in the doorway before she could make any move to rise. "I'll find it," he said. As he ran down the passage her voice followed him sadly.

"It's not to say Drayton's there now."

But he knew that already; the words that went with him were more disturbing still. *Malicious, more like . . . that's the sort he is . . .*

CHAPTER 17

Jenny had sounded remote when he spoke to her on the telephone, not like herself. Maitland stood now on the wet pavement, not far from the telephone box, and waited for Larry to join him. Common sense told him that it was quicker than trying to hire a car, or looking for the railway station; his sense of fairness added, with a faint flicker of humor, that to deny Truscott a part in the proceedings would be to frustrate him to an extent that would probably warp him for life. But in spite of his impatience he was thinking mainly as he waited of all the things there hadn't been time to say to Jenny, and though he turned up the collar of his raincoat he was hardly aware that he was getting wet.

It was surprising really how little traffic there was. He considered this vaguely after a while and decided that the weather was quite unpleasant enough to deter most reasonable people. He was keeping an eye on the cars as they swept up and passed him, but the Jaguar's outline would have been unmistakable and he was momentarily taken aback when a long, sleek American car, twice as large as life, drew in to the curb, until he realized that he was an obvious target for anyone wanting directions. But it was Jenny who reached across to push the door open, Jenny's voice that said impatiently, "Do get in, darling. Hurry!"

He had had time now to see that she was alone. "Wouldn't the car start? And what," he added suspiciously, "have you done with Larry?"

"I'll tell you," said Jenny, "as we go." The car was in motion again almost before he had scrambled in beside her. "There's a map on the seat, Antony, and a flashlight in my handbag. Tell me where we're going, and look up the route."

"I'm going to Sunbury, but—"

"Oh, then that's easy. Putney Bridge and the Portsmouth Road. But you'd better have a look to see if the Bypass would be quicker. I don't really know the way after Kingston."

Antony was struggling grimly with the map. "I can listen at the same time," he said. "To begin with, whose car have you stolen?"

"It's Mr. Taylor's new Oldsmobile, don't you recognize it? I've always wanted a chance to try it out. Not one of the cars he hires, of course."

"That's what I was afraid of," said Antony gloomily. Jenny gave a small, triumphant crow of laughter.

"I can't tell you what a relief it is not to be sitting at home," she said. "I borrowed it, of course; I mean, he knows I've got it. I knew you wouldn't mind when you understood."

"If you're under the impression that you've explained anything—"

"I'm afraid you won't like it very much, darling. It's why we have to hurry, you see." The Oldsmobile was sweeping on with a smooth disregard for the speed limit. "I'm just getting the feel of her," said Jenny.

"You'd better take the Bypass when you get there. After that I'll tell you." The map was folded as he wanted it now; he leaned back and looked at the road ahead. "What won't I like?" he asked. He was aware of her tension as if it were a tangible thing.

"Ten minutes before you phoned," she said, "there was another call. A man's voice, asking for you. Somehow he sounded . . . not one of our friends . . . not business either, at least I didn't think so. I suppose I was nervous; after all, it might have been Drayton again. I gave Larry the phone and he said he was you. Of course I listened." She paused, braking, as a truck swung without warning out of a side street just ahead.

"There's one born every minute," said Antony unemotionally. The Olds swept forward again, passing the truck, which had decided that, after all, it wasn't in a hurry, and for the first time he felt the power of the acceleration, pressing him back against the seat. "Who was it on the phone, love?"

"It was the man who'd been shadowing you."

"Is that how he announced himself?"

Jenny kept her eyes on the road, but she heard the tremor of amusement in her husband's voice, and was no more deceived by it than he was by her chatter. "He said his name was Hilton, or Hinton . . . something like that. And he said, 'Maybe you've seen me around, Mr. Maitland. I've been sort of watching over you these last few days.' Larry didn't understand, of course, but I nodded at him and he pretended he did. So then the man said—I can't remember the exact words, darling, but he said he hadn't known why they wanted an eye kept on you, and he didn't hold with kidnapping, and now that he knew what had happened he'd tell you where I was. That's a bit of a muddle, but do you understand so far?"

Compared with some of Jenny's explanations, this one was clarity itself. "I suppose Larry fell for it," Antony said.

"Yes, he did. I *told* him to wait for you. But it was an address in Sunbury, the same one Mrs. Arnold gave you, I suppose. I wasn't sure about that. If it was a plot, or just a message to get you out of the way, I mean."

"They want me to go to Sunbury, I expect." No use repining that the time he had spent with Mrs. Arnold had been wasted . . . and perhaps, after all, it hadn't. The extra knowledge of Drayton's character . . . "That explains a lot, doesn't it?" he said.

"You mean, why they tried to kidnap me? But *you'd* have suspected the message, darling. Wouldn't they have thought of that?"

"Very likely. But I'd have gone just the same."

"Yes, I know." She was silent for a moment, and then added, "What I didn't know was whether this would have made any difference about calling the police."

"What did you do?"

"Nothing."

"That's good. We'll stick to our original plan. If you telephone at the same time as I go in—" His voice was even, but he shivered as he spoke, and spread the map on his knee again to hide the movement, and switched on the flashlight. "There'll be no harm they can do then, and perhaps a lot of good. I suppose that young idiot rushed off on his own."

"I couldn't stop him. And I must say, Antony, I take back every word I said about him being correct."

"Do you though? I'm not blaming you, Jenny . . . or him. I think I know how he felt. He took the Jag, I suppose."

"Yes, we'd been to fetch it, it was waiting in the square. So I rang Mr. Taylor right away, and he brought this round for me. And when you phoned—"

"You did your best to deceive me."

"I *did* deceive you," said Jenny indignantly. "What's worrying me," she added in a subdued tone, "is what will have happened to those two by the time we get there."

"Perhaps the unorthodox nature of Larry's approach will put Drayton off his stroke," Antony suggested. "I feel sure he will blunder straight in, with no precautions at all."

"Well, what will you do?"

"Much the same, I suppose." He sighed at the thought. "I may or may not still be expected. After that I shall—er—engage Drayton in conversation until the police arrive; unless any more suitable course of action suggests itself."

"Antony—"

"I'm armed, love. Don't worry."

"No, of course not."

He went back to the map for a while, but presently—having got the route, as he hoped, by heart—he sat back again and turned his head to watch Jenny's profile. Oddly enough, she seemed to have her serene look again, but it was difficult to see in the intermittent light of the street lamps. It was waiting about while other people did things that troubled her composure; the thought hit him suddenly, and his voice was apologetic when he broke the silence. "I'll have to ask you to wait again, love, for the police."

"Yes, I know. I won't—I won't make things difficult, Antony," she reassured him. He was quiet for several minutes before he said:

"It shouldn't be very long."

After that there seemed to be no more to say. They were warm and comfortable, and he was even beginning to get dry again; it was raining steadily now, the tires swished on the wet road, the windscreen wipers moved in hypnotic unison. He thought of Mrs. Arnold, with her merry face and the fear in her eyes . . . at least Jenny didn't know how good a cause they had for fear. He daren't think of Jo, with her grown-up ways and her childlike naïveté. . . .

"Do you think she's still alive?" Jenny asked him.

The words hung between them for a moment, cold and brittle as glass. That was imagination again for you, giving fear a shape, making of it something you could touch. He said roughly, "Don't ask such damn silly questions!" and knew as he spoke that the answer was as revealing as any admission he could have made. But he still hesitated a moment before he said, honest with her at last, "I'm sorry, love. You see, I haven't the least idea." And after a while he added, "I'm afraid—"

She dropped him at the end of Clapton Road, and drove on towards the town to find a telephone. He thought as he turned away that for a parting in the face of danger it must have been as unemotional as any on record, because as he kissed her it occurred to him to wonder if she had any change, and his query had the obvious result of making her unsure about it, and sending her scrabbling through her handbag until she found her purse.

It was a wide road, ill lit, with houses on either side. Not new houses, if you were to judge by the heavy wooden gates and the thickness of growth that screened them from the passerby. Now, in the darkness and the rain, it was indescribably dreary. He kept to the left, having formed the impression that the river was on that side; and he kept to the shadows, though he wasn't expecting trouble yet, and paused only for so long as it took him to decipher the names on the gates as he passed.

Laurel Bank . . . it was the laurels, he supposed, that were dripping moisture down his neck as he stooped to read the words. *The Orchard* . . . one plum tree, at a guess, that had last borne fruit in 1938. *Elm Hurst* . . . *The Shrubbery* . . . one honest man, at least. *River* . . . no, not River View, *River Cottage*. And here was the end of the road, a dead end, with a fence across and a hawthorn hedge beyond for good measure. Which probably meant his sense of direction had failed him; the road led down to the Thames, and only these two end houses —River Cottage and its neighbor on the opposite side—had grounds that went down to the water. If the other wasn't River View . . . but, of course, it was. There was no sign of the Jaguar, and he wondered for the first time if Larry, perhaps, had not after all arrived ahead of them.

The double gate where he had found the name opened onto a short drive with a garage at the end of it and the side door of the house close by. Lots of white paint, and very well lighted. Not a good bet for someone with clandestine business; even if the house and its occupants were an elaborate cover, the wicket he had passed a few yards back was more likely to be the one used by Drayton and his associates. A secretive little gate, leading to a narrow flagged path between high hedges. He eased it open, paused a moment to let his eyes adjust to the darkness, and then began to move along the path, soft-footed, but at a fair speed.

It twisted away from the house, as he had half expected,

winding claustrophobically between what felt like walls of yew. And then suddenly he was in the open again, with a wide lawn stretching away ahead to a dark mass of trees. He still couldn't see the river, but he could hear it now, murmuring gently to itself. There were no lights at all from his right, where the house should have been; perhaps its name was no more than a figment of some estate agent's fevered imagination? But the flagstones led down at the edge of the grass to a low building with a steeply pitched roof and one lighted window. If that wasn't the boathouse . . .

At any other time he would have shared Jim Arnold's enthusiasm; the setting, at least, was delightful, and it was as solitary as the most confirmed misanthrope could have desired. The noise of the river was louder now; there were lights that were probably no further away than the opposite bank, but they had an air of remoteness, blurred by the rain. Seen from the landward side, the building had a squat air; it was cut into the bank, and no higher here, he guessed, than the original loft had been. An annex had been built out at the back, with two windows. The lighted one was probably the kitchen, but the curtains were tight drawn; the other might be the bathroom. In the angle formed by the annex and the wider wall behind it there was a door, with a narrow flight of wooden steps leading up to it.

He couldn't even be sure that Drayton was expecting him; it all depended on whether Larry had arrived, and what he had said. The door would be locked, of course. If not, it was an invitation he'd think twice before accepting. The bathroom window should be quite easy to open, but getting through it would be another—and noisier—matter. The best way was probably through the boathouse, always supposing it was rented with the apartment and connected with it . . . and surely that must be the whole purpose of the place. And it was no use wasting time wondering what approach Drayton would expect him to make; you could work that out, on the lines of a double or treble bluff, for a month of Sundays, and still be wrong. The bank fell away steeply here, and he half walked, half slithered down to the water's edge.

Leaning over the retaining wall he could look back into the boathouse; black as pitch, of course. He could swing himself in, and trust to there being a catwalk, but it would have to be from the other side so that he could put his weight on his left arm. More time wasted! He swore softly to himself, but he was already moving to circle the building. There was no sign of a direct entrance to the boathouse from the grounds.

It was tricky in the darkness, but the footway was there all right: narrow, and slimy with moss, but still passable. Halfway along he paused and fumbled for Jenny's flashlight, and saw in the narrow beam a stout cabin cruiser with the black water slapping against the hull, and a wider staging of dry planks across the back of the boathouse. He flashed the light again when he reached the platform, and saw the steps of rough timber in the corner. He was halfway up before the thin band of light shining under the door at the top became visible, and it was too late then to worry about the reception committee. He got a grip on his uncle's automatic and went quietly up the remaining stairs. His left hand groped for the doorknob, and found it without much difficulty. He stood very still, listening; but what was there to wait for, after all? If his death was the only object of the exercise . . .

It was odd to find himself hoping he hadn't been wrong about the streak of viciousness in Drayton's character, a cruelty that could not be satisfied by the mere act of killing. All he needed was a little time; time, and the opportunity to protect Jo when the police arrived . . . if, indeed, she was still in need of protection. It was, perhaps, this last uncertainty more than anything else that made him hesitate before he flung open the door and stepped across the threshold, almost blinded until his eyes accustomed themselves to what seemed to be a blaze of light. But instead of the shot he had half expected there was only Drayton's voice, smooth and self-satisfied. "You must take my word for the fact that I am armed, Mr. Maitland. If you attempt any drastic action I shall certainly shoot your friend," He realized then that he had been holding his breath, and relaxed deliberately; only then it was more difficult to hold the automatic steady.

The original loft had not been subdivided in any way, and it made a spacious living room only spoiled by a subtly un-lived-in air. But that was a later impression; at the moment Antony noted automatically—because a line of retreat might be useful—the two doors on his left that led, presumably, to the annex; and the heavier door beyond them that he sup-posed to be the one he had seen from outside. There was cer-tainly enough to fix his attention in the tableau that confronted him. Facing him, but a little to his right, Larry Truscott was seated in a chair which had been dragged out from under the dining table; John Drayton stood behind him, one hand hidden, the other clamped across Truscott's mouth.

So much, then, for plans; Larry's expression, and something strained in his attitude, seemed to argue that the threat had been a valid one. Antony took the setback philosophically enough, though it would have given him great pleasure to shoot the gun out of Drayton's hand. He had hoped, but not expected, that the opportunity would arise. "Deadlock?" he said. And then, "Where's the girl?"

"Hardly that, I think." Drayton ignored the more urgent query. "On the whole I should be happier if you dropped your gun—no, better toss it into the armchair over there, out of harm's way. Otherwise—" He released Truscott as he spoke, and straightened himself, but his right hand remained invisible and his meaning was obvious even before he added, "Now that you're here, his presence is really an embarrassment. Of course, you might argue that he hasn't long to live in any case."

Larry said, "Don't listen. It's Jo that matters," and was silenced by a violent blow on the side of his head.

"Is she here?"

"See for yourself," Drayton told him, and gestured towards the other end of the room. It was all Antony could do to keep his eyes from following the movement. He wanted so badly to know. . . .

"He says she's alive," said Larry desperately. "He says she's drugged, but she hasn't moved—"

"You seem to have forgotten, Mr. Maitland. We were dis-cussing the disposal of your weapon."

Antony started to say, "I'll keep it," and was stopped by the look in Drayton's eyes. To anyone else he could have said, "If you shoot Truscott I shall kill you," but suddenly he was uncertain. He had thought, casually enough, "He must be mad," and he was pretty sure now that wasn't true. But neither was he sure that Drayton was completely rational, that on this one point—where his power to hurt was called into question—he would react in a normal way. On the other hand . . .

He couldn't risk it. "I expect we could talk more comfortably," he said, "if we all relaxed a little." The automatic fell harmlessly into the cushioned lap of the chair Drayton had indicated.

"Are we going to talk?"

"About the girl. Where is she?" There was no point in watchfulness now; he turned as he spoke and for the first time saw the divan bed under the window where Jo was lying. There was an alarming limpness about her, and she did not move at all. Her fair hair was spread out across the dark cover. "Is she alive?" he asked, and saw the fury leap in Larry's eyes at the indifference his tone achieved.

"For the moment." Drayton's look was cold and penetrating. "Not your wife?" he said.

Antony smiled. "My dear Drayton! A child of eighteen."

"For all I knew . . . she's a pretty little thing," said Drayton casually.

"I told you—" said Larry, and was again cuffed into silence.

"You also told me Maitland had no means of knowing where we were," Drayton remarked. "I suppose you hoped I'd relax my vigilance. I've a good mind—" Again his meaning was obvious, but he contented himself with another blow; Truscott shook his head in a dazed way.

"Do you know who she is?" said Antony clearly.

"A friend, I suppose, since you've troubled to come after her."

"A girl I hardly know. I admit," he added, "it was an understandable mistake on your part. But one you may regret."

"Why should I? She's served her purpose. It would be sensible, I suppose," he added reflectively, "to kill you first. But after the trouble you've caused me I'd like you to see them die."

"You're missing the point. Her name is Marston." He saw Drayton stiffen, and added quickly, "She's William Marston's granddaughter."

"I don't believe you!"

"You have a most distrustful disposition," Maitland complained. "I'm telling you the truth." He paused, to let the statement sink in. "You're not going to be very popular, are you?" he asked.

"That can be remedied." The blaze of anger had been momentary only; Drayton spoke now with a controlled viciousness that made his next words all the more terrifying. "At least I shall have the pleasure of dealing with you, and your friend here—"

"His name's Truscott. I don't think your principal wants him killed either. I mean, in that case, who's to take the blame for Ross's death?"

It was a queer thing about Drayton, the sudden capacity for stillness that carried no suggestion of repose, but instead an indefinable menace. He said now, softly, "What do you know of my principal?" and Antony felt the short hairs rise on the back of his neck.

"Quite a lot. It was his idea—wasn't it?—to frame Truscott for the murder."

"Somehow I don't think he'll worry . . . so long as he's dead."

"And before that, Bromley." Time was running out; somehow, before the police arrived, Drayton must be induced to make a move. Standing where he did, with his gun at Larry's back, he was more or less invulnerable. "There was never any real intention, was there, of getting away with the d'Albret emeralds? Only of making sure that Bromley got the blame."

"And if you're right?" Drayton was shaken inexplicably by laughter. "You don't know how funny that is," he declared.

"Tell me then."

But the invitation was hardly needed. "We couldn't have done it without his cooperation. You do see that, I expect."

There was an odd little silence, as though he were genuinely interested in Maitland's reply. Larry made an abrupt movement, which ceased as the gun was rammed more firmly into his back. Antony said slowly:

"I don't think I quite understand you." And as he spoke one more piece of the puzzle fell into place and made the words a lie.

"That's what's so funny." Drayton wasn't laughing now. His eyes were hard and intent. "He was doing a reconnaissance for us, that's why he cultivated the girl. But he'd never have stepped out of line and done the job himself; that wasn't what he was paid for."

Once you knew, it was all so clear. Bromley protesting his innocence in all good faith, and probably never realizing—such is the human race's capacity for self-deception—that there was an element of justice in his conviction. And Sykes had told him quite plainly that the Association used scouts as well as operatives. He lowered his eyes for a moment and met Truscott's frantic gaze. Larry said, as if they were alone, as if in some way he was in need of reassurance:

"It isn't true!"

"I think it is."

This time Drayton ignored the exchange. He was watching Maitland's expression . . . cat and mouse, thought Antony resentfully, and smiled at him. Drayton said harshly, "Not so clever, was it? You wouldn't have mixed yourself up in all this, if you'd known. Not worth dying for—"

"There is still Ross's murder. Someone must answer for that."

"If Truscott shoots you and then disappears—"

"Yes, you do find the cabin cruiser useful, don't you?" Antony seemed to be considering the question seriously. "You know, I can't think what his motive would be; and if our wonderful police have a fault it's a stubborn addiction to having the motive explained." He shook his head in a regretful way. "Not good enough," he said.

"That's my worry, isn't it?" The scene was not, perhaps, going quite to Drayton's liking.

"You haven't considered the humor of the situation. All this trouble, and I honestly don't see how you're going to get away with it. Besides, you're forgetting Jo—Miss Marston. *He* may forgive you for doing away with Truscott; the girl's a different matter."

Drayton's left hand clenched and unclenched slowly. A muscle twitched at the corner of his mouth. "Is that your idea of a joke?"

"It has its amusing side," Antony admitted. And this time the derisive tone had its effect. Drayton thrust Larry aside with hasty violence, and took the three strides across the room that brought him face to face with Maitland. Truscott picked himself up and would have followed, had he not encountered a glance that stopped him effectively in his tracks. Antony, seeing the revolver not quite steady in Drayton's hand, was profoundly grateful for the hesitation . . . the situation was not one that called for the tactics of the football field. Drayton wouldn't need much encouragement to pull the trigger; it might even be his own words that proved the final straw, but that was a risk he had to take.

"You daren't kill her, but you'll never feel safe again," he said deliberately. And then, his eyes still on Drayton's, "She's coming round, Larry . . . see what you can do for her." And as Drayton's stare wavered for an instant he brought his hand up sharply and caught him under the wrist.

Even at that moment, when he would have been the first to admit he wasn't entirely calm, the sound of the shot seemed unduly loud. The gun clattered to the floor some two feet behind and to the right of Drayton; Larry made a dive for it; and Drayton himself crumpled slowly, his body as slack as a marionette when the guiding hand is removed, until he was huddled on the ground at Antony's feet.

And the door in the corner, which none of them had seen open, closed quietly. A moment later the key scraped in the lock.

CHAPTER 18

Jenny had found a telephone box without too much delay, and dialed 999 with a feeling of unreality. It was only when she had relayed her message, in a high-pitched voice she hardly recognized as her own, and was back behind the wheel of the Oldsmobile again that reaction set in. Her hands were unsteady and her whole body was shaking; she was surprised to find that she was very cold.

But Antony had told her to drive back to Clapton Road and wait for the police, and she knew herself that she must do this. The voice at police headquarters had been businesslike and impersonal, but she couldn't quite believe in the efficacy of the message; in any case, she hadn't attempted to direct them to the "sort of side gate" that Mrs. Arnold had mentioned. Time enough to show them when she'd had the chance to reconnoiter and wasn't so likely to confuse things.

She found herself driving rather cautiously along the main road, with no recollection of having put the car in motion, and gripping the steering wheel like any novice. She tried to concentrate on what she was doing, without becoming tense again, and found it surprisingly difficult. After a while she began to think about the war, and memory was for a moment so vivid that she almost expected to see searchlights cutting the dark sky. She couldn't think what had put her in mind of it, but at least it was something to think about and she did so rather fiercely.

There had been a special ambulance drivers' course, and she had enrolled for it as soon as she was old enough; and though the blitz had been well over by that time there were still the incendiary raids to come, and the doodle bugs and the V–2s. Her colleagues had done their best to give her the easy runs— Mr. Taylor, whose Oldsmobile she was now driving, had been as well-meaning as any of them—but things didn't always work out quite as they intended. And always there had been the tension . . . that was what had reminded her, of course. Only then it had been easier, because as long as you were alive you knew you weren't dead, or your load of casualties either. But now her thoughts were with Antony, and anything might have happened since she dropped him at the corner of Clapton Road.

Even so, it was better than waiting at home.

She had memorized the turns as she came, and it wasn't difficult to retrace her route. Clapton Road looked sad and unwelcoming; even the bright swathe of the headlights did little to lessen the gloom, showing only dark trees and darker shrubbery, and wide puddles lashed by the rain. She drove on, and passed the lighted entry to River View, and came to the dark driveway of River Cottage with the wicket opposite that must be the one. . . .

The open gates of River Cottage offered a convenient turning place. As the Oldsmobile nosed in, shuttered windows were illuminated . . . a summer place not yet in use? And parked demurely at the front door, the familiar shape of the Jaguar. The drive circled a center flower bed; she came back to the gates again and pulled up where she could watch both entrances to River View.

The rain came down steadily, drumming on the roof. She wound down the window, and felt the cool air on her face and the splash of moisture. There was very little wind, the bushes stirred only gently; on her right an oak tree, its branches still unblurred by greenery, stood gaunt against the sky. Traffic was a faint hum, something from another world; some hardy soul with an open window was playing a beat record, but that too seemed far away.

And then she heard the shot.

Afterwards she wondered why she had been so certain; at that distance it wasn't a very distinctive sound. Her first thought was that it was Antony doing the shooting, and it was only a moment later that doubt struck home, and with it fear. She had the door of the car half open when the police car came up the road.

It drew up outside the lighted entrance to River View; one man was out in a flash and disappeared through the gate, the driver followed more slowly. The best thing was to tell them. . . . She snapped her door shut again, started the engine, and was just easing forward into the roadway when she saw the man come out of the wicket gate.

Perhaps it was not altogether to be wondered at that she jumped to the immediate conclusion that Antony was dead. It was only after a moment that a cold anger took the place of sick despair; if that was Drayton he wasn't going to get away with it.

A middle-sized man, dressed like a thousand others on a wet evening in spring. Even the fact that his hat was pulled down over his eyes might denote no more than a dislike of the weather. He came through the gate cautiously, but without hesitation, took in the police car with a quick glance, and then came briskly across the road towards the Oldsmobile. The two policemen were just coming up the drive again, their voices clearly audible in the stillness.

The man who had shot John Drayton wasted no time cursing his luck. The Oldsmobile, coming from a neighboring house, was sanctuary; seeing it turn from the driveway, the police would never connect it—any more than he did himself—with River View. And once he was back among the bright lights again there was nothing to connect him with what had happened . . . nothing at all. . . .

This had all happened so quickly that Jenny still had the engine idling, the car edging its way forward. He had the rear door open almost before she realized it . . . a girl alone . . . so his luck was holding after all. "I should like you to drive me to the main road, my dear," he said. She'd hardly recognize him again after that quick, startled glance: eyes shadowed by the brim of his hat, scarf pulled well up across his mouth and nose. "Don't turn round again," he told her, "and don't do anything foolish. I could knife you in an instant, and be out of the offside door."

Something in the calm tone carried complete conviction. As if that wasn't enough, he let her feel the prick of the knife at the base of her neck.

Larry hadn't seen the movement of the door. He stood now with the revolver in his hand and stared down at Drayton's body, and then raised his eyes to meet Antony's with a bewildered look. "He's dead. But you—you couldn't—"

"No," said Antony. If he spoke curtly it was because he was only just realizing that he was still alive. "He was shot from the door," he added, and went across and rattled the knob. "Someone who had a key; it's locked now on the outside. I just saw a gloved hand . . . and—that's kind of him!—he's left us *his* gun too."

It seemed to have been tossed down casually, not far inside the doorway. Larry peered at it disbelievingly, and then glanced back at Drayton again. "Is there anything we can do?"

"For him? Nothing." The need to dissemble had gone now, and his voice was hard.

"I don't understand anything," said Larry despairingly.

"We'll try the kitchen window in a moment. But first, there's Jo—"

Her eyes were wide open when he reached her, but he did not think she had shifted her position at all. After a moment her lips moved; there didn't seem to be any words, but the look she gave him was frightened and questioning. He said, "All right now," and was aware of relief when her hand twisted under his, faintly returning its pressure. Then she was looking past him and her whole expression changed; he thought it was as if some part of her had died, and then condemned himself for being overfanciful. But however it was, she stared for a moment and then rolled over, burying her face in the crook of her arm, and began to cry.

Antony went back down the long room and knelt by Drayton's body. Larry was saying in an agitated way, "No, look here, Jo, you mustn't—" and he wondered whether she had been awake long enough to hear what was said about Roy Bromley, or whether one of them would still have to tell her.

Drayton had been shot through the head, a nasty mess, but it meant the contents of his pockets were unharmed. Loose change, key ring, handkerchief; cigarette case in the hip pocket, slim, elegant, expensive; breast pocket, a well-filled wallet, he didn't stop to count the notes . . . a paying-in slip, *Northumbrian and Wessex Bank, Piccadilly Branch, Credit to the account of John Drayton* . . . a folded bill, unpaid, from a firm of tailors. Well, that was that. Better see what the prospects were of getting out.

He was wrestling with the kitchen window, which didn't seem to have been opened since last it had a coat of paint, when he heard a step on the flags outside followed by a thunderous knocking on the door. He went back into the living room to explain to the police as best he could that if the key wasn't on the outside they'd have to break their way in.

Jenny started the car smoothly, and didn't realize until later that if her passenger hadn't been preoccupied he would have been suspicious of her apparent calm. Not at all the reaction of an innocent passerby. Her skin crawled at the thought of the knife, but she wondered if she was being very cowardly as she drove past the two policemen—who were walking now towards the wicket gate—without trying to attract their attention. She thought that the man on the back seat had slid down out of sight, but she wasn't under any illusions that he had relaxed at all. It was like having a bad-tempered rattlesnake, poised to strike, and she didn't want to die.

One part of her mind told her, drearily, that it wouldn't

really matter . . . if Antony was dead. The other struggled, superstitiously, with a faint flicker of hope. She put up a hand and adjusted the driving mirror; there was one on the fender that told her all she needed to know about the road behind, this should give her a chance to keep an eye on her passenger's movements.

A second later he slithered back onto the seat again. He seemed to have been giving some thought to his position, or perhaps he was just pleased with her docility. "I think perhaps it will be best if you drive me back to town. Holborn, say . . . Holborn Kingsway underground station. Will you do that?"

"But—" said Jenny, because it had just occurred to her that she oughtn't to seem too eager. The beginnings of an idea were stirring in her mind.

"You really haven't much choice, my dear." She was coming to hate that easy, arrogant voice.

They had reached the end of Clapton Road, and she made the turn before she answered. "V-very well." That sounded convincingly frightened, but it made her think of Antony when he had lost his temper, and for a moment everything else was blotted out; perhaps if she'd tried to hold him back, perhaps if she hadn't made that foolish, quixotic pact with herself never to interfere . . . She looked up at the driving mirror, and found herself staring straight into her passenger's eyes. She had just time to think, I might not be able to describe him but I'd know him . . . I'd know him anywhere! when a gloved hand came over her shoulder and pushed up the mirror until it lay flat and harmless against the roof of the car.

"That was foolish," he told her, and let her feel the knife again. But she knew, as surely as if he had spelled it out for her, that in that moment his plan had changed.

It would no longer be safe for him to leave her alive.

But she gave him no hint of her awareness. "I'm s-sorry," she said. And then, "Which way?"

"Which route do you usually use?"

She remembered in time that he thought her a resident, or at least a visitor at River Cottage who had probably made the

journey before. "The Kingston Bypass," she said, and hoped
she could remember the way. It probably wasn't the most
direct route, unless you were starting from Fulham, as she and
Antony had done, and she was inventing an aunt at Putney by
way of explanation when he said:

"That will do," and she heard him move and thought he had
relaxed again in the corner behind her.

So for a while she was concentrating on retracing the way
they had come. And even when they were on familiar ground
again she kept the speed down, the big car purring gently under her hands with hardly a hint of the power that was waiting
to be called on.

He did not speak again until they were passing the ceme-
tery at Putney Vale. "We shall be stopped by the traffic," he
said, "and you may think that makes you safe. Believe me, my
dear, I could kill you in an instant and be lost in the crowd."

She had thought of this already; he might have been surprised to know how fervently she believed him. The only question now was how far he meant to go with her, but she daren't
make her move too soon.

The car swept on, and the silence was heavy between them.
Past the end of Roehampton Lane, across Telegraph Road,
and so to the junction with Putney Hill. A policeman in the
High Street, his cape gleaming in the rain; though she could no
longer see her passenger, Jenny felt an uncomfortable sense of
identity with him, as though she had known him a long time
. . . long enough to be sensitive to his moods. So now she felt
his watchfulness, but even so she wondered whether the time
had come to act. Fewer people . . . a smaller chance to lose
himself in the crowd; but still too many, and the constable was
on the opposite pavement, and if she stopped the car she had
no doubt at all he would use the knife. It was fantastic to think
that he could do so in almost perfect safety. A car draws up to
the curb: no passerby stoops to peer inside, the people in the
still-flowing traffic have their own preoccupations; after a moment a man steps out . . . no alarm . . . no fuss . . .

But even though she saw all this clearly her nerves were raw
and the risk would have been almost welcome; it was only

some inward stubbornness that held her to her course. She passed the constable with never a glance, and heard the almost inaudible sigh from the man in the back seat.

"Good girl," he said. And Jenny snapped at him suddenly, as though it was the only point at issue between them:

"I'm not a girl."

She heard him chuckle, pleased with himself now, sure of her. It was funny that his mock politeness irked her more than his threats. She drove grimly and very steadily over the bridge, and made the turn into King's Road; but presently, at his command, took a left turn that would take them to Fulham Road, and so along Brompton Road into Knightsbridge . . . which wasn't where she wanted to be at all. The traffic flowed, and checked, and jerked forward again; she went with the stream, the Oldsmobile obedient to her lightest touch, three hundred and seventy-five horsepower, leashed, well-mannered, ready to her command.

Once or twice she had a glimpse of her passenger's reflection in the car window, a shadowy figure, leaning back apparently at ease. But the snake simile came into her mind again; she found it disagreeable, but it would not be dismissed.

When they came into Piccadilly he leaned forward, tense now as he had not been before; she could feel his breath warm on the back of her neck. She tried to forget everything but the steering wheel under her hands, and the fact that she must be thankful the theater traffic hadn't yet joined the rest; it was bad enough without that.

She had never known it could take so long to get along Piccadilly.

As they neared the Circus he spoke in her ear. "You know the best way?" he asked, and saw her nod. Even when the street became one way she had stayed in one of the center lanes, not daring to edge too far over to the right, and this seemed to satisfy him. The lights were red against them and he sat back waiting. Jenny waited too, and the cross stream of traffic flowed past unbroken . . . two taxis, a Humber, a shiny Daimler with diplomatic plates, another group of taxis, a fractional opening . . . and all of a sudden a thousand demons awakened and with a scream of protest from the tires the car leaped forward.

Jenny had a moment of pure exultation, feeling its response. Then the wheel was spinning effortlessly . . . thank God for power steering . . . the constable on duty had his mouth open and his hand raised in futile remonstrance . . . there was a gap, and she took it, and she was through. . . .

CHAPTER 19

Twenty minutes after the men from the patrol car gained entrance Maitland was still trying, and now rather desperately, to convince a skeptical policeman that neither he nor Larry was responsible for Drayton's death. The argument hadn't been helped by the discovery of a spare key to the front door hanging on a nail in the kitchen. The constable had phoned his station, of course, and a lengthy conversation had ensued. "We're staying here till the Inspector comes," he told his companion as he replaced the receiver. "Better make the girl a cup of tea, I'll keep an eye on these two." He turned an unfriendly eye on Antony, and made a sort of shooing motion with his hands. "Just stay down that end of the room, out of harm's way. Then we shan't quarrel, see."

Out of harm's way . . . Drayton had used that phrase too. Out of reach of any of the three weapons, which were being left *in situ*, presumably for the Inspector to see. Jo was sitting cross-legged on the divan now, with a blanket round her shoulders; she was pale and heavy-eyed still, and all her movements were languid. Larry hadn't moved from his place beside her;

there was a stubborn look about his mouth as though he were just realizing the complexities of the situation.

Antony backed towards them. "The tea can wait," he said. "Do you mind, Jo?" he added over his shoulder. "Then your colleague could fetch my wife. She's outside somewhere in a dark red Oldsmobile."

"Your wife? I don't get any of this," the constable complained.

"It was she who called you."

"Oh . . . well. We'll wait till the Inspector gets here, and see what he thinks about that." There was a certain doggedness about him as he went back to his questions, as though he had given up hope of making any sense of the answers.

Oddly enough, Maitland never heard the local Inspector's name. He arrived ahead of his own experts, except for the doctor, who—after an extremely cursory inspection of Drayton's body—marched down the room and took possession of Jo, intimating only too clearly to Antony and Larry that their presence at the bedside was not required. As they moved away Maitland realized for the first time that the three men who had come in behind the Inspector were not, after all, from the local force; though he hadn't the remotest idea what Chief Inspector Sykes, Inspector Conway, and Sergeant Mayhew were doing so far from Central. Nor could he say that he was altogether pleased to see them. Conway was pursing his lips and looking disapproving; not altogether, it was to be supposed, because he—like the others—appeared to have been through a shower bath. Antony turned to Sykes and suggested hopefully:

"Perhaps you can convince these chaps here I haven't murdered anyone."

The Chief Inspector was looking around in his placid way: at Drayton's body, at each of the three guns in turn. "Now, Mr. Maitland," he said automatically. "I'm here by courtesy, as it happens. Perhaps Inspector Conway—"

"Look here, how did you get here, anyway?"

"It's a longish story, and 'appen it should wait. Properly speaking, the Inspector brought me. And the idea seems to be to ask you a few questions, Mr. Maitland, not to answer yours."

"He says——" the constable burst out; but continued on a lower key when they all turned and looked at him. His report was accurate enough, and his obvious suspicion understandable, but Antony was aware of Larry, beside him, bristling with indignation, and shot him a warning look. "And he says it was his wife who called us," the policeman finished. "And she's somewhere outside."

Four pairs of eyes turned inquiringly to Antony, and Inspector Conway spoke for the first time. "We saw no one."

"An American car a mile long. You must have seen that, at least. It's a dead end street, she couldn't be far away."

Sykes contented himself with shaking his head. "There was no one," said Sergeant Mayhew heavily. "No one at all."

"But she wouldn't have gone, she was waiting for you. That's what I can't understand. Unless she went to phone again. That's probably it," he added, in a tone of relief. "She'll be back by now."

"You'd best have a look," said the local Inspector. He didn't seem unduly awed by the amount of outside talent that was crowded into his manor, only a little thoughtful. The constable went out with obvious reluctance. "Now, Inspector Conway, do you still feel this business ties in with the case you were speaking to me about?"

"There are points of contact," said Conway slowly, his eyes on Larry Truscott. Antony's temper boiled up again suddenly.

"The connection's here," he snapped, indicating the dead man with a gesture. Conway gave him one of his less friendly looks.

"I've been wondering about that," said Sykes. "Who is he?"

"John Drayton."

"Well now, that explains things, doesn't it?" (Unexpectedly, the local Inspector threw up his hands in a mute gesture of despair.) "I was telling you, Conway," Sykes went on imperturbably, "about Mr. Maitland's theory that Drayton might somehow be mixed up with the Association."

"You were." He acknowledged the reminder without taking

his eyes off Antony's face. "You say this man kidnapped Miss Marston."

"He did."

"In mistake for Mrs. Maitland."

"That's right." His glance flickered to Sykes's face, and found it equally stony. "I thought at first it was to put a stop to my inquiries until he could make a getaway; but it turned out to be quite simply a trap."

"Into which you walked, all unsuspecting." That was Conway at his most sarcastic; and his smile didn't render his tone any more palatable.

"H-hardly that."

"It's all very well to sneer—" Larry growled. Conway ignored the interruption.

"You say you arranged for the police to be informed. It would surely have been simpler to have got in touch with us in the first place."

"No, you see—" He paused, looking down at the dead man, and his face was expressionless. "He m-made certain threats," he said. "I wanted to get here first."

"You were angry, weren't you?" said Sykes gently.

"B-bloody hell, of c-course I was angry! What do you take me for?" He glanced at Conway, and then back at the Chief Inspector again. "I didn't come here to kill him, if that's what you mean."

"Just what had you in mind, Mr. Maitland?"

"I hoped to get a chance to disable him . . . and I'm not such a bad shot I'd have done that by shooting him through the head. Besides"—he nodded towards the chair where the automatic was still lying—"that's mine. It hasn't been fired."

No one made any move to check the statement. Conway said sourly, "Have you a firearms license?"

"Oh, for heaven's sake! We're talking about murder. It would be even more reprehensible, I suppose, to shoot a man with an unlicensed gun."

Behind the Inspector's back Sergeant Mayhew allowed himself a grin. Conway said, unmoved, *"Is* it unlicensed?"

"I haven't the faintest idea. You'd better ask my uncle." The constable had been gone for several minutes now; surely he'd had time to find Jenny and bring her back with him?

At this point the doctor brushed past him. "She'll be all right. Give her some more tea, hot and sweet as you like, then get her home." The second and more domesticated constable disappeared, presumably to do his bidding, and he went down on one knee, laboriously, beside Drayton's body. His lack of interest in anything but his own concerns could not have been more clearly indicated.

Sykes had taken advantage of the interruption to do another tour of inspection; the rain dripped gently from him with every step he took. He said now, looking at Conway, "The third gun is a bit of a puzzle, you know."

"I've been wondering," said Antony bitterly, "how long it would take you to get round to that." Jo had come down the room behind the doctor, and now she pushed herself in between him and Larry, and tucked a hand under his arm. "I could have used the weapon I brought with me, and called it self-defense; I could have shot him with his own revolver, and said it went off in the course of a struggle. Why on earth should I have troubled to invent this singularly implausible yarn?"

"You're forgetting Mr. Truscott's presence," said Conway to Sykes, who nodded slowly.

"What about that, Mr. Maitland?"

Jo's hand was not quite steady. He squeezed it absentmindedly. "Conway's opinion of me seems to be rising, if he thinks I'd stick at a spot of perjury to save a friend embarrassment. Either of the situations I outlined would have served that purpose equally well."

Sykes shook his head. "Miss Marston was also present."

"Leave her out of it," Larry growled.

"I don't think she was in a position . . . when did you wake up, Jo?"

"I heard some of your talk. I didn't see anything. I'm sorry."

"Get her statement tomorrow," said the doctor without looking up.

Conway opened his mouth to retort, but before he could

speak the door opened and the constable came back. "I couldn't find her," he said, and all Antony's fear, which had been submerged for the moment in anger, came flooding back.

He took a quick step towards the door. "Let me look."

"I tell you, sir, there's no car there but ours."

"Well then—" The constable's solid figure barred the way; he might tackle one man, but not five, and where would it get him anyway? He turned, and let his eyes sweep deliberately from one of the detectives to the other. "This nonsense has gone far enough," he said. "You'd better do something to find the man who shot Drayton, because probably Jenny's with him. And she wouldn't be driving him for love."

"You think *she's* been kidnapped now?" Conway made no attempt to hide his disbelief.

"I prefer it to the alternative, that he took the car by force." He looked at Sykes. "Put out a call, at least," he said. And then, in a dead voice, as though he had encountered an insuperable difficulty: "I don't know the registration number."

Conway was looking sardonic. Sykes said, "No harm in that, at least," but there was no telling what he really thought of the suggestion. Sergeant Mayhew went across to the telephone, enveloping the receiver in a vast handkerchief before he removed it. "A dark red Oldsmobile," he said. "Do you know the year and model?" He sounded as if he was enjoying himself.

"An Oldsmobile Ninety-eight. I don't know the year." The information could be obtained from the helpful Mr. Taylor, but that would take time; he wouldn't suggest it yet. He stood waiting in silence for the call to be put through, until a cough from Sykes recalled his attention.

"You can't leave it there, Mr. Maitland. When we find the car—"

"If we find it," said Conway.

"You spoke of 'the man who shot Drayton'; but according to your own story you didn't see him."

Jo was behind him now. He heard her draw in a quick breath as though something had hurt her, and wondered for a moment if she knew what he was going to say . . . only, of course, she couldn't. "I know who it was though. I think—

this isn't proof. Inspector—I think, because of the relationship between the two men, that he was Drayton's chief . . . the head of the Association."

"Why should he—?"

"For the same reason that Drayton killed Ross: because he was coming under suspicion. Not only was he no further use, but he could be a threat to his principal's safety."

"From what you have told us, he also saved your life."

"That wasn't part of the original program. Larry and I were left alive because Jo Marston was here. He didn't want to upset her more than was necessary."

"An unusually thoughtful gentleman," said Conway skeptically.

"It meant rather a lot to him. I'm sorry, Jo . . . I'm sorry," he added, and turned and pulled her back, rather roughly, to his side. "As for the rest, he could afford to be magnanimous: he thought Drayton was the only person who could identify him, you see."

"Wait a bit . . . wait a bit! You're saying that all this, from the theft of the emeralds on, was Association business."

"Not exactly. Not in the way I think you mean." He paused, and cast an anguished glance at Sergeant Mayhew, hunched stolidly over the telephone. "I'm not explaining very well, am I? The man behind all this, the man who arranged everything —you laughed when I suggested this before, Inspector—I think it was David Warren."

Sergeant Mayhew turned ponderously from the telephone and clapped a hand over the mouthpiece. "They said to hold on," he informed them. "There's a report just coming in."

A matter of seconds after Jenny first put her foot down, and after a kaleidoscopic vision of the traffic which was proceeding in a more decorous fashion down the Haymarket, traffic signals leaped up to meet her, for the first time giving her the right of way. All the power of the huge engine was hurling them towards the corner, completely spoiling the evening of a young man in a new sports car who had hoped to impress his girl friend with its paces. Jenny braked hard from eighty-five to a mere forty and swung the Olds left into Pall Mall East. Though she hadn't had time to think of her passenger, she saw now this was the best thing she could have done; he had recovered from the first shock—more quickly than she had expected—and decided forthwith that the back seat was no place for him.

The turn sent him back hard into his corner again, and took his breath for a moment. In the ensuing seconds he was probably more aware than Jenny was of the stir their passing occasioned. Then she was taking a zigzag course, swerving roughly enough to keep him out of mischief and finding time to pull down the mirror into place again. Coming up to Trafalgar Square he had another bad fright—again the traffic coming in from their right seemed a solid mass, filling the road—but Jenny aimed the Olds for a gap between the back of a bus and an oncoming cab, drove the accelerator to the floor and kicked the automatic change into emergency passing gear. Again the tires screamed and the cab driver, deciding he wasn't ready to die, pulled his vehicle round in a circular turn to the right, leaving a minute space through which the big car stormed triumphantly.

She had switched her headlights to high beam, and now she put her finger on the horn and kept it there as she saw-toothed through the traffic in a way that hardly endeared her to her fellow drivers, though it gave rise to a good deal of imaginative profanity. A policeman making his majestic way along the pavement started to move out into the road, but quickly thought better of it, retreated to the curb, and began to run in the direction of his telephone.

Gaining the right-hand lane as the result of a complicated and suicidal maneuver, Jenny found the signals at red on the next corner and her car boxed in; but the pavement was clear, and there was only a taxi ahead of her, waiting for the light to change. She pulled the car onto the pavement without hesitation and cut across the corner. The Olds leaped in the air as it bumped across the curb at forty miles an hour, and the man in the back cracked his head on the roof and began to think long thoughts about death . . . preferably Jenny's. But she, pleased with her stratagem, proceeded on her way, leaving the night hideous behind her with shouts of protest and the blaring of motor horns.

A police driver, witnessing this lawless behavior from his position in a line of stationary traffic in St. Martin's Place, hauled his car out of the stream and roared in pursuit with his bell shrilling indignantly. His colleague, seizing the microphone, began to broadcast, in a voice that quivered only slightly with the excitement of the chase, a description of the Oldsmobile and the direction in which it was heading.

Once again the big car demonstrated its extraordinary powers of acceleration. ("A Grand Prix driver, I'd say," said Constable Hallett into his microphone. "Gone mad by the looks of things.") The police car in pursuit had the effect of bringing other traffic to a halt, and Jenny got a clear run across the head of Northumberland Avenue and into Whitehall. With the Oldsmobile given its head, the hydraulic box shifted into top at seventy-five, and for all Constable Grisholme's skill as a driver, the official car began to fall back.

If Jenny had had time to think, she might have stopped then; but it was as well she didn't, because the man in the back seat was far too angry to have considered his own safety if the faintest chance had offered of laying violent hands on her. As she came to the War Office she caught up with the stream of traffic that had crossed the lights ahead of her, and found the road packed solid to the center. The slight check as she pulled the Olds onto the wrong side brought the police a little closer; and the two cars—one with horn blaring, the other ringing a frantic alarm—stormed down the road, scattering pedestrians, bringing oncoming traffic to a standstill, and causing a certain amount of fidgeting and snorting even from the well-trained troop horses of the Household Cavalry.

Back on her own side of the road again, she took a second to glance into the driving mirror, and as the speedometer passed sixty-five she saw her passenger start to climb over the back of the seat into the place beside her. This time she let him achieve a precarious position halfway across before she braced herself against the wheel, stood on the brakes with both feet, and arrested the forward progress of the car so violently that he was flung forward, completely helpless, hit his head hard on the underside of the glove compartment, and disappeared under the dashboard.

Terrifying noises from the patrol car indicated that Constable Grisholme, finding his way blocked, in best racing tradition had utilized Richmond Terrace as an escape route. The car skidded into the opening with all wheels locked, crashed into reverse gear and shot back into Whitehall with its bell still clamoring incessantly, and took up the chase just as Jenny gave the Olds emergency passing gear again. A moment later, braking hard, and with the rear of the car overshooting and a final scream from the ill-used tires, she entered Derby Gate crab-fashion, and screeched to a stop outside Cannon Row Police Station.

Constable Grisholme's arrival was almost as dramatic.

The next few seconds after Sergeant Mayhew spoke were the longest yet. Sykes was looking puzzled, Conway openly disbelieving. Antony couldn't have cared less about either reaction; like Jenny earlier, he had a premonition of disaster. He stood very still, waiting, and when Conway spoke he didn't seem to hear him; only when he felt Jo shiver he pulled her closer, and then tried to tug the blanket more closely round her shoulders.

The sergeant was listening now, grunting occasionally. Damn the man for an unemotional blockhead, there was no telling anything from those grunts, they didn't even register surprise. But when at last he turned he looked first at Maitland, and said, "It's all right, don't worry," and grinned at him; and only then reported more formally to his superiors.

"An Oldsmobile just arrived at Cannon Row after some pretty hair-raising driving, or so I hear. A woman driver"— his eyes flickered for a moment to Antony's face again— "broke all the rules and arrived without a scratch."

"That'll be Jenny," said Antony, and relaxed for the first time; for the moment he was almost incurious to hear the rest.

"That's what she says," Mayhew agreed. He was stolid

again, unimaginative, inhuman, but Maitland would never see
him now without the slow grin that had transformed his face
a moment before. "Seems a bit confused though," the sergeant
added. "Says the man in the car with her shot her husband."

"But he wouldn't have let her drive him——"

"Boot's on the other leg," said Mayhew, and paused a moment as though contemplating this unoriginal phrase with
pleasure. "She says he forced her . . . he says, How could
he? No weapon. They found an open penknife in the back of
the car . . . fiddling little thing, not particularly lethal. But
if you ask me," said Mayhew confidentially to Antony, "it's a
good thing your missis shook him up as she did. He might not
be able to stab her, as she says he threatened—steady on now,
sir, I told you it was all right—but the thing is he'd taken his
tie off."

Antony made no comment, but he released Jo and moved
away a few paces to sit down rather limply on the nearest
chair. His bones appeared to have turned to jelly, and he rather
thought he was going to be sick; but somewhere beneath the
surface of his mind a faint, rueful amusement was struggling
for recognition.

"Well, if he meant to strangle her——" said Conway, and
broke off because he hadn't really meant to imply that it was
unreasonable not to have done so.

"Didn't have the chance, from what they tell me. Not with
her doing eighty down Piccadilly, and ignoring the lights, and
cutting corners, and driving down the wrong side of Whitehall," said Mayhew with relish.

Conway said, "Good God!" more weakly than Antony had
ever thought to hear him speak. Sykes looked at him with a
dawning amusement in his eye.

"Well, I never," he remarked mildly. "And the passenger——?"

"He's howling for blood." Mayhew had forgotten himself
again. "Says he never saw her before; says she offered him a
lift when he was trying to get a taxi in Knightsbridge, and then
drove like the devil right through town; says he's a respectable
citizen."

"His name, man . . . his name!"

"The one Mr. Maitland mentioned just now . . . Warren. Says he's something to do with one of the big banks."

"Yes, I see." Though Conway was momentarily speechless, Sykes had regained his normal placidity. "Are they holding him? They'd better do that until we get there."

"They're holding them both," said Mayhew, and again exchanged a conspirator's look with Antony.

"Yes, well, ask them to give Mrs. Maitland a message . . . tell her her husband's unharmed," Sykes told him. He turned to Conway. "Perhaps if we went back to the Yard we could get all this sorted out," he suggested.

"Perhaps we could, Chief Inspector," said Conway sourly. From the sound of it he viewed the prospect without much pleasure.

CHAPTER 20

It probably does not need stressing that counsel is unlikely to appear to the best advantage in court when he has been up all night, and Maitland would have been the first to admit that it was largely due to Derek Stringer's promptings that Mr. Enderby's brief was dealt with the following day without open disaster.

He got home at six-thirty and Jenny came into the hall to meet him. "If you want to go straight to bed, you can't," she said. "Inspector Sykes is here."

He became aware of the murmur of voices from the living room. "Is he talking to himself?" he inquired.

"No, of course not. Uncle Nick's there too."

Antony groaned. "Just what I needed," he said, "to make my day complete."

"Well, but, darling, you'll have to talk to them." Jenny might sound anxious, but her eyes were sparkling and there was an indefinable air of well-being about her. He looked down and grinned and said ruefully:

"I suppose I must."

Sir Nicholas had his favorite chair, Chief Inspector Sykes sat opposite him with his back to the window. Both looked very much at home, and quite prepared to stay all night if necessary. "I call this the limit," said Maitland, avoiding his uncle's eye. "How you can sit there, Inspector, drinking my sherry, when you as good as accused me last night of shooting Drayton—"

Sykes eyed him indulgently over the rim of his glass. "Would you say that was such a bad thing?" he asked innocently.

"I'd have thought so if Conway had charged me."

"Well, it didn't come to that, Mr. Maitland."

"No thanks to you," said Antony, unappeased.

"In point of fact," Sir Nicholas interposed smoothly, *"not* your sherry, Antony. I brought the bottle up myself."

"A peace offering, I suppose," Maitland inquired disagreeably, looking at him for the first time. He had not seen his uncle since about six o'clock that morning, and the memory of their meeting rankled; by no stretch of the imagination could it have been called an amicable one.

"Something like that," agreed Sir Nicholas equably.

Jenny had quietly been refilling their glasses, and now she brought one to Antony. "I explained what really happened," she told him.

"That should be quite sufficient to sever diplomatic relations for good and all," said Maitland, unimpressed.

"I assure you, my dear boy, quite the contrary."

Seeing her husband's sardonic look, Jenny went on in a hurry. "He quite sees it wasn't *at all* your fault—" Antony gave her his sudden smile. "And anyway, darling, if I can forgive the dreadful things he said to me—"

Maitland placed his glass carefully on a handy table, and pulled her down onto the sofa beside him. "But you deserved to have dreadful things said to you, love." Jenny laughed back at him.

"Well, I'm not in prison either," she said.

"Just be thankful Inspector Conway isn't a traffic cop." Sir Nicholas winced slightly at the colloquialism, but with real nobility refrained from comment.

"Constable Grisholme," said Jenny with her chin in the air, "said it would have gone to his heart to charge me. He says it's one thing to break the rules, and quite another to drive dangerously." She glanced at Sykes, and then back at Antony again. "I've got a date with him," she said.

"Have you though?"

"Next week, when he's off duty. He wants to drive the Olds, and Mr. Taylor said he could."

"There's magnanimity for you," commented Sir Nicholas dryly.

"And talking of magnanimity," said Antony, "so far as I recall our session this morning, Uncle Nick, you spoke for a quarter of an hour without repeating yourself once, and without ever giving me a chance to say anything for the defense."

"I was worried about Jenny," said Sir Nicholas meekly.

"Considering that she was home by then, cooking breakfast—"

"No, really, darling, that sounds too like Charlotte," Jenny protested. "You know," she added, seeing his blank look, "the heartless female who went on cutting bread and butter."

"I *don't* know. Would you say heartless?"

" 'Charlotte when she saw his body carried past her on a shutter—' " said Chief Inspector Sykes helpfully. Antony, who was not feeling very bright, gaped at him. After a moment, however, he picked up his glass.

"I suppose we may as well conclude a peace treaty. I'll even forgive the Chief Inspector," he offered handsomely.

"That's remarkably good of you, Mr. Maitland." Sykes's tone was warm with gratitude. Sir Nicholas said nothing, but stretched out his legs across the hearthrug and leaned back in his chair. "I thought," the detective added, "that you might like to hear what's been happening today."

"I shall probably fall asleep before you're halfway through." He broke off, and eyed Sykes with a dawning interest. "You never told me how you got to Sunbury last night. *All* of you," he said reproachfully.

Sykes seemed suspiciously ready to discourse, which only meant, reflected Maitland cynically, that he wanted something in return. "I was a bit worried," he said, "about that chap who was following you."

"You didn't behave as if you were."

"Well, after I talked to you yesterday I sent a man round to your chambers to have a look, and of course your fellow wasn't there."

"I ought to have suspected right away there was something queer about that. I mean, he was smart enough to keep out of the way of the police, but a complete flop as a tail."

Sykes acknowledged this with one of his sedatest smiles. "There was nothing else to do, after that, so I didn't do it. I don't mind telling you, Mr. Maitland—"

"I know. You thought I was pulling your leg."

"Well, I wondered. But I was kept rather late last night, and then I stayed a bit longer to read a pile of reports I ought to have looked at earlier; and the long and the short of it is there was one from a plainclothesman who was working on quite a different matter. He reported casually that he'd seen one of our regulars as he passed through Kempenfeldt Square on Sunday evening. Name of Hinton. That made me wonder."

"I hope it also made you ashamed of harboring unjust suspicions."

"I thought I'd have a word with him, if I could find him." said Sykes, admitting nothing. "And as luck would have it he was at home, and we had a nice little talk."

"I can imagine."

"Very obliging, I found him," said Sykes pensively.

"If you succeeded in making him more afraid of you than he was of Drayton—"

"Now, don't go getting any wrong ideas, Mr. Maitland. It's one thing to be scared of a chap you think's invulnerable; quite another when the police are on to him . . . or so you think."

"It all sounds extremely fishy to me," said Antony frankly.

"Well, be that as it may, he told me about the phone call he'd just made, and where Mrs. Maitland was—as he thought. Of course, according to him he was practically an innocent by-stander, but we understand each other well enough, he didn't waste too much time on that lark. As I had the story it seemed

straightforward enough, I didn't know then about the complica-
tions; and if you'd gone off to Sunbury it seemed I'd best be
getting there too, if only to see there wasn't murder done. Only
it was Inspector Conway's pigeon really, so I picked him up on
the way, and we had a proper heart-to-heart in the car on the
way down,"

"And after all," said Jenny, "there was a murder. And I
hold no brief for that horrible man," she added severely, "but
it does seem rather hard that he should be tried for killing
Drayton."

"That's not what you're holding him for, is it?"

"He's booked on the 'receiving stolen goods' charge," said
Sykes, faintly regretful. "Plenty of evidence there, once we got
a search warrant, and it seemed better than dragging Mrs.
Maitland in to make a complaint."

"I'd have been glad to," said Jenny, bristling.

"Best keep out of it, love," Antony advised. "You never
know with magistrates; once he'd heard the evidence he might
have committed you." He added, his eyes on Sykes's face, " 'It
is understood that further charges are pending.' "

"Something like that," the detective acknowledged.

"But Drayton was a Monster," Jenny declared unanswera-
bly.

"I shouldn't worry, love. I'm not saying Warren got any
pleasure out of killing, but what Drayton did was done at his
instigation. He gave him a free hand. And whoever else sheds
tears for Warren, I'm not likely to," he added thoughtfully.

"What I'd like to know," Sykes told him, "is how you came
to have his name so pat last night."

"I explained that too, when we talked on the telephone
yesterday. Or weren't you listening?" He looked at Sir Nicholas. "All the same arguments I gave you on Sunday," he said.

"There were four names then," said Sykes. "How did you
decide—?"

"I never thought Eversley had the right temperament—"

"Dangerous reasoning," said Sykes, shaking his head.

"—and once Giuditta confirmed that he was hard up—personally hard up, I mean—it didn't seem very likely he was run-

ning a business on the scale of the Association. Angelo was a different matter; a formidable character, for all his affectations. And for all he seemed completely wrapped up in his films, that might have been a blind. He could have let Anglo-Italian go into the red, and been rolling himself for all I knew. The only thing I really had against him as the kingpin of the whole affair was the fact that he told me Ross had had a go at blackmail. I could have been wrong about that, he might just have been trying to divert attention from the Association; but I thought—I still think—it was nothing more than an attempt to interest me in Eversley, to the latter's embarrassment."

"Why should he want—?"

"Personal reasons, Inspector. I don't think he seriously thought Eversley had killed Ross, or stolen the emeralds, or anything. But he wouldn't have been sorry if I'd entertained the idea for a while."

"I see," said Sykes, who obviously didn't. "That left you with the Bank people—"

"Yes, and it was the coincidence that bothered me," said Antony. "Not until after Ross was murdered, of course. That meant—as I saw it—two men had been accused of crimes they hadn't committed, and on perfectly good grounds too; which seemed a bit steep. No, I know Conway hadn't got as far as arresting Truscott, but it was perfectly obvious he was heading that way. Now, I may have been arguing from a faulty premise in Bromley's case—"

"You were," said Sir Nicholas, with a good deal of satisfaction.

"—but at least I was right about his being framed. Anyway, I was expecting someone to raise the point at any moment, but nobody did; not even you, Uncle Nick. At first I thought the connection must be something to do with their work; it was only later it dawned on me that their affection for Jo was an even more potent bond, and then I began to get hints there was someone else in the running. Giuditta said, 'It wasn't only the younger men'; and you told me, Jenny, that you thought there was someone her grandfather had in mind. When I pressed you, you couldn't remember why you'd said that, only that something Jo said had given you the idea . . . and when I started thinking on those lines, of course, I saw what had been staring me in the face all the time: the fact that Grandfather would never have discussed Jo's affairs with me with a third party present, unless it was someone he felt had both an interest and a right to be there. I haven't spoken to W.M. today—"

"I have," said Sir Nicholas. "Somebody had to."

"Well then?"

"You're quite right. He has old-fashioned ideas—which I cannot bring myself altogether to deplore."

"Really, Uncle Nick!" said Jenny, revolted. "You'll be saying next that marriages should be arranged."

"No, I wouldn't go quite as far as that. Mr. Marston, however, certainly felt that an older man would be better able to cope with Jo's vagaries. And he was probably quite right," concluded Sir Nicholas annoyingly. Antony glanced from his uncle to his wife, and seeing Jenny all ready to do battle, remarked placatingly:

"Your theory about Grandfather was almost right, love, and if I'd known what Uncle Nick's just told us I'd probably have settled for it right away. There was another point in its favor— the message left for Larry to meet Jo on Friday night; but at first I thought Jo was fibbing about that, just as I knew, once I'd been to the Bank, that Bromley was lying when he said he knew nothing about the emeralds . . . he must have known them as part of the AngIt security. But that didn't mean his whole story was untrue."

"To return to the point—" said Sir Nicholas.

"I don't . . . oh, yes. Grandfather was well placed to know that Jo was dining with the Valentis, but Warren told me himself that W.M. had mentioned the fact to him. And once I started thinking about him, quite a lot of things fell into place. For instance, the way Ross was stabbed—the sort of trick a left-handed man might have played, but it was unlikely Jo had told her grandfather that Truscott was left-handed. Then, Warren knew about Bromley's financial situation, and probably didn't believe the story that he'd been sending money home; that was an important part of the case against him."

"I still don't understand quite how Warren came to be mixed up with the Association."

"He *was* the Association, Jenny."

"But still—"

"I can guess," said Antony, giving his uncle a look in which even an unprejudiced observer must have seen provocation. Sir Nicholas gave him a smile that was almost unnerving in its benignancy. "It was probably all because he enjoyed the war."

"Now really, Antony—"

"Well, Uncle Nick, he did. And though he was doing well in the Bank I don't suppose he found it completely satisfying. It provided scope for his ability, perhaps, but not for his energy. Suppose while he was Accountant at the Piccadilly Branch he began to get interested in the working of one of the accounts— Drayton's—because he noticed that the deposits were irregular and inexplicable; no harm in that, he was just making an occupation for himself. Then one day he read in the papers about a jewel robbery, and perhaps he noticed the report especially because he thought: 'Now, if I had the disposal of them I'd know just where to get the best price'; shortly after there was one of the usual cash credits to Drayton's account, and it may have struck him as an amusing coincidence. Next time there was a job pulled I expect he kept an eye open for a deposit, but still I don't suppose he really believed—"

"You've made your point so far as I'm concerned, Antony. No need to labor it."

Maitland grinned. "With that encouragement I can move to my next assumption. No one could deny Warren's nerve, and when it had happened once too often I expect he tackled Drayton. Something like: 'If that's all you got for the Everett diamonds'—or whatever it may have been—'you've been done.' After a bit of sparring they could have come to terms . . . Warren to arrange a more profitable disposal of future hauls, for a fee. The formation of the Association would follow logically, with Drayton supplying the knowledge of the underworld and the necessary contacts . . . don't you think so, Chief Inspector?"

"I should not," said Sykes cautiously, "care to go quite so far out on a limb as that, Mr. Maitland. All the same—"

"You agree with me. Of course," said Antony shamelessly. "So there they were with a nice, profitable sideline, and Warren was doing well in his career. He'd really nothing left to wish for . . . until he fell in love with Jo. And perhaps it was because here was something he couldn't just put out his hand and take, or perhaps there was some deeper reason; anyway, she began to be an obsession with him . . . and Marston encouraged the idea. So when she fell for Bromley—"

"Was he already on the payroll?"

"Oh, yes, I think so. I expect that Warren—who must have been a fair judge of men—got Drayton to recruit him as soon as he knew he was in financial difficulties. The theft of the emeralds was planned, and then he went and spoiled everything by falling in love with Jo. So Warren scrapped the idea of a real theft, substituted a fake one, and arranged for Bromley to carry the can."

"I should like another glass of sherry," said Sir Nicholas in a failing voice. Jenny got up to comply with this request, and said over her shoulder:

"Was he really in love with her?"

"I'm afraid he was. I only hope—"

"Don't be so silly, darling. Jo was already falling out of love with him when she came to see you, only she didn't know it then."

"Was she?" said Antony, startled.

"That's why I told you it was so important . . . don't you see? She wouldn't want to throw him over while he was in prison."

"Oh," said Antony blankly. And for the first time that evening exchanged a sympathetic look with his uncle.

Jenny came back to her place again. "Go on about what happened," she said.

"I was a bit out in my ideas here, about Ross being unpopular with the Association on account of his failure to get away with the emeralds. But we know now he was working on the side as a blackmailer, and if Drayton had found that out he'd hardly want him to be interviewed again by someone with a suspicious mind. Drayton had heard of me from Jim Arnold, I should think, but that isn't really important. Anyway, say he'd decided to liquidate Ross . . . don't you think Warren would have given him the go-ahead, for his own reasons? He must have heard from Grandfather about the two young men who were competing for Jo's favors, and here was a chance of getting rid of them both at once."

"It doesn't sound very—very rational, darling."

"Now, there I can't agree with you, Mrs. Maitland," said Sykes, suddenly. "A ruthless man . . . a powerful man . . . he only had to say the word, remember, he didn't have to take any action himself until it came to killing Drayton."

"And that was dramatic irony, or something," Antony went on, "because I think Drayton was killed for the same reason he gave for wanting Ross out of the way: questions were being asked. And there was the additional reason that he was the only one who knew who the head of the Association was."

"But . . . everything that happened last night—"

"Drayton arranged that, and *then* told Warren. Wouldn't you think that was the way of it?" he appealed to Sykes. "It probably signed his death warrant, because it showed he was getting jittery, or trigger happy . . . it must have always been a rather nervous business dealing with him. Like keeping a savage dog. If you'd been there, love, instead of Jo, we'd both have died—because I don't suppose Warren had any objection to profiting by the arrangement—and afterwards he'd have killed Drayton. As it was, he didn't want to upset Jo by leaving her there with three dead men; I'd mentioned her name just before Drayton was shot, so Warren was in no doubt of her presence. And I daresay he hoped the plan he adopted would be almost as embarrassing for me as the original one. Which it might have been, except for your efforts, love."

Sykes laughed suddenly. "I wouldn't have missed seeing Conway's face when he heard what she'd been up to," he said. "Not for a thousand pound."

"It was good value," Antony admitted.

"Nothing else would have convinced him," said the detective. He considered that for a while, and then added honestly, "Or me, for that matter. But first you said 'Warren,' and then Mayhew told us . . . All the same, Mr. Maitland, there's a lot of work to be done yet."

"I'm sure there is," Antony agreed, in the complacent tone of one who was in no way concerned. "And when you've got your case complete you can come and tell me how far off my guesses were from the truth."

"I'll be glad to do that." He picked up his glass and drained it, and put it down with an air of finality. "I told you the search warrant was helpful; that's because he felt himself safe, I expect. And we think we've got a line on his contact abroad."

"Already?"

"It was you saying he'd been at Arnhem, you see. Seems he didn't get away across the river like some of his mates, but was hiding up with the Resistance for a month or two after that. I got all this from Mr. Landor, at the Bank. Well, you know yourself, Mr. Maitland, some of those types—"

"Biggest villains unhung," said Antony, hiding a smile. "I hope you're on the right track, Chief Inspector."

"So do I," said Sykes, getting to his feet. He stood a moment, thinking perhaps of the labors ahead. "So do I," he repeated, with the fervency of a prayer.

Jo and Larry Truscott were walking in the park. The air was soft and damp, and the world smelled of growing things, and to both of them the darkness felt friendly. "He didn't say a word," said Jo. "I think his spirit's broken."

It might have been more clearly expressed, but her meaning was obvious to her escort. "I don't understand," he said, "how he could ever think that you and Warren—"

"Well, he did." The thought seemed to depress her. "So you see, I really am a jinx, Larry. Everything was my fault."

"Don't be a little fool," said Larry. Comforted, Jo tucked her hand under his arm.

"Well, I've been sensible all day," she told him. "Grandfather was upset, you see, but his feelings are a bit mixed because he has a sneaking feeling it was all my fault. At one point I rather thought he was going to suggest my ending my days in a nunnery, but I kind of sidestepped that one."

"You weren't to blame for anything," Larry insisted, ignoring this digression.

"After that there was the police. I had to make a statement. And I must say it was pretty beastly, Larry . . . last night, I mean. I'm glad you were there."

"You never told me how it started. I got an awful fright when we got back and found you gone."

"That was too silly. The phone rang, so I answered it, of course, and a man said 'Mrs. Maitland?' but he never gave me time to say I wasn't. He just went on as if it was urgent, 'This is St. George's Hospital, there's been an accident and your husband is here. A car has been sent for you, so please come straight away.'" She paused, and smiled. "Jenny *says* she'd never have fallen for it."

"Well, I must admit," said Larry reluctantly, "she was right about the other message . . . the one about where you were. And I might just as well have waited, only I expect I'd have gone mad, doing nothing. But you were saying what happened to you."

"The man rang off without waiting for me to say anything, so I thought I'd better go down and explain to the driver—"

"You took your coat."

"Well, I didn't know how long I'd have to wait. But there was a car outside already, and I went across and a man leaned out of the back as if to speak to me, and there was no one about so he grabbed me and pulled me in with him, and then he put something across my face and I went to sleep." Larry muttered something, fortunately inaudible. "Yes, I know, it was horrid. The doctor said he gave me an injection later, but it doesn't seem important now, does it? I mean, it's all over."

"It's over . . . in a way," said Larry. "Did you go to see Mr. Horton, or didn't you have time?"

"No, I managed it, late this afternoon." She didn't seem to have anything to add to that, and after a while he prompted impatiently:

"What did he say?"

"Oh, he'll try to do something for Roy, but it will have to wait till the police have completed their inquiries," said Jo, very offhand. Larry stopped short and said furiously:

"And what then?"

"It doesn't make any difference really." She pulled her hand free and waggled her fingers at him. "Are you quite blind, Larry? I took off his signet ring."

He took the hand and held it still. "Is that what you want, Jo? To forget him."

"I expect you think I'm a traitor." He couldn't see her expression, so he moved a little until the light from a nearby lamp fell on her face. She said fiercely, "I don't care if you do. I wouldn't have gone back on my word when he was in prison; but it's different now—isn't it? Now I know it's fair."

"He didn't actually steal anything, Jo."

"Don't you think what he did was just as bad?"

"And I think he's really in love with you," said Larry stubbornly.

Jo snatched her hand away. "Oh, for goodness' sake!" she said crossly. "Do you think I should stick to him then?"

"If it will make you happy."

"Not because it's my duty?"

He flinched a little from the scorn in her voice. "You don't owe him anything, Jo, that you don't want to give."

She looked down, away from him, scuffing the path with her shoe. "It isn't a sin to change your mind," she said. And then his hands were on her shoulders, shaking her.

"Is that what you've done, Jo? Tell me, is that what you've done?"

"It's nothing to do with you," she told him sulkily.

"You know damn well—" There were tears in her eyes; he'd never seen Jo cry. And he couldn't stay angry with her, no matter how she provoked him. He tilted her chin, and kissed her gently; and thought—but he was very much in love—that her smile was like sunshine after the rain. It occurred to him dimly that someone might have used the description before.

"I *thought* you did," said Jo, obscurely but with great satisfaction. "But I'm not made of porcelain, you know."

Later—how much later?—they were walking arm in arm across the damp grass. "I might never have known," said Jo, at peace with the world, "if Michael hadn't been killed."

"What difference could that make?"

"Well, when they thought you'd done it—"

"If you mean you were sorry for me—" Larry might be besotted, but he wasn't going to put up with any nonsense like that.

"No, of course not. That's the whole point. I couldn't be sorry for you, because you weren't sorry for yourself. But I *was* miserable. And then I began to think about Roy, and somehow he didn't seem to come out of the comparison very well. I mean, it was dreadful what happened, but not so bad as being accused of murder. I thought he wasn't—wasn't sufficiently resilient, and it put me off him rather."

"I'm glad, of course, but I can't help feeling you're being a bit hard on him," said Larry, secure now in his own happiness. "I say, Jo, have you thought about the future at all? That contract of yours, for instance . . . is there anything in it about getting married?"

"I notice," said Sir Nicholas, after dinner, "that Sykes still attributes your knowledge of the Sunbury—er—hideout to the good offices of his friend Hinton."

"He knows I was out when the message was delivered, but I promised I wouldn't tell anyone about Mrs. Arnold, sir." Antony was relaxed now, and inclined to be somnolent.

"You told me," his uncle pointed out.

"That's different. Besides—"

"Something will have to be done about that family," Sir Nicholas agreed.

"It will, won't it?" said Antony, thankful that the point had been taken. He couldn't help feeling that his uncle's patronage would be more useful than his own.

"By the way, I meant to ask Sykes about that. The use of the apartment above the boathouse, I mean."

"It was rented by the owner of River View to a youngish man—I forget his name—who described himself as an artist."

"Do you know that, or did you just invent it?"

"I was talking to the Chief Inspector for some time before you came in," Sir Nicholas reminded him.

"So you were. And this artist—"

"Made only occasional use of the accommodation, so far as his landlord knew. Nor did he know of any visitors."

"He wouldn't need any, as a general rule. Take out the boat —first stop *Gaiety Sal*—pick up whatever Drayton happened to have on hand—next stop Port of London, some friendly vessel bound for the Continent." He broke off as he caught his uncle's eye. "Am I right?"

"Surprisingly so," Sir Nicholas admitted reluctantly. "The man was quite easily traced; he used his own name, though I think Sykes said he wasn't an artist. He named the ships that were generally used, and as you might expect was horrified at the idea that he'd been smuggling stolen goods."

"As you might expect," said Antony. And, after a pause, "He may even get away with a lightish sentence if nothing else turns up to his discredit."

Sir Nicholas finished his coffee and got to his feet. "You both need an early night, I'd better go," he said, a little reluctant to leave the comfort of the fireside. But halfway across the room he turned. "One other thing: you remember that I felt constrained to purchase an automatic pistol after those unfortunate events last year—"

"Yes, of course," said Antony uncomfortably.

"I never informed Mallory that I had done so," said Sir Nicholas.

"I didn't suppose you had."

"You've missed the point, Antony. Mallory would have reminded me that the license should have been renewed at the end of July."

"You don't mean to say . . . Uncle Nick, you can't mean—"

"With all his preoccupations," said Sir Nicholas pensively,

"Inspector Conway found time to mention the matter to me. I understand, in fact, that you had recommended him to do so. It is not, strictly speaking, his province, of course—"

"Of course it isn't!"

"—but I should not be at all surprised to hear in due course from the proper authorities."

"Ten quid, at a guess," said Antony, grinning.

"So I understand." Sir Nicholas moved to the door, and paused with his hand on the knob. "What I am wondering, my dear boy, is this . . . which of us do you think should pay it?"

Antony showed no immediate disposition to go to bed when his uncle had gone, and when Jenny started to get up he pulled her back again. "I think he's forgiven us, don't you?" he said.

"Yes, of course. But why were you so cross, darling? You ought to know Uncle Nick by now."

He thought about that. "One thing and another," he said vaguely after a while. "First . . . well, you might have been kidnapped, Jenny . . . and Drayton . . . it doesn't bear thinking of. And just when I thought you were safe I heard you were racketing about in that damned car."

"I enjoyed it," said Jenny stoutly. "And I don't suppose I'll ever get a chance like that again."

"I expect I was angry with Uncle Nick because I knew he was in the right of it," said Antony, determined now to complete his examination of conscience. "I let you get involved . . . well, anyway, love, it won't happen again."

"Why not?"

"Because I've made up my mind to stick to the paths of rectitude. Nothing unorthodox. Nothing—what was it Conway said?—beyond the proper discharge of my professional duties."

"And no damsels in distress?" asked Jenny wickedly.

"That's right."

"Darling, how dull. But you shouldn't tempt me, I might take you at your word."

"You can . . . I mean it."

Jenny pondered. "I love Geoffrey, you know—"

"I beg your pardon!" said Antony blankly. The change of subject seemed a little drastic.

"Well, I do. *But*," said Jenny, "I can't help seeing he's frightfully sensible. And I expect the two things go together."

"What two things, for heaven's sake?"

"Well, being sensible and—and not raising the devil occasionally," said Jenny, frowning with the effort to make her meaning clear. But then she looked at him and smiled. "So if keeping out of trouble means being sensible too . . . and rather dull . . . I think you'd better not make any more good resolutions."

Reprehensibly, Antony never attempted to point out to her the illogicality of her argument.

But it was Giuditta who had the last word, when they visited the penthouse apartment at Montague Court one evening and the gist of the above conversation was relayed to her. And how the reticent Jenny ever came to do such a thing will never be explained; she wasn't given to casual confidences, but perhaps, like her husband, she found their new friend sympathetic.

"There are some men who make an excitement, just by coming into a room," said Giuditta. "And I am afraid your Antonio is one of them. There is nothing to be done." A dreamy look came into her eyes. "But I would not change my dear Angelo—"

Her dear Angelo was singing lustily somewhere offstage; presumably in the kitchen, because it was he, and only he, who could make the coffee to that peak of perfection . . . "Have you noticed what he's singing?" said Antony, grinning at her.

It would have been difficult not to notice. *"Qual piuma al vento, muta d'accento e di pensiero,"* sang Angelo. No doubt the aria had frequently been better rendered, but seldom with greater feeling.

"It may just be because I quoted it last time I was here, and that put it in his mind," said Antony doubtfully.

Obviously Giuditta did not pale, but she succeeded in conveying the impression that she had done so. She tilted her head to listen. "Do you mean, Antonio *mio* . . . he knows?"

"I think it would be best to assume so." To his relief she showed no sign of taking offense; for himself, he still thought Angelo a force to be reckoned with, which was why he had felt it only fair to warn her. . . .

Giuditta sighed. "I had hoped . . . but he is not foolish, you see," she added, turning to Jenny confidingly. "And you were quite right to tell me, Antonio." Two slow tears trickled down her cheeks. "It is well to know the worst," she added bravely.

"If he hasn't said anything—" Maitland was already regretting his impulse.

"But of course he will not say anything until the film is completed. He would not wish to upset me," said Giuditta, as though the fact should be self-evident. "Then he will be angry . . . *very* angry," she repeated, perhaps thinking him not sufficiently impressed; and she shuddered. Antony's ever lively imagination immediately presented him with the picture of a dismembered corpse at least.

But if he had any real worries on this score her next words dispelled them. "But then I shall tell him it is all over," Giuditta said, more cheerfully, looking up at him with such innocent candor that there was no question at all of doubting her. "And I shall tell him that never again . . . never—" She paused, and looked from one of them to the other, obviously satisfied with her rehearsal. "He will forgive me," she asserted, "because he knows—you will understand this, Giovanna—that always I do as he says."